THIS PLACE CALLED
ABSENCE

THIS PLACE CALLED ABSENCE

LYDIA KWA

KENSINGTON BOOKS
http://www.kensingtonbooks.com

KENSINGTON BOOKS are published by

Kensington Publishing Corp.
850 Third Avenue
New York, NY 10022

All Kensington titles, imprints and distributed lines are available at special quantity discounts for bulk purchases for sales promotion, premiums, fund-raising, educational, or institutional use.

Special book excerpts or customized printings can also be created to fit specific needs. For details, write or phone the office of the Kensington Special Sales Manager: Kensington Publishing Corp., 850 Third Avenue, New York, NY 10022, Attn. Special Sales Department. Phone: 1-800-221-2647.

Kensington and the K logo are Reg. U.S. Pat. & TM Off.

Library of Congress Card Catalogue Number: 2001091609
ISBN 0-7582-0147-8

First Printing: March 2002
10 9 8 7 6 5 4 3 2 1

Printed in the United States of America

To the memory of my maternal grandmother,
Yong Chan Leong

Freedom. It isn't once, to walk out
under the Milky Way, feeling the rivers
of light, the fields of dark—
freedom is daily, prose-bound, routine
remembering. Putting together, inch by inch
the starry worlds. From all the lost collections.
>   —"For Memory," Adrienne Rich, 1979

We shall not cease from exploration
and the end of all our exploring
will be to arrive where we started
And know the place for the first time.
>   —"Little Gidding," T.S. Eliot, 1944

EACH TIME MY HAND
UNLEASHES CHANCE

田

November 11, 1994. The twentieth Remembrance Day of my life in Canada, but only the ninth one in Vancouver. I count the number of years I've been here this way. Back home in Singapore, nobody commemorates the world wars. Back home. After such a long time away, I still catch myself thinking that.

A few blocks away, in Victoria Park, a small ritual is well underway. I hear the trumpets blaring out their bold and soulful tones, while the trombones slip-slide lazily through their bass harmonies, to the occasional rasp and beat of a side drum. *Brrak, pah-pah-pah, bom-om-om, brrak.*

Plodding thuds from upstairs. My friends Dominique and Gerald—whom I've nicknamed Dom and Gerry—are home. I think of them as human equivalents of the cartoon cat-and-mouse team, scurrying about in their domestic dramas. They're frequently dropping things, or walking too heavily, as if they don't realize how well sounds carry.

I can imagine the Canadian Legion band members, decked out in military regalia, their hands sheathed in angel-white. The usual glint of brass dulled by today's overcast winter light. Sombre coats of the audience huddle together, offset with red poppies, the field of flowers that announce, *we will hang onto a burst of life.*

Some hands in the audience are cosily hidden in gloves, while others are stubbornly naked to the elements, or more likely, stuffed with resignation into pockets. A hymn drifts through to me, familiar from childhood. *Abide with me.* At funerals back home, I'd heard the hymn too often sung with maudlin emotion. Now, hearing it again, I cringe.

It was one of Father's favourites. He loved to sing hymns, having grown up in a semidetached next to a small Methodist church on Chapel Road in Katong, back in the 1930s. He picked up the melody and some of the lyrics from straining his ears at the window. Didn't matter if he missed some words, because he enjoyed filling in the gaps. For example, this one: *What a friend we have in Jesus, all our screams and riffs to bear, what a privilege to bury everyone who hates our guts.*

I'm still adjusting to living in Dom and Gerry's house. It began as a temporary solution three years ago. I needed to leave the house Kim and I had shared as quickly as possible. But then I stayed on in this ground-level apartment, happy enough with the easy companionship of these friends, satisfied with looking out onto a shared garden at the back of the house. A perennial herb garden in the sunny area, with woodruff and hostas and alpine plants in the shade. A bald patch of soil next to the garage that becomes our vegetable garden in the summer. Two plastic lawn chairs, tastefully forest-green under a hawthorne tree.

Father would have liked this Remembrance Day ceremony, had he made it to this country. He would have risen early, put on too many warm clothes, drunk a cup of scalding hot Ceylon tea, thickened with condensed milk, then briskly walked out to the park, already having warmed up his voice in preparation. He might even have spoken to some people—offering phrases from his stash of *Daily Bread* booklets, Christian tracts that he picked up as a young boy from the Methodist church and that he kept hidden from the disapproving glares of his atheist father. This was around the time Grandmother Neo had become very sick. All those years into adulthood, Father squirrelled the booklets away as if they were pornographic material. Along with power tools, do-it-yourself magazines, records, and ten years' worth of *Reader's Digests*. The shelves and the old clothes cupboard in the store-room were choked full with his things. My brother Michael and I called it his mad collection. Wide-eyed Father, whose hunger seemed never to be satiated.

I had been thinking about Father's mad collection three months ago when I stepped out of the air-conditioned taxi, and walked into the even colder funeral parlour, direct from landing at Changi airport. There he was, laid out in his open coffin, neat in a plain grey suit and navy blue tie, the scars inflicted by the coroner thinly visible along the top of his scalp, running behind his ears, disappearing down his neck into the pearly pink satin of the eight-hundred-dollar box. The scars were like a trail cut with a scythe, a clearing in the woods. I was grateful for those scars: they reassured me that it was true, something irreversible had happened. Not a figment of my imagination.

Most visitors to the parlour couldn't look me in the eye, act-ing as if I'd killed him myself. As if my years away from home were to blame for pouring those pills down his throat. Others flung their sweaty bodies at me, clutching at my neck or my back, as if I was supposed to grant them pardon or relief. I wondered what people thought, especially about my lack of emotion. Most of them would have known I worked in Vancouver as a clinical psychologist. They must have expected someone more obviously empathetic, more emotionally demonstrative. My voice was calm during the eulogy. I also made sure I didn't linger too often by my mother's side. I stayed away from Mahmee as much as possible, letting her direct her grief to others. My brother Michael was cry-ing on his wife Susan's shoulder a lot of the time, and I kept thinking to myself, *Lucky boy*.

Father keeps dying in my imagination. While working his weekend shift, patiently walking a potential customer through all the deluxe features of the new 1994 model, pointing out the safety advantages of air bags. His co-workers hear incoherent, garbled sounds, turn to catch the final seconds of his fall as he crumples onto the cool, Italian marble floor of their showroom, scratching the new red car with the metal hook of his watch strap as he falls.

Of course, his death was nothing like that. It was more invisible, as indecipherable as a shadow glimpsed around the corner. Uncle Samuel, Father's older brother, phoned me at work. Monica, the receptionist, interrupted a therapy session by knocking at my office door.

"Sorry, Dr. Lim," she whispered to me when I opened the door, her lips turned down at the edges with nervousness, "urgent phone call, long distance."

Uncle Samuel's clear voice clicked in after a pause, "Wu Lan? Wu Lan, is that you?"

"Yes...." My heart started to thump loudly. Which one of my parents? Who?

"Your father passed away ... this morning ... please come home soon."

Come home soon. It was mid-August, during the lull when many people were away on vacation with their families, enjoying the final freedom of summer. The same people who would, after the Labour Day weekend, feel their anxieties catch up with them and insist on being seen immediately. I lied to my colleagues, served them the fantasy version. A heart attack, sudden and unforeseen. On the plane my uncle's words raced through my mind, "Sleeping pills, two bottles. The autopsy will be finished by the time you get home."

The music coming from Victoria Park has stopped. If I were dead and watching my funeral, I would find my silence intolerable—not only to be deprived of the ability to speak on my own behalf, but, even worse, to hear the living go on and on about what they don't understand. The person's already dead, so why keep driving the point home? Wonder what Father thought of his funeral, of the speech I made. It was brief. Not much I felt I could say. I focussed on his stability as a provider and family man, these truths being easier to confess than some others.

When I got back from Singapore, it was more difficult than I had anticipated, to be back at the office, sitting in my chair, facing clients' anxieties, with clammy hands and a pounding heart, feeling as if the floor would give in under me. A voice from a place just below my right ear insisted: *Ask if they've lost someone to suicide.* I heard my clients' voices rattle through the small office, but they seemed very far away, at the end of a hallway or a tunnel, some conduit that diminished sounds while conveying them. Everyone at work was sympathetic, although many couldn't hide their surprise. It was the first time anyone at the organization had a nervous breakdown. I hate the term. It makes me sound like a walking bundle of jumbled, confused nerve endings. And that is simply not the way I usually am.

"Yes, a leave of absence. Give me a year. I'll be back, promise."

Ben, our president, replied, "We need you, Wu Lan. Get well soon."

Lots of people lose their parents. They cry, they get mad, they talk about it. Then they go on with their lives. I feel as if I've walked up to the edge of a cliff, in a slow, deliberate trance, the pebbles crunching softly underneath my shoes. Look down into that total and infinite absence, the abyss, unable to turn back, unable to jump.

Lan-Lan, you think too much, must let things go. Drink cooling things, I send you.

Mahmee tries in her own way to reassure me. I wonder what she'll do with his clothes, the rest of his mad collection, his second-hand Morris Minor. I surprised everyone including myself when I asked for a few of those *Daily Bread* booklets. I've been hoping I would find an answer there, some clue as to the kind of person he really was.

At my desk in the living room, cleared of all paperwork, I spin the wooden toy top again and again, watching the colours blur, imagining myself deep in the centre of the top. The faster the circular motion, the more illusory everything becomes.

Appetite, sleep, movement, the animal demands, days and nights blurring.

Two loud knocks on the outside door. It's Dom, cheerful and rosy-cheeked, sporting her very floppy beret pinned with a red poppy.

"Do you want us to get you anything from the supermarket?"

"No, I'm fine."

"You don't mind if we use the car again later tonight? Think we'll catch an early show downtown and go somewhere for dinner."

"Go ahead." I smile approvingly at her. She and Gerry are still romantic after all these years. She winks and scurries back upstairs. I don't shut the door immediately. In the dull winter light, it takes some effort to recall the garden's summer vibrancy. And yet it is easy for me to remember my maternal grandparents' garden in Singapore. Memory is a strange thing. I spent many afternoons playing in Kong-Kong and Mah-Mah's front yard. I was a five-year-old who liked to sprawl out on the rough sandy ground, squinting up at the clouds as they waltzed through their various disguises. Snakes, prowling tigers, old men with long beards, women with fast-deforming babies in their arms. I admired the clever clouds, how swiftly they transformed.

My sadness about Father's death is a bit like that feeling I had for clouds. When a favourite shape disappeared, I gasped in regret, promising myself I must remember its former glory. Yet I inevitably forgot. What lingered as I got up from the ground after an afternoon of cloud watching was a physical sensation that returns to me today, thirty-six years later, a sweet ache between throat and sternum, a silent, tender witness.

* * *

LEE AH CHOI

Inhale opium smoke, erase that dull ache in my chest. Erase everything. Here at 61 Upper Hokien Street. My cubicle, Number 2, next to the front room. Sum Tok told me when I first came, this brothel is special, used to be a mansion, I should be proud to belong. A British merchant built it for his family, lost it to Chan's father in one night of crazed gambling. Now Chan Ah Ng runs us, gambling our lives away to any man who can pay. Chan, our kwai kung, devilish father. And Sum Tok, our kwai po, wicked den-mother. Yes, this is a mansion, a temple of hell, where bodies must crush other bodies in a pyramid of greed.

So I should be proud? The eldest daughter who dutifully sends money home. A daughter sold to this new country, and to this mansion where Sum Tok sits in the waiting room below, her gnarled fingernails clinking against abacus and pipe, while she surveys books filled with our names and how much money we make each day.

Yes, I'm supposed to be grateful for this new life, for the hungry ones who pass by, peering through windows on the ground floor, searching for merchandise they can run their coarse hands over. But it makes no sense to be grateful. Better to follow the pull of greed. If Lan Ho in the front cubicle is lucky, a regular will buy her as his concubine and then I'll take over. My sisters have been here longer, but they reassure me. *Your youthful face, oval, still so smooth, eyes wide and wider with allure, how could you not succeed?* Tease and flatter. How polite they are to the newest addition.

A room with its very own window. Looking out onto the street. Imagine. It'll mean more money per client. I dream of saving enough for that lilac silk purse inlaid with pearls, eyes of the phoenix, and black velvet shoes from Shanghai, the kind women wear to banquets with their rich husbands. I dream of gold bangles as thick as my thumb, of expensive hair ornaments that glitter like stars in my sea of black.

In my village near the town of Xiaolan, the wealthiest man, Liong Soon Fatt, travelled to Guangzhou to buy the finest red silk for his wife and daughters. At fourteen, while planting rice seedlings one afternoon, my feet drenched deep in wet mud, I stood up to glance at the banner of red he held up high, as he jumped off his horse-drawn carriage. Ever since that time, I've been dreaming of a better life. A life without mosquitoes sucking on my bare legs, without mud caking the roughened soles of my feet, a perpetual, cracked border of dirt rimming my rolled-up trousers. I want a life of silk softening all the bitter edges, until the bitterness can no longer be tasted on the tongue.

I don't understand why many want to return. Oh no, not to the fields and back-breaking labour! Not to that prison of duty to infant mouths and an ugly husband.

No, I tell myself, I mustn't think too much about that. Now, this is my family, my life. There is Chan who owns all of us, then sisters and mother who keep their eyes trained on me. Ah, Sum Tok, she too had been an ah ku, now she's our kwai po, keeping the books, not having to service customers any more. The men who leave must contend with her, as she guards the only exit downstairs. Pay, her glassy eyes and upright back command, as she sits, empress in her blackwood-and-marble chair. Any trouble, and she has the muscle of the samseng at her command. · Those gangsters! How they can crush arms and skulls so easily with their savage hands.

But Sum Tok doesn't know that tucked underneath the straw mat of my bed, there's two hundred dollars saved from secret tips. Delicious and precious. What will I buy with it?

I hear the rickshaw coolie's bell. Three quick *triing-triing-triings*. Punctual as usual. Sum Tok is letting me visit the gambling den tonight. She knows I stand a good chance of bringing a rich client home.

The coolie takes me to the one I frequent most often. The small room is crowded with mostly labourers and a few of us ah ku. There is a handful of wealthy merchants and shop owners, the towkays who like to cast their fate in with us common people. The smoke of cigarettes and opium is a thick haze blanketing us against this world of sharp risks and swiftly changing fortunes.

A group of coolies are playing Chap-ji-ki, but I'm hungry for the feel of the hard edges of the dice in the hollow of my hand. I roll it, my body thrown into each moment my hand unleashes chance. Nervousness coats the surface of my tongue, chalky taste of face-powder mixed in with sweat. Men like the way greed animates my face. They pause in their gambling, cast sidelong glances at me, their eyes flashing ravenous as the night.

Chat Mui from Number 64 down the street is not here yet. When I saw her this afternoon she said she wasn't sure if she could come tonight. She prefers mahjong. I was startled the first night I saw her face. My attention had strayed briefly, while someone else was throwing the dice. There she was, thirty feet away, oblivious to everyone, even her client for the night, as if all the world existed in the thin mahjong strips in her hand. I saw that her fingers were older than mine, clutching and tossing with a tenacity bred from many years of hardship. Her eyes burned with fever. Whenever she lost that night, I heard her low curses clearly even in the midst of all the raucous voices. She was speaking with an accent I recognized. When she rose from the table, I grabbed my wooden chips, a meagre sum, and walked quickly towards her. Chan wasn't watching, his attention focussed on action at another table. I don't remember what exactly I first said to her, but soon I found out that her village in China was only fourteen li away from mine. Tall and lanky, her body sways with the music of the opium in her veins. Her eyes are unlike mine. They don't conceal her fury.

I enjoy watching her. A private pleasure. When we talk, we return to Toisanese, shedding the impositions of other dialects.

She isn't here tonight. I sweep my gaze through the den once again. Who can I charm this time? Who will return to the brothel with me?

CHOW CHAT MUI

My mother taught me to hold my head up high. "Let your mind be drawn up towards Heaven," she used to say. "Just because you're tall, doesn't mean you shrink down with shame." Don't know where she got that from. Maybe my grandfather, the village storyteller. Even at eighty, he used to sit for hours into the night on a low stool, telling tales about military heroes and wise men while puffing away on his bamboo water pipe. The nights hummed with a chorus of cicadas, masking the sly movements of strangers hiding in the fields. By the light of a single kerosene lamp, he spun his tales with a lazy, confident drawl, the drawl of a mouth missing half its teeth. The moths fluttered towards their ferocious deaths. Whenever I think of moths, the sharp smell of kerosene returns.

I remember Grandfather's kindness. He didn't seem to mind three granddaughters and no grandsons. Not a harsh word for us. But my father was different. He was an angry man who came home late at night after drinking at the inn. Laughing one moment, swearing and hitting my mother the next. Coming into bed in the early morning before the rooster crowed.

I grew tired of living like a captured animal. I was a chicken in a wire cage, slaughtered nightly without bloodshed. At least chickens only die once. I'd heard stories about the North, how the war against the foreigners was not going well, about a mysterious drug called opium. Then there were stories of the Nanyang: the southern ocean and the countries in that region. I heard about Singapore, how it was a land without mountains, a flat landscape completely surrounded by water. I thought to myself, what would it mean to look out towards the horizon and not see mountains, what would it be like to live outside my father's cage?

Finally at twenty-one, I grew tired of waiting for some man to marry me. Always the complaint, *too tall*. I decided to run away with my cousin. Ah Loong and I met in that deep blue darkness before dawn and set off in the direction of the nearest town. It was nearly dusk when we entered it, passing by rundown watchtowers, sentinels that reached up towards Heaven. Ah Loong whispered to me, as if afraid to be heard, that the towers were built in the days of intensive feuding, the Gaos and the Lius killing each other over land and water rights. "When the Gaos caught a Liu, they would crush his head on a grindstone until he was dead. When the Lius caught a Gao, they would steam him in a pottery jug until the eyes popped out. Like a dumpling."

That was just like Ah Loong! Even when we were younger, my cousin fought against his fears by making up the most terrifying stories to tell himself and the rest of us children. His belief? If we can survive the terrors of our imaginations, we can withstand the frightening world around us. I shuddered at the thought of a pair of steamed eyes. Would our fathers know where to look, would they come for us? And would my father blame Ah Loong for taking me away from him?

We spent the days begging for food, and at night we slept in stench-filled alleys, with rats and cockroaches crawling over our stiff bodies. Mosquitoes buzzed, eager for our blood. There were many nights of cold, hard rain. Fists of water pounding us. I passed for a man because of my height. Some days we cleaned stables and fed horses, eating their grain, just to put something into our stomachs.

We were biding time, keeping our ears open for any news of departures to the Nanyang. Then one day we saw a crowd gather at a wall across from the local inn. People were straining to look at a large piece of paper pasted across it. We asked a man to explain what it said.

"For those who want to go overseas, meet here tomorrow, the ninth day of the fifth month, 1900, at six," he said.

A woman of about my mother's age waved her snot-ridden handkerchief at us, urging us to be brave, to become adventurers seeking our fortunes in Southeast Asia. How excited we were! The thought of crossing the vast South China Sea. We were naïve, and hopeful.

The next morning, there were hundreds of us—who knows how many were young women like me in disguise?—a throng of people barely keeping in a line, a creature writhing with nervous anticipation. The putrid odours of fear, the cowardly green smell of piss-soaked trousers, the bruise of bodies fighting for sheer breath. That was all it took, fear and utter desperation to reduce us to acting like pigs. We all fought for the right to be herded away.

There were a few older men and women in their forties or fifties, calm in the midst of our confusion. Their hands were tightly clamped onto the arms or necks of young girls, hands that drained innocence. One of the men in charge asked Ah Loong for his name, wrote it down, told him he would have to pay for the voyage by pulling a rickshaw, three years of labour needed to pay off the debt.

Then it was my turn. He must have suspected when he heard me speak. Ripped off my jacket. Ah Loong tried to fight them, but they took me down to a nearby alley. I heard their grunts and roaring laughter above me, while my body sank into the mud. When they were done, one of them stuffed some papers into my hand and told me I could go, that thanks to them, I would be able to find wealth in the new country.

They piled us into an army of horse-drawn carts, to begin the numb, winding journey to the city of Guangzhou. I saw clouds trailing orange and purple through the sky. A good omen for travel. We passed through the city in the early hours of the morning, eventually stopping at the docks. Then we sailed, starving, in the hold of a junk for endless days like nights, with the suffocating smell of human waste. Air no longer neutral or free. My mother's words echoed in my head. I spat without caring where it would land. I spat whenever her gentle admonitions came to assail me. Shame, what did she know of it? One of the men sitting near me scratched lines into wood with his long fingernail, one mark for every day. By the time we reached Singapore, there were twenty-seven marks. When I stumbled out of that stinking hold, my legs had to learn again how to hold me up.

Easy enough to fool the colonial officers, telling them we had come, brother and sister, to look for the rest of the family. Easy to find the streets where the greatest hunger resides, where men and women slave to buy back some morsel of freedom.

Now, in 1908, on this street alone, there must be nearly forty brothels like the one I work and sleep in. Seven of us here, not counting my kwai po Wong Ah Yee, her cruel son Wong Ah Sek and the servants. Is it possible? I've been an ah ku eight long years already.

First a chicken then a pig now an ah ku. . . .

* * *

In the washroom I peer into the mirror. An early-morning image of myself splattered with toothpaste specks. I rarely clean this surface. Everything else in the apartment is tidy and spotless, as usual. Some days I see Mahmee with her large moon eyes, stunned gaze, and the thick pout of the lower lip protesting the slightest inconvenience. Other days, especially since the suicide, I've started to see Father in the mirror more and more often. His narrow face. The tensions that stretched from the crown to just below the chin, culminating at his Adam's apple. The eyes that shrank with suspiciousness, the lips often dry and cracked. Too much heat in the body.

This face. Today for some reason I feel as if this face in the mirror, this reflection, is not mine.

Here in Canada, I don't need to hunch forward for my whole head to be visible in the bathroom mirror. In this country of the Tall Ang Mos, I'm considered of average height, although certainly not of average looks, being dark-haired, with unplucked eyebrows, soft brown eyes, and a nose that's unassuming.

Back home in Singapore I was considered an anomaly because of my height. Lanky as a teenager, at five foot six, when

15

half my classmates were below five feet. "Here comes the Towering Inferno!" the bullies in the class would exclaim. Is that why I sometimes catch myself hunching when I'm very tired? In this regard, I take after Father, while poor Michael, much to his male chagrin, takes after our dear mother. A thick sensual fleshiness now dangerously on the edge of portliness.

Father was a Dragon, Mahmee a Pig. And they bred a Snake in me, while Michael was born in the Year of the Dog. Which could explain why Michael and Father were the most troubled in their relationship. Michael was often the target of Father's scathing outbursts, whereas Mahmee knew how to handle Father with her indirect strategies, and sought emotional cushioning from friends and acquaintances. Sneaking in a few phone calls while Yen, her husband, was at work. Babbling hurriedly, and then becoming passively pleasant when the man of the house arrived at the end of the day. And me? I took pride in how I dealt with Father. Shrewd and concealing, evading his, or anyone else's, attempts to understand me or my motives.

I open the cabinet door. On the top shelf, Q-Tips, a tensor bandage for the knee, a tube of antiseptic cream leaning into a small bag of cotton balls, and a brown plastic bottle of hydrogen peroxide. The middle shelf is completely different: orderly, almost militantly so. Bottles of pills, all with the labels facing front. Left to right: acetaminophen, ibuprofen, vitamins A, B6, B12, C, E, and zinc lozenges. If I swallow all these pills, the worst thing that'll probably happen is that I'll get a bit nauseated. They won't be able to kill me. Lowest level: toothbrush, toothpaste, dental floss, unwaxed. I grab the toothbrush and begin to brush my teeth.

What does a body feel when it has ingested hundreds of sleeping pills? What does a body know after it has been taken too far into a choice that prevents escape?

Father's difficulty sleeping was an extension of his waking restlessness. While sitting at a table, legs crossed, his top leg would twitch with nervousness, and those vibrations often travelled to the table. Hence his rationale for the brandy in the evening, feet up on the ottoman, head receding into the beige crochet piece covering the top of his armchair.

So many ways of killing oneself. Just the other day, standing on the platform at Broadway station, waiting for the Skytrain, it occurred to me that all it would take was one split second. Irreversible. Fatal.

But it isn't that kind of dramatic dying that holds my deepest attention. Anonymity intrigues me far more than the newspaper headliners. The silent dying that eventually collapses a person in the middle of the afternoon while sipping strong black coffee, casually glancing out the window, or while waiting for the bus.

And the death that someone like my father eventually chooses, bottles of sleeping pills. I'm relieved he chose pills. Had he decided he was going to kill himself when he phoned me less than forty-eight hours before he overdosed? All he said in his message on my answering machine was "Wu Lan . . . it's Father . . . I want to talk to you." When I got home from work and heard this message, I couldn't believe it. Mahmee was the one who usually phoned, who passed the phone over to Father only after she had satisfied her curiosity. I was shocked to hear his familiar, tight voice, yet I wasn't jumping to phone back. I thought, I'll phone on the weekend.

I never will know if I could have made a difference. What if I had been home when he called? If only I didn't hesitate, let myself interrupt him at work, what with the time difference. When I saw him in his coffin, his closed eyes, his lifeless body accused me. But I've told no one. Not even Mahmee or Michael.

His wordless, private suicide. Unlike the horror of public spectacles. I remember the revulsion I felt as a teenager when I stared out our kitchen window, down at the sight of a woman who had jumped off the top floor of the block of flats behind us. She was a speck, an insect, a collapsed heap of bones and muscle. Bodies vibrated with anxiety and shock around her. I wasn't upset only by the way she killed herself. I was disturbed that she exposed strangers to her tragedy in such a public way. Even though I'd laughed at Mahmee's and Mah-Mah's tendencies to quote superstitious beliefs, I couldn't help but worry that the woman's ghost might linger in the spaces nearby, in the parking lot, the corridors, infecting the nights with her unspeakable despair.

But Father took the slow path, building up to the silent finale. Hennessy, Johnny Walker, Barcadi Rum, and the pills he used to help him sleep: Valium and Imovane. Hardly betraying his intoxication with any kind of inflammatory behaviour. Except when he lost it with Michael. Towards Mahmee and me, he was usually distant and polite. Except sometimes late at night, if he was still up watching TV in our living room, and if I was on the way from my room to the kitchen or the washroom, he would try to engage me in conversation. That was when he let his defences down and could be maudlin. Talking about his mother, my Grandmother Neo, with the soft hysteria of a child who had permanently lost his way.

With the toothbrush back in its place and the cabinet door closed, I walk into the kitchen. There are so many weapons of destruction here. Knives to expose the inner body to the rest of the world, to cut one loose from secrets. The gas oven, à la Sylvia Plath. The bottle of Javex. I open the refrigerator. Stare blankly at the eggs lying loosely contained in the separate chambers of the refrigerator door. Until I settle on one egg, its brownness bland yet comforting. The pink stamped words on it seem out of place: FREE RANGE. A paradox. This egg, beseiged by its own helplessness, at the mercy of human interference. Waiting, all it can do, waiting to be consumed.

I pick out a couple of eggs, leaving that particular one alone for now, and make myself a breakfast omelette with onions and tomatoes. I'm just starting to eat when the phone rings.

"Lan-Lan? How? Everything okay?" Her voice comes through with a sudden, shocking loudness, a consequence of her impaired hearing.

"Mahmee. No need to call so often!" I shout back to make

sure she hears me. She's been phoning practically once a week since I returned to Vancouver from the funeral.

"Don't worry lah! You sleeping okay? Anything bother you?"

I sigh quietly, feeling exasperated. What do I say to her? *Oh yes, Father killing himself.* Instead I mumble, "Fine, nothing. Fine." But I feel guilty, caught in the act, as if Mahmee might have sensed I just had been punishing myself with numerous recollections of the past.

"Your father . . ."

"Yes?"

"He still come kachau me."

"What do you mean?"

"He come, Lan-Lan, he come late at night. I don't like." Her voice now sounds small, with a timidity I've seldom heard from Mahmee. I figure out, with the sixteen hours' time difference, that it must be past eleven PM Singapore time.

"Are you taking those pills your GP gave you?"

"Crazy?" Her voice is loud again, ending the question at a slightly higher pitch. She continues, "You think I want to take pills after Father wipe himself out like that?"

What can a daughter say to that? Mahmee asks me once again about my health, and after a few more reassurances that I'm fine, we hang up.

Even though it's already been several months since the suicide, neither Michael nor his wife Susan have tried to talk directly with me. Mahmee herself tells even more stories about the past, as if this is her way of dealing with it. Sometimes I get a note in the mail. Or it's a little speech on the phone. I wonder if she's going to send me an audio tape next time. I'm guilty of avoiding the issue. Ironically, for someone who works in this trade, a crucible for confession of secrets and illusions, I don't find it easy to talk about my deepest experiences. The more painful or profound an experience, the less I'm able to speak of it. I'm waiting for someone else in my family to take the initiative, to broach the topic of Father's suicide. Had they seen any warning signs?

But that's ridiculous. If any of us had known or suspected, could we have made a difference? The rest of my family has to bear the guilt of having been right there and helpless. And I? It was difficult going back to seeing clients after returning from the funeral. If I couldn't help Father, how could I help my clients? Of course I tried to reason with myself, but it didn't help. It didn't change the way I felt.

I'm guilty of distancing. First, I left the country. Then I came out to Mahmee, Father and Michael in a joint letter, announcing not only that I was lesbian, had been for thirteen years, but also that I was living with Kim, my lover at that time. It wasn't until I believed I was in a stable relationship that I felt ready to come out to them. Shortly after I sent them the letter, Michael called me up, said he didn't understand how people became homosexual, but he respected that I needed to, as he put it, "separate from the herd."

Ever since the "Big Shock"—that's how Mahmee refers to that time—she has kept talking about her longing for a grandchild. And Father's response? He had never said a word to me about the letter. Such a silent, sullen man. But he loved to sing, didn't he? And he loved his mad collection.

* * *

MAHMEE

Lan-Lan so secretive. Once in a blue moon, she say something. Rest of the time, quiet. A bit like Yen. Lucky she not a drinker. Burning tears come to my face thinking how bad-tempered my husband was, and my chest feel like a lorry come along and crushed it. When my daughter speak, she say so little, as if she stand very far away from me, on a beach on the other side, calling out to me, but her shouting reach me only as softly as the pillows I sleep on every night. You have to shout, Lan-Lan, I tell her all the time. I'm deaf from old age. Don't hear too well. Phone line make it worse, thousands of miles of noise.

Imagine, she don't want to get married. Now I don't dare ask if she had any intercourse, God forbid, I don't even want to think about it. What do women do together? This my child? A beautiful woman who don't want . . . I don't understand. What she do with women? That person she lived with all that time, I don't even get chance to see her face and question her!

A lot we can tell from the face. Good fortune, bad fortune, cunning or honesty, short life or long one. Everything in the face.

But Lan-Lan far away in Canada, and I don't see her face, cannot tell many things. Can only guess from letters, from phone calls.

Now Yen gone. I spend time in our flat talking to myself a lot. Try to keep busy. Not used to empty flat. Floors get dusty so quick, must clean all the time. Yen's mess in storeroom, I don't want to look. Too soon, too much!

I cannot sleep. I thought it help me to call my daughter. But what she do? Tell me to take those pills! Will he come again tonight to bother me? I don't want to close my eyes. He always disturb me just when I'm about to fall asleep.

* * *

LEE AH CHOI

It was late in the afternoon and the cicadas were loud. I was outside our mud-brick hut taking dry clothes off the line. A woman had come to speak with my father. I could hear that she wanted both me and my sister Ah Fong, but for some reason—I could not hear all that was said—I was the only one sold. For the price of three sacks of rice. She handed him a piece of paper, said she would come collect me in a few days' time. She told him I would be able to return once I finished paying back the money for the passage. At twenty I would be a kong chu, with no rights over my own body. What choice did I have? That auntie now owned me.

The day I was taken away, it was raining. A light, quiet drizzle, green fields momentarily blessed, my brothers and Ah Fong crying in the doorway, my mother with arms outstretched blocking their squirming attempts to reach me. She looked through me as if her eyes couldn't find me, while my father was a mere shadow retreating into the house. The large, smooth hand of my owner's greed grasped my small, cold one. I remember how her grip never left my body for more than a few minutes at a time. Even now, thinking about it, I can feel the pressure of her touch on my shoulder. In the junk, she coached me what to tell the officers when we reached Singapore. *Looking for my parents and brother who are here. Yes, she's my auntie. No, I'm not going to become an ah ku.* All I could do was repeat the words. Holding down that choking feeling in the throat. Some of the men in the dark, stinky hold of the junk watched me rehearsing my story with eyes that wanted to drown me in their gaze.

What a miserable voyage across the South China Sea. There were too many of us squeezed together with hardly any room to lie down to rest. A few curled up against the pile of coals at one end. One day, towards the end of our journey, there was a horrible accident. The coal ignited spontaneously and caught the skin and clothes of a girl. She burned down to a char right in front of our eyes, while the others closest to her frantically scrambled away from the disaster. The horrid smell as the flames consumed her! Nowhere to run, except against and over each other's bodies, until we all sensed the end of the danger.

The sailors fed us gruel that was even more watery than what I ate in my parents' home. In the first week, my stomach cried out in need, like a petulant child, but towards the end of the journey, it became hard like a fist, turned into itself.

I remember how crisp the air was when we stepped onto the wharf in Singapore, finally free to enter the city. The air smelled of fresh grass and wet bark. Must have stopped raining just before the junk reached the harbour. It was July 1906. Has it been only two years? In the horse-drawn carriage from the harbour, I was so nervous that all I could do was keep staring down at the road as we were moving along. Where was she taking me?

The streets were muddy and dark red, something I'd never seen before. Darker than earth, and more slippery with the rain.

The chaotic sounds of many strange languages swirled around me. I was frightened. It was all I could do to keep looking down until the carriage stopped and a man's voice boomed, "Welcome, welcome!" That was how I met Chan, a short, dark man with a gold tooth right in the front. In the early morning sunlight, the tooth flashed boldly at me.

The auntie hustled me through the entrance, following after Chan. He led us into a large hall. Along one wall there were a couple of elaborately carved chairs with a piece of marble the shape of a half moon set into the back. Above the chairs was a silk hanging crowded with all kinds of birds I'd never seen before. I looked up at the ceiling. A large, upturned flower of shiny shapes. My mouth must have gaped for such a long time that Chan laughed.

"Never seen one before? Chan-de-lia ahh! Named after me! That's why I win the house from white man."

I heard tittering from somewhere off to the left, ahead of me. Some faces peered at me from behind the spindles of a staircase. Then I heard a crackling voice call out to me from another part of the room. I turned towards this voice. She was partially hidden in the shadows.

"Eh, come here and let me have a better look."

When I moved closer, I could smell something strong coming from her person. Like smoke from a wood stove, but sweeter, as if sugar was leaking from her clothes into the moist air.

"From now on, I'm your kwai po. Understand?"

Later I learned from the sisters the name they secretly used for her. Sum Tok, a heart full of poison. None of us knows her real name, so why not call her what we see in her? But to her face we address her as Kwai Po, our den-mother.

So quickly I was exchanged, passed from one set of hands to another. Chan made some loud smacking noises with his lips. I shrank away from him, more out of shock at the unfamiliar gesture than anything else.

Sum Tok called out to the women on the staircase, "Come meet your new sister!"

There were five of them, all so different. Two actual sisters who'd been sold together, Sui Yuen and Sui Peng, fair-skinned with small mouths and eyes that disappeared easily with each smile. Ah Leen, whose hair was braided and rolled up into buns on either side of her head. Lan Ho, the most attractive of them all because of her wide hips and tottering walk. I recognized that walk. My sister Ah Fong had it. Finally there was Loke Kum. How could I forget? I disliked her from the very first glance. Her mouth was in a permanent pout, while her eyes betrayed no hint of liveliness.

After the quick introductions, I broke down in tears, thinking of my old home. I felt the heat and oiliness of hands descend, trying to comfort me. I was nudged up the stairs and shown to my cubicle. There was a bed along one wall, a spittoon underneath it, a few hooks hanging from a pipe that ran along the ceiling. An empty kerosene lamp sat on a wooden crate next to the bed. Who had lived here? I turned to ask someone but they all had left noiselessly. A rat scampered out from under the bed and into the hallway.

I'd never had a room to myself before this cubicle. I sat down on the bed and placed my cloth bundle down beside me. I decided I would sit there until someone came to tell me what I had to do next.

Chow Chat Mui

The younger ones make fun of me. "Too ugly, too tall, too sour-faced, you dried-up cunt!" They even call me mui-tsai, pretend I'm just another domestic servant. They've no idea what it's like to be a dirt rag for so many years. So what if I don't keep myself as clean as them? Can't fool me, they're scared of looking ugly some day. Clean on the outside, but deep inside, they're full of dirt, the bitches!

I don't care what they say. Let my face remind them of their fate. Besides, an old rag like me knows how to keep strong. Seen many pretty ones succumb to the sex-disease, or to their own foolish excesses. Taking opium as if they're invincible, as if opium could erase those cuts the disease makes on their skins.

I don't look into the mirror any more. Doesn't matter, I don't get the rich clients. This dirt is my outer skin, ever since that time I rose up from the mud eight years ago, after the men tore into me. My skin soaked up an extra shadow then.

I still remember that first day here. When we reached Singapore, the officers came on board and questioned us. A burst of questions barked at us. After our successful lies, Ah Loong and I were pushed down the gangplank along with the crowd. The sun was setting, a heavy, ripe melon. I saw a man grab Ah Loong's arm and lead him down the wharf. My cousin whipped his head around to catch sight of me. I had never seen him so terrified as he looked then, his eyes almost popping out of his face. I tried to follow, but there were many people pushing, adding quickly to the distance between us. I panicked. What would I do without Ah Loong?

I didn't have time to sink too deeply into my fear. A tall, large man grabbed me by the shoulders and turned me towards the other side of the street.

"Over there! Women to the other side!" he bellowed at us.

I looked and saw a row of rickshaws and horse-drawn carriages, mostly empty. A few men stood nearby, staring at the crowd of people leaving the junk. It was then that my eyes were drawn to a man in one of the rickshaws. He sat upright in the seat, while the coolie squatted a few feet away, smoking. The man wore an unusual hat. Light yellow with a narrow brim, and a strip of black cloth around it. His black and white shoes gleamed in the last rays of the sun. I'd never seen anyone dressed like that before.

It seemed to take me forever to cross the street. Along with the crowds, there were also the bullock carts to be careful of, as they ambled along, the animals large and foul-tempered. I turned my head in the direction where I last saw Ah Loong. He was gone. Absorbed into the moving mass of deepening silhouettes. Where could I go now? My legs felt awkwardly stiff, like pieces of bamboo. I almost fell forward as I approached the rickshaw. The man had climbed out and was now standing.

"Looking for someone?" he asked in a unfamiliar accent, but I understood what he was saying. I must have looked stupid, with my mouth half open, my hands crossed over my chest, and my cloth bundle slung over my left shoulder.

"Looking for my cousin. Down there." I pointed nervously.

"Oh, another rickshaw coolie." He laughed, a succession of thunderous bursts. I felt the urge to run away. Run back to the junk and beg to be taken back. But the man did something so shocking that I was rivetted to the spot. He pulled out some coins from his pocket and threw them down at my feet.

"Money for you. Take it."

"But why? I don't understand."

"You come from a village near Guangzhou?"

"Yes. . . ." My eyes flitted from his face to the ground where the coins lay, and back to his face again. A young man, my age, a good-looking face with animal eyes that flashed in the night. Except the skin on his left cheek was like the rough bark of a tree, crinkled as if it had been chewed up. But his eyes. I saw my grandfather's look as he told those stories by lamplight.

"You have your papers from the other side? The homeland?"

I nodded.

"Give them to me. I will keep them, and make sure you earn money to pay for your journey."

"How? What must I do?"

He walked up to me, didn't touch me, but stood so close I could smell his clothes and his breath. I'd never smelled anyone like this before. Sweet airiness of smoke and fragrant night-flowers, scents that promised adventure. He whispered carefully into my ear. Things I had to do to men. Or let them do to me. What he was saying reminded me of what my father did. I didn't even know this man, and here he was telling me all those secret things. I started to giggle, and then, from somewhere deep inside, a loud, bellowing laugh. My body shook under the recollection and the irony. Some things hadn't changed, even though I had made the long, difficult journey. Ah Loong and I escaped under such trying circumstances, then to lose each other the moment we land in Singapore, and this man was asking me to do the same things my father wanted from me!

He was taken aback. "Wah . . . such spirit!" His hand reached out and squeezed my breast.

This was how I first met Wong Ah Sek. I bent down to pick up the shiny coins.

* * *

I watch *Last Tango in Paris*. Missed it when it first came out because it was banned in Singapore. I switch off the TV just as the credits come on, and catch myself sighing heavily as if suffering from an inner revulsion. Like the nausea that's triggered by the sight or smell of a particular food.

Something about the connection between sex and death. An instantaneous and gut-wrenching sensation, when I realized that Father was about Brando's age in the movie when I left Singapore for Toronto. Unfortunately, Maria Schneider's luscious body wasn't enough to ward off the upset from this association. The memory of Father in his coffin flashed through my mind.

The way Father and Mahmee related to each other in front of us, we would never have suspected they were sexual beings. Other than the one time I saw them groping behind the door when I was about eight, I'd never seen them display any affection towards each other.

I push myself to imagine my parents in bed. Did he please her? Did she enjoy sex with him? These prove to be unsatisfying fantasies. I get up and switch on the lamp at my desk. Glance at the photo: Kim and me together the day we became lovers. I can't quite remember that person I was, the one who looked so absolutely vital and happy. Ah, the drug of being in love. It had kept me going for a long time, kept me unaware of Kim's dissatisfaction. "Lan, I want a family, a husband." But why did she have to pick Daniel? It has been difficult in these past three years, going to work and seeing him practically every day in the coffee room, at staff meetings, in the hallway between therapy sessions with our clients. No longer spending time together talking about our work, the way we used to.

Kim. I loved her sunny, energetic nature. She had a talent for finding something positive to say about almost every difficult situation. But when she heard from our mutual friends that my father had committed suicide, she left a message on the answering machine that was awkward and filled with silences.

I keep telling myself it's time to put the photo away. It's covered with a thin veneer of dust. I turn the photo face down and switch off the light.

I wake up to fragments of a dream. Father asked Maria Schneider if she had remembered to deposit the salary cheque. The way he would every month with Mahmee. When Maria tried to touch him or walk towards him, he withdrew the way a child does when he expects to be slapped or pinched. In the next fragment, Father was no longer in the room, but it was me instead, sitting in an armchair draped with a crimson fabric. Naked, legs crossed, leaning towards Maria, who was dressed the way I used to for work, in black pants and jacket with a fuschia silk shirt underneath. She sat on the floor facing me. I plied her with questions, "Why did you sleep with him? Were you in love with him?" and then the last question, "Why did you leave me?" I can't recall any of her answers. In fact, she mumbled, sounding uncannily like Brando.

I climb out of bed before too long, not wanting to get bogged down thinking about the dream. At nine-thirty, I'm out the door, catching the bus to the library. It's been a challenge to relinquish sole ownership of the car, but I've also liked sharing it with Dom and Gerry. Two days after Remembrance Day, and it's as if the ritual never happened. Only one red poppy on the whole bus. The moving room buzzing with ordinary lives. I eavesdrop on the conversation between two young men, Gen-X types. Both of them have stylishly cropped hair, treated with expensive hair products to give the just-so details of structure, spikes and shine. The cloying smell of Calvin Klein fragrance. *To Be*, or not. The white guy sports a thick layer of mud along the edges of his Doc Martens, and wears a dark blue bomber jacket over loose jeans with a loud "Diesel" label flashing from his bum. The Asian guy stands at almost right angles to his friend. Extreme faux macho. I catch a flash of the white letters "D & G" on his open black jacket, over a black knitted crew-necked top and black jeans.

"Did you watch it live? The building gave way like a pack of cards."

"So I heard. Pretty amazing, huh?"

"A few well-placed sticks of dynamite in the basement. That's where you've got to score, man, deep down in the bowels."

"Yeah, right."

That was a few weeks ago. I'd watched a news snippet on BCTV. A twenty-three-storey apartment building at Alberni decimated in a matter of seconds. The shocking transformation into a ton of rubble.

I study these two young men's faces with a touch of curiosity and envy, especially the Asian guy. Apparently when Father was in his early twenties, he was a very sought-after bachelor. Slim, with chiselled features and bright, penetrating eyes. Mahmee liked to describe the man she had married in this way. This was not the father I remember. Father's eyes had been distant, as if they belonged to someone else, or to another time and place. They squinted down to pinhole size, as if at the overbearing sun, whenever someone in the family did something he didn't approve of. This was enough to warn us to apologize, or change our behaviour quickly, if we wanted to be spared his annoyance.

I remember one particular incident. The principal of Michael's school phoned and spoke to Father. Michael had been caught smoking in the boys' toilet. When he arrived home, walking through the door with his schoolbag strap flat against his forehead, the weight of his books counterbalanced by his jaw-clenching determination, Father didn't go up to speak to him, but waited in the living room, in his armchair. He began with his squinting, then in a very controlled voice, he addressed me, ignoring Michael's presence. "You haven't watched out enough for your brother, and now he's going to get lung cancer, thanks to your neglect." His face reddened, his mouth tensed into a thin, unwavering line, and his body became very still and stiff, as if refusing to be moved by anyone else's presence.

Secretly I was angry, but I merely shrugged my shoulders, feigning indifference.

Mahmee finally said, "Yen, he try something new, all teenagers try, you remember yourself at fifteen?"

Father glared at her, his eyes momentarily flashing with a directness seldom seen, and then, slipping into Singlish: "Me? Got to be kidding! I too busy trying to stay alive during the war, what you think? I was living on leftovers from pineapples I sold. You forget!"

Then he turned back to face Michael and said, "You! Bodoh or what? Tobacco eat up your lungs and your wallet!"

Michael broke down in tears and went into his room. Mahmee followed to comfort him. I stayed seated at the table, staring at my fingernails, bitten to ragged edges. Then I opened one of my textbooks and pretended to read. I always kept my cool. That was how I fooled them into believing Father never got to me.

Maybe Father the bachelor was happier than the man I knew. I look back at the Gen-X boys, wonder if they have steady girl-friends, how many times a week they have sex. I sigh, feeling a growing heavy ache spread across my toes and creep up my legs.

At the corner of Burrard and Robson, a gust of wind sends down a sudden shower of dancing leaves. I glance up at the library. Very soon it will be haunted with absence, all its contents moved to a new location. Then it remains to be seen if the people in power will decide whether to demolish it or to let it be occupied with another kind of life.

In the musty comfort of the library, I return to the journal in which I had found the article about a month ago. What had drawn me then? It concerned women who had left Mainland China and Japan from the late 1800s to the mid-twentieth century, women who landed in Singapore and were indentured to the sex trade to pay off debts. Some had been sold by their families, while others willingly sold their bodies. Many of the women had committed suicide in response to the utter misery of their livelihood and the suffering they experienced from diseases like gonorrhea and syphilis. Looking at the article again, I reread the first few lines, explaining that the term "ah ku" was a polite way to address a Chinese sex-trade worker. I hadn't known that before. This second time I read the article, I wonder if the author, a social historian, has published anything else. I locate one of his books. It's newly bound in red, the pages still pristine white. I sit down clumsily on a library stool, making a loud, awkward land-ing. A woman giggles to my right.

She is a youngish post-hippie type, probably in her early twenties, with a carrot-dyed buzz cut and lots of silver on both earlobes. Her ugly neon green and yellow plaid pants hang down from small hips like two postal tubes. I stare at her until she speaks up.

"Aren't books sexy?" Another giggle.

"Yes," I say tentatively, not feeling ready for this direct challenge. She isn't my type yet a prickly sensation arrives at the back of my neck. She's come quite close and is peering over my shoulder, breathing into my book. I shut the book abruptly, and startle both of us. "Excuse me, but—"

"Do you think I'm too forward?"

I remain silent.

"You had the most interesting expression on your face as you were looking at the book. I couldn't resist."

I stare at the curves of her left ear. "Oh? What kind of a look?"

"Mmm . . . very, very deeply engaged. And engaging." She pouts charmingly and continues, "Are you from Hong Kong?"

"No. I'm from here."

"Oh, just that the accent. . . ."

"I left Singapore twenty years ago. I'm Canadian now."

"Is that why you're reading a book on . . . ," she cocks her head to read, "*Ah Ku and Karayuki-San: Prostitution in Singapore 1870-1940?*"

"I guess so."

"I live nearby. Why don't you come by? We'll have tea, and you can tell me more."

I follow her out the door of the library, after checking out the book. Her name is Stephanie, and she lives only a few blocks away, in the heart of the busy West End. We walk along Robson, holding our coats shut against the wind. The crowd bustles around us with their brand-name shopping bags, their assortment of blank or focussed expressions, body perfumes drifting in and out of my range of smell. I don't care about the chill. All I care about right now is the possibility I can slip out of my clothes and into the arms of another human being, and lose this aching sensation.

* * *

MAHMEE

My daughter away from home a long time now. Twenty years. She say she wants to come back but every year, same story. Not good enough jobs here in Singapore for her qualifications. Still not understand why she left Singapore. At first, I told her, stay here, study at the Uni, why go? Michael stay, study Econ, then he work good job. Marry Susan, hard-working girl, soon can have my first grandchild. But I tell Michael wait, one hundred days at least, three hundred even better. Then we can take off our mourning patches. Sometimes I hide mine in my handbag when I go out, put it back on at home. As long it go with me everywhere. I don't like strangers know what happened to him.

At our market nearby, people like Mee Rebus man who used to see Yen go twice a week, sometimes more, to eat his mee in the morning, now he of course wonder what happened. I tell him Yen go away on business trip, then I quickly rush off in case he want to know more.

The ones who know he died, they a bit nosy but what I say, he died peacefully in his sleep. Most people not professional busy-bodies. I don't like too many difficult questions. If I have to, I lie.

Lan-Lan said must go study psychology in Canada, only four years, then come back be a reporter. So what happened? Another school gave her money to study some more. What good is it for a girl to study many years, no man wants her afterward, I used to say. Look at her now . . . no man wants her, I was right. Why she do this to herself?

Too much studying make her brain go funny. Like the dirty water in the drains after monsoon. Or maybe she has wind in the head, make her do strange things. Does she dry her hair after shampoo? That wind is dangerous. I don't know if wind in Vancouver worse or what, but if it is humid and hair wet, then head can catch wind, became weak.

Big Shock. First the letter where she tell us her horrible secret, how can? I still keep that letter, take it out to look at it once in a while. My Lan-Lan doing strange things without man in her life. Don't understand. I don't tell her how khek sim I am, my heart so sick with worry. She is like me now, no hubby to wake up to, no one to cook for, just talk to myself all day all night. Good thing Michael here, and Susan always cook something tasty for Sunday dinner. Wu Lan, be a good girl. Eat well, sleep well, take Brand's Essence of Chicken. Must remember to say that in the next letter.

* * *

LEE AH CHOI

My kwai po Sum Tok arrived with a beautifully embroidered red robe draped over her arms, carefully extending her fingers so as to keep her nails away from the precious material.

"Downstairs, to the end of the hallway. Next to the kitchen. A tub of hot water is waiting for you. Go clean yourself thoroughly."

She placed the robe down next to me and left. I followed after her. The sisters were nowhere to be seen. Kwai Po returned to her throne, and nodded in the direction I was to go. An old man was hunched over a large steaming tub, towels in hand. A woman's undergarments were draped over his shoulder. I blushed with surprise, and he gestured to me to take off my dirty clothes. I shook my head in protest.

"All right then, I will turn my back, and hand you the towels and clothes when you are ready."

I had no choice. I walked to the other side of the tub and, half-crouching, I slowly took off my clothes. The water was scalding hot. I screamed. The old man extended an arm backwards with a small washcloth.

"Here, scrub hard," he admonished.

Then the large towels. Two of them. And the undergarments, which were a bit loose on me.

"Upstairs," came his next command, without looking back, as he hobbled away and turned into a room off the kitchen.

I walked past Sum Tok, who was no longer sitting erect. She was reclining on a fancy bed, her head on a dark red bolster, her eyelids half-closed, sometimes flickering. The empress was gone, and in her place, an ordinary peasant savoured a few moments of rest. Her hands were curled like an infant's around a pipe. Smoke escaped from one end of it, one cloud trailing another, while her lips sucked at the other end. Puff, puff puff went her aging, flabby cheeks.

"Eh, now for the flower plucking!" She cackled at me, like a hen gone mad before an impending storm.

When I entered my cubicle, Chan was waiting for me on the bed. "Time for your new life, I will show you, come." His gold tooth flashed again, this time with a greedy menace. He grabbed my arm, pulling me towards him. He held my face in his hand with a firm and painful grasp. My legs trembled. Then the earth began to shake and echo with every move of his body against mine.

CHOW CHAT MUI

Silence in the house. Everyone still asleep. I look out the window in the hallway.

The new land! So flat, without the mountains familiar in my childhood. Still not used to the absence of those sleeping dragons, grand and immovable. They say that this flat land once swelled with lions. Where are they now? I squint, half-hoping they'll suddenly emerge. Instead, I detect a haze in the distance. Omen of yet another hot and humid day.

I look down at the alley. No one there. Ah Choi must be still asleep. I can hear her if she's taking her daily morning bath in their courtyard, because she likes to sing.

Back to my cubicle. My haven. Little has changed. The same narrow bed, only inches longer than my body. As a tap tang, it took me four years to pay for the passage from the homeland to this new country. Now I pay for food and lodging and a new set of clothes each year. I pay my dues to Wong Ah Yee, Ah Sek's mother, and she pays the samseng to protect me. What are they but a nuisance to us? Hired hoods, watching us like hawks. Their eyes must tire of staring at an old rag like me.

When I first began as an ah ku, under the spell of opium and Wong Ah Sek's charm, I thought my escape was complete. I'd never known such freedom. The ways my body opened, the ways I learned to use it to pleasure a man. Ah Sek taught me how to be bold with a man's lust. An ah ku is powerful in ways that a wife never could be. I learned the various positions of sex acts, that there are many ways for a woman and a man to lie together. Not the routine ways my father touched me, while I lay still, doing nothing. The more I learned, the more hopeful I became. I had acquired the powers that would guarantee my freedom. In a world where men's hungers are never sufficiently satiated by their well-mannered wives. Phee! Those women who cannot stand the smell of their armpits and their wet sex mouths!

Whenever I learned something new from Ah Sek, I rose up from the mud of those strangers who used me that fateful day in 1900. Something else . . . do I dare admit it? Tenderness, a soothing breeze, stirring a woman's body, when she's loved. I thought Ah Sek was devoted to me. Surely he would urge his mother to take special care of me. Foolish, I acted as if it was going to last forever. I should have guessed why his mother gave him that name: forever hungry, forever eating. He devoured my sex until there was only vileness left. Many women have had their turns with Ah Sek since he trained me. It's Sew Lan these days. A woman learns after eight years, watching the man's actions, that she mistook his necessary acts of survival for something personal, as if his attention meant she was special.

* * *

We take the clunky 1950s elevator up to the eleventh floor. Its black buttons are scratchy from age, the white in some of the numbers faded or completely gone. The elevator door opens with a double jolt. I follow Stephanie down the hallway, with orange and brown checkered carpeting, to the last door on the right. The living room has a pale yellow couch stacked with piles of books. Two ashtrays filled with cigarette butts sit on an armrest. No, Father definitely wouldn't have approved. And with that thought, I feel triumphant. I am supposed to be here, it was the right thing to do.

"So, do you live alone?"

She laughs lightly and touches my wrist. "No, I don't."

I wasn't expecting this.

"He's very . . . uh . . . cool. You'll see, just wait."

She strides up to the bedroom, knocks once, then enters. I try to see who's in there but can't. A muffle of voices.

The living room walls are covered with lots of newspaper clippings, mostly classified ads, and profiles on people famous in the arts or politics who had died recently. There are also charts, each with a circle on the top half, with different symbols within its divided segments. On the lower half of each page, columns with the same symbols and abbreviations, PLU, URN, SAT, NEP, and so on.

She emerges from the bedroom followed by a guy. He's probably not much older than Stephanie, same body type. A clean-cut blond, his blue eyes liquid and dreamy, partially hidden underneath small gold-rimmed glasses, his lean body sheathed in a wine-coloured Indian blouse, and loose indigo silk pants.

"Dale, this is—"

"Wu Lan."

"Oh. As in Maxine Hong Kingston's *The Woman Warrior*?"

It takes me a few seconds to figure out what he means. "Oh no, that was Mu Lan."

"Stephanie says she found you in the library, looking lonely." He smiles a slight but comfortable smile, as if he just made the most ordinary comment on meeting someone for the first time.

"What are these?" I ask, staring at Stephanie, then Dale.

"Astrological charts. That's what I do for a living."

"Looks quite complicated."

"Yes and no. I could do one for you, if you like." He raises an eyebrow, perhaps to emphasize some doubt that I would be interested.

She walks towards me, brushing past him, and touches the inner crease of my right elbow. I release a soft sigh and, to my surprise, feel tears come up to my eyes. How foolish of me to follow a stranger home. And with her boyfriend here, I feel even more exposed.

Stephanie takes my hand gently in hers and whispers, "Come with me."

"What about . . ." I look at her then at him, wondering what they mean by all this. With pulse racing, I follow her without resisting. I need to surrender, to stop worrying what to do next.

The bedroom is bare except for an amber beaded lamp on the floor and a queen-sized futon on a black bedframe. The curtains are drawn shut. Light filters through, softly permeating the simple space with a netherworld feeling. It reminds me of that sensation I sometimes have swimming underwater for a long time, an inner stillness, confident that the presence of others would not be able to upset that peace. Would Dale say that's because I'm a Pisces? Or perhaps he isn't that literal. I hear him moving about in the living room, then the opening and closing of the main door to the apartment.

"Lie down and let me hold you."

"Where did you learn to be so brassy?"

She doesn't answer. I take off my coat and sit down on the bed, and after a few minutes of resistance, place my head on the purple pillow. She takes off my shoes and hoists my legs onto the bed. My legs feel heavy, far away and disconnected from my tired brain. During the sixties there used to be a weekly TV program in which a magician levitated his assistant by first lifting her feet off the ground, then waving his hand over her legs. Voilà, she was no longer earthbound, but a bird riding on the crest of a rising air current.

Her hand strokes my hair, a slow, calming rhythm. The magic trick isn't working because my body is only becoming progressively heavier, sinking into the bed. I close my eyes, feeling a tug towards sleepiness. Tears begin to seep through my eyelids, roll down my face, finding their way into my left ear.

"I lost—"

Too carelessly, the words spill out. I stop myself from finishing the confession. This would be too much, to admit that my father's death is enough to make me do risky, irrational things, like following a stranger home, ending up on her bed in tears.

She remains silent, but her hand is attentive, present, as if it has become an organ of receptivity, brushing my hair for thoughts, as if they would leak out of my brain and be caught up in her kind hand.

* * *

Lee Ah Choi

I stared at his gold tooth in his dirty, wide-open mouth when he pushed me down onto the straw mat. His hand pushed against my belly and moved down quickly to separate my legs. The red robe slipped off the bed and onto the floor. His breathing was so heavy that it squeezed out all the air in my chest. The painful glitter of his gold tooth as he pushed himself into me!

Imagine, sitting in the cubicle like a piece of wood for hours after Chan had plucked my flower. A storm had overtaken me and churned its wicked disasters through me. When he left, I sat up slowly and retrieved the red robe from the floor. I wrapped my shivering body in it. The storm was so strong and sudden that I had to be very still afterwards to survive its wrath.

I'm no longer that frightened girl. I was twenty years old and very naïve. Now I'm just another one of Chan's dainty blossoms. Opening to each night's demands. But the day is mine, to wander the streets nearby. I don't stare at the streets as I did that first day with such bewilderment. Now I teach myself to find the gold and the money lurking in men's eyes. Much to find for those of us who know how to look.

But in this heat that won't be cooled by winds, my vision is clouded by a perpetual haze that floats above ground, stretching ahead of me for miles. I must strain my eyes so! Red dust stirred up from the streets by strong winds. Whose idea to make streets like this? When it rains, the street is a red stream, and when it's dry season, we choke with the dust. Why couldn't they let the earth remain underneath our feet?

I know these streets of Chinatown well. I'm sure I can find my way through them blindfolded. This afternoon I walk down past North Canal Road to Boat Quay to be intoxicated with the smells and sounds of a busy river. Tongkangs ply the river, or line up side-by-side, moored. Cradles lulled by gentle waves. A few bullock carts crowd right at the edge, the animals impatient while the coolies load up with goods from the boats. In my black samfu, without makeup,

I easily pass for an amah, just an ordinary servant of the household. But a coolie unloading large bags of rice from one of the tongkangs recognizes me, and calls out to me in jest, "Ah ku, hey ah ku, how much, how much?" I wish he wouldn't do that. Spoiling my precious hours.

Down to the Mercantile Establishments. Closer to the ocean, how its expanse conjures up memories of my strange fate. What would have happened if my father hadn't sold me? The thought of breaking my back planting the rice seedlings, of eating melon gruel for days and days, of living so close to Liong Soon Fatt's wealth, and not being able to taste it as my own. . . .

I watch the junks sway with squeaky splendour as they enter port. The wealth of my old country stored within these wooden wombs. Exciting to watch wealth from a distance, to anticipate the arrival of dreams. Deep in the holds of the British trading ships lies opium from India. In wooden boxes, dirt pellets like rat droppings to lessen our suffering. Ah, they might look dirty, but underneath is gold. A country of addicts, and pellets of riches for the colonial government's fat pockets.

The wealth of this young country. As if all the world favoured her with its generosity. Let me enjoy some of that. You labourers and coolies, you who hurl out insults in the daylight hours, yet call out passionately for me in the night, share your hard-earned money with me. You self-made towkays, you gluttonous merchants, you red-faced, lust-licking government officials. . . .

On the way back to the brothel, I turn into Circular Road. I'm hungry for hints of luxury. A memory trail of Soon Fatt's red silk still flows strongly through my veins. In the jewellery shop, a woman fingers beautiful merchandise that the clerk, Mr. Ong, has drawn out from under a glass showcase. Heavy gold rings from Europe bearing jewels that catch the glint of sunlight. Silver bracelets and earrings from India. Behind the showcases, lined up on shelves that stretch up to the ceiling, brocades and silks from Siam and China. Mr. Ong ignores me without any hesitation whenever a married woman is in the store. He averts his eyes from me as he smiles at the rich woman. I suppose he assumes it is all perfectly reasonable. After all, why would he expect me to buy anything when I'm alone? Ah, but when I'm here with a rich client. . . .

One day, I'll spend some of my savings here. It will be the day some man wants to take me away from the brothel as his concubine or, better still, as his wife. Then I'll stride proudly into the store and boss Mr. Ong around. But he doesn't know that right now. That's why he's turning his greedy back on me. What is it? Does an ah ku deserve less? What's the matter with him?

CHOW CHAT MUI

These young ones, they dare act like lions! Roaring and strutting. I say, watch out for the hunters in the bushes, watch out. Since I came here, some of my sisters have died from the dreaded disease eating up their genitals and wombs, others from hanging, or from being beaten to death, or from opium overdose. So many ways to lose life. As for me, in a few months, I'll be thirty, very old for an ah ku. I'm proud of surviving.

There are the ones who get to marry. Can't believe a Malay man applied at city hall for a marriage licence for an ah ku. The wedding is going to take place in that brothel next month. The woman has to swear she'll never return. She has to say the final goodbyes to family on that day—kwai kung, kwai po, cook, amah, sisters. She gets to escape and, if she continues to be lucky, die from old age, unlike most of her sisters.

I wonder what kind of man would want an ah ku for a wife? I've seen some Malays look at me with their raw desire. They don't mind my tallness. If a Malay man would offer to free me from the brothel, would I go with him? There would be gossip, sneers, and ugly looks of disdain from Chinese men and women. There will be crude jokes from the British bosses. What kind of freedom is that? And if I were to have children, how would they be able to hold their heads up high? Impure blood. Shame visited on their heads because of their parents' foolishness.

Never had one for a client yet. I wonder. Their dark skin, their different smells. We try to keep to our own. But, of course, if a Malay insists, Ah Yee wouldn't turn away money. It seldom happens. The lines are drawn, the invisible lines that separate our allegiances. We serve our own, while the British and the Japanese and some Malays go to the karayuki-san. Sometimes, I hear the strong, earnest voices of the Malay men singing or chanting prayers, sounds carrying a fair distance from their mosque. The music of their voices makes me restless. . . . They were here in this country long before us. The orang laut, the ones who tamed the seas, who fished and hunted, respecting the gifts of their Allah. They have stories to tell. I know a few words and phrases in Malay. *Pergi manah? Ini brapa ringgit?* Where are you going? How much money?

I catch snatches of stories. A word, a few lines, in the hallway, out on a street corner, here on my bed. A murmur, a groan, a scream. Sounds indistinguishable from the din in my head. *Malay men have cocks shaped like hooks, they'll grind a woman down.* Is he joking? My Chinese client with his little firecracker, what does he know?

Nothing simple left any more. That place I used to call home, place of mountains, hazy. So hazy.

* * *

I must have fallen asleep. I open my eyes to the beads of the lamp glowing as if radioactive. The room is cooler. The light from outside has faded substantially. I shiver, registering a sudden movement of air.

"You mumbled something." She's peering down at me, her face inches away from mine. Her hair looks a darker shade of orange, melting into the shadow behind her. Panic presses into me, cold as a blade.

"What did I say?"

"Couldn't make out the words, it was a different language. If you're still tired, you can sleep here. Spend the night."

I jerk my neck and shoulders slightly up from the bed. "I've never slept with two . . . I don't know."

She looks at me, slightly amused. "Well, you can just sleep, you know."

"No . . . no, thanks."

"You started to say you lost. What did you lose?"

I drag myself up from the bed. The magician has gone on strike, leaving me to fend for myself.

"Oh. A bit complicated to explain. I, uh, I need to go now."

I put on my coat and shoes, stumble to the door, and open it. In the living room, the floor lamp is switched on, casting a ring of light upwards on the ceiling. A ring of Saturn, but no sighting of Dale. I glance back quickly at her, then make my way to the apartment door.

"Wait, your book."

She holds it up, her arm stretching out at me as if offering a bait. I walk towards it, but she folds her arm inwards, drawing it close to her body.

"We're not weird, you know. Just because you're freaked out about something. We believe in being ourselves, that's all."

"I'm sorry. I'm not used to acting this way."

"What? Following your instinct?"

I look into her eyes, lit by extraordinary fieriness. In my twenties, I didn't have even a tenth of her gall. I gingerly retrieve the book from her embrace and, after a moment's hesitation, cup my other hand very close to the side of her face.

I'm turning the doorknob when she says, "See you around."

On the bus back home, I look at the photographs and maps of Singapore in the centre section of the book. There had been no photographs in the article I read a month ago. But here in the book, there are rickshaws lined up on either side of Sago Street, their wooden bars resting on the ground. Some coolies sprawled on the seats of their vehicles while others are standing. Weary bodies resigned to waiting for business. Another photo displays a Smith Street ground-floor barbershop that used to be a brothel. The caption indicates there are words carved into the window frame upstairs, words of praise for the ah ku who lived there. Smith Street. We must have passed by that shop many times on our family jaunts to Chinatown.

Words on a window frame. I would hate to be exhibited like that. I look up from the photos. Outside, along the last two blocks of West Hastings before Main, the dusk bodies of street people, stick people, the hustlers, hookers, dealers and users. Moving under neon signs and the light masking of rain. Anonymous pawns on a shadowy chessboard. Hordes of people board at the Main Street stop. The bus smells of fresh green vegetables, fast-food grease, and the sourness of poverty. Punctuated by a waft of combustible alcohol fumes. Wet coats and umbrellas drip and jostle against bodies. The fluorescent lighting in the bus casts a yellowish pall on faces, some of them more wrinkled with stories than others. On the front seat at right angles to me sit a couple of elderly Chinese women, obviously well acquainted with each other, chatting in Cantonese about their sons and daughters. I can make out a few sentences. A boast here, a complaint there. One of them, with grey hair rolled up in a bun, is dressed in a subterranean blue cotton top, with a quilted brown jacket over it, her earlobes distended with the weight of large jade earrings. The honeyed orange of 24-carat gold set with green moons. The other one wears her hair cropped short, just above the shoulders. She too wears gold earrings, but they're not set with any gems. They're shaped like daisies. Her outfit is a conglomeration of pink wool scarf, green sweater, black wool bomber jacket. And white running shoes.

My maternal grandmother Mah-Mah dressed very differently from either of these women. A traditional Nonya, she wore lace blouses with sarongs and rolled her hair into a sanggol siput. Snail bun. She and it crawled leisurely through life with nonchalance, a certain ease and laziness. I wonder if Mah-Mah had adventures in her youth. Mahmee doesn't tell us much about those aspects of Mah-Mah. Is that why I have more fascination with her than Father's mother, Grandmother Neo, who lived only into her early thirties, dying tragically of cervical cancer? Father never stopped talking about her, about not having a mother, about my grandfather being too harsh and unavailable to do the job of two parents. And so on.

Mah-Mah. She left Bandung in Java for Singapore in 1927, when she was seventeen, to marry a merchant she hadn't even met yet. The marriage had been arranged by her parents in 1909 when Mah-Mah was still in her mother's womb. They had made a special trip to Singapore, and hired a matchmaker who found a wealthy merchant family with a ten-year-old son my great-grandparents agreed to betroth Mah-Mah to.

The bus now passes by the Pink Pearl restaurant, nearing Clark Drive. I flip through the other pages. Portraits of two ah ku. Their faces are quite different. Both of them have neatly coiffed hair, sit up stiffly, their feet crossed at the ankles. Maybe that was a standard pose. Women, cross your feet please. Show that you are bound at the ankles, even if your feet might not be bound. Yet one of the ah ku displays an eternally defiant look, as if she were at any moment going to strut out of range of the camera's gaze and race off to some wild party. That glimmer in her eyes, and the slight downward turn of the right side of her mouth, a charming lack of politeness. Reminds me a little of Stephanie. The other ah ku, on the contrary, looks vacant, staring as if not knowing what or whom she's staring at, her head tilted slightly forward, chin down, the life submissively absent from her eyes.

As the bus makes its turn south onto Commercial Drive, the elderly woman with the pink scarf scurries to get off the bus with her several bags of groceries. She loses her balance and crashes against the slim, willowy woman standing next to her white boyfriend. The anger shoots out as sharp as a bolt of lightning.

"Ngei ka mah! Kum choo loo," the young woman hisses, through claret-coloured lips.

The rain pours down. As I step off the bus, I pull on my hood and tuck the book inside my Gore-Tex jacket, cradling it with the crook of my arm. The world is now a dream awash in refracted images. Truths are bent through the minuscule pools of rain on my glasses. The occasional Vancouver Specials with their ugly 1950s rectangular façades of brick and stucco transform into dark, wavering cardboard houses.

When I step into my apartment and switch on the overhead light in the living room, the sight of my clean white desk is shocking. It's as if I'm seeing for the first time its stark loneliness. The only thing on it is the photo frame, still flat on its face. The tears saved from earlier on return. Sounds sneak out of me, choked syllables and half-stifled moans. My body feels heavy with tiredness. At least Dom and Gerry aren't home yet so I don't have to worry about being heard.

I wipe my glasses, then pull off my wet socks, massage my cold, sore feet and tuck myself under a blanket on the sofa. I light a cigarette and inhale deeply. I nudge the tip a few times with my thumb. This habitual gesture always leads to an instant relaxation. When I sense that I'm ready, I open the book to begin reading.

Floods, famine, mass migration of people out of China, particularly the southern provinces. The influx of migrants into Singapore that rose steadily from the 1880s until the early twentieth century. At the back of the book, there's a table with the names of ah ku who committed suicide, their brothel addresses, dates of their deaths. One of the columns carries the heading "Suicide Due To." *Overdose of opium. Asphyxia from drowning. Jumped from second floor window. Lysol poisoning.* Nothing much has changed, these means of eliminating oneself. *Suicide due to.* The true causes buried beneath the means, hidden from outsiders' eyes.

I wish I could be under their skins, to know what it was like. Did some begin in a hopeful spirit? Were others disillusioned from the very start? I already had begun to imagine details about

the ah ku after reading that article, but now here were photographs, images that compel me, spur me on. I look at the two
portraits again, waiting for inspiration.

Time passes. The rain is light at first, fingers tapping, then
more insistent and percussive. Beating out its own music on the
roof of the shed. I'm so tired. I remember the soft hand stroking
my hair only a few hours ago and close my eyes.

* * *

LEE AH CHOI

I understand duty, but I also understand red silk. Why must fin-
ery belong only to the wives of men like Liong Soon Fatt? Did I
not don the embroidered red robe after Chan plucked my flower?

I stroke her hair while she rests beside me, her head on my
lap, eyes closed, her mind and body temporarily lulled by opium's
power. Still I see her fiery eyes. She told me the story of how she
had escaped with her cousin. She sold herself into a new life,
while I was sold by my family. The difference between a tap tang
and a kong chu. Lucky Chat Mui.

Opium releases memory from her, brings to the surface her
slurred recollections. Her low voice whispered the story, until her
mouth drew closer and closer to my ear. Oh sweet breath, hot
with honesty. Her willowy form bent down until wisps of her hair
brushed my neck. At that first shiver, I saw the trail of red silk and
felt its heat flow through me once again.

Who fooled whom first? How did we come to our first kiss?

I have never seen other women kiss each other. I dare not ask,
for isn't it a strange thing? No one pays us for this pleasure. How

naïve I'd been that first day in the brothel when Chan smacked his lips at me. When he plucked my flower so callously, delighting in my terror. But now I've learned that men want women to open their mouths to them. Open, keep opening, then they feed our sex mouths with their urgent liquid.

But what about this kissing between Chat Mui and me? And the heat that travels from her eyes to my hands as I reach for the back of her neck?

She wants to unfold me. She wants me to surrender the way I don't to men. She wants a kind of nakedness that no one else can see.

CHOW CHAT MUI

Sex. My body wars with the scum of their bodies rubbing and spilling disease, sinking me deeper into mud. Keeps me far from rest. Sex, like every moth drawn to the light, and the burning that destroys it. Inevitable. And ridiculous.

I've met all kinds of firecrackers, their noises exploding short and loud without the lies of romance. They flop then they fly, hovering at the edge of my disaster. Men with their eyes closed, with their minds numbed. Who can deny such base needs?

Men with rattling coughs, with their diseased hearts thumping in their cocks. Tuberculosis, syphilis, opium. Always at the edge, their hearts threatening to give out, cheating death each time they come, and survive their brief passage through slumber.

Ah Choi. You listen to my fantasies, yield your lips to my fire. Disgust with my diseased body doesn't hold me back. Is this sex? Without the thrusts of men, our skins must be sufficient to show desire. Our tongues and fingers find ways to travel into each other. One day I will wake up with a firecracker large and hot enough to match the way I feel. . . . Would that frighten you away, or would it draw you even more assuredly to me?

* * *

MAHMEE

Yen, why you come still and bother me? Even in death you don't leave me alone. How many times already? Lose count. Maybe five, maybe more. You come, you go, still do whatever you please. Hah, nothing changed!

Fed up, fed up. How many months you dead? More than three. Nearly one hundred days. Why is your ghost so strong? Maybe because you still have too many things to come back to. So last week I finally throw away some of your collection, take up too much space. Junk! I give your clothes away, and still you come to my bed, like you still my husband? And not say too much. Stand at the foot of our bed, roll your eyes up to the ceiling, then look back at me, like you want something. What you want?

You used to laugh at my mother, Ah Mak, and me, say we stupid to believe in ghosts. And now you become one big hantu, with no words. But I remember, not to worry. Try to scare me? Ah Mak told me when I was young girl, if I see one, don't pretend I don't see it. Do two things. Tell it I see, then show no fear, because if I do, it will take over.

You do enough all those years to kachau me, Yen. Now, you think you can still keep bothering me? Go away, I not afraid of you. See?

* * *

LEE AH CHOI

She has left for her brothel. In the late afternoon, before it's too late, I venture out again, in my black samfu. I didn't want to tell her that my night sweats and chest pains are getting worse. I must quickly get more medicine. From Upper Hokien I turn into South Bridge Road, where the Tamil businesses are. The men sit or squat among jute sacks of spices, three grades of basmati rice, and dried chilies. Men with bright eyes, betel-stained teeth, and gleaming black legs peeping out from their dhotis. In the textile and jewellery shops, the upper-class merchants are more formally dressed in beige linen jackets over longer dhotis. Here and there, a few Chinese shops stocked with porcelain wares, paper lanterns, temple papers, joss-sticks, and herbal medicines.

I go to the yi sun in one of the corner shops. A tiny but neat hovel. Can't escape detection, his fingers on my wrist picking up the presence of many men's energies coursing through me, eating at my insides. The yi sun prepares a few more packets of medicine for me.

The medicine helps me sometimes. Surely this sex disease can't be too serious. I heard that a long time ago there was a rule made by the British governor that all ah ku and karayuki-san had to be checked monthly. Forced examinations. They wanted to know which sex disease, gonorrhea or syphilis. I say such diseases are all the same! How humiliating to be herded into the clinics like animals. The governor said it was for our own good. What good is it if we're kept from making a living? Luckily this is no longer a rule. Sum Tok wouldn't be happy if they reverted to the old strictures. At least now, we have a choice. We can go to the hospital or the clinic if we want. Our dear colonial surgeon Dr. Mugliston and his private clubs: Pin On Tong, Po On Tong! I don't want his Western medicine. That fancy English stationery I've seen other ah ku clutch nervously in their clammy hands. I know it's their ticket to cheaper prices at the dispensary. Corrupt man. We know about his greed, we hear it through gossip, him coolly proclaiming that he and his wife "have to live," that his life insurance has to be paid, and that he has to save enough to make up for having no pension to live on when he is past work.

"Live"? Ha, ha. If he only knew what it's like to have no pension and to live like an ah ku. Let him wake up one morning trapped in a diseased body, mired in the worst of sores, the ceaseless itching of his lower parts!

I'm fine. I want to keep working, I want the front cubicle. It takes a lot of money for a kong chu like me to buy freedom, compared to those tap tangs. That first auntie who brought me here, she lied about how many years of labour. She never told my parents that the costs were far higher and keep rising, the money to pay for protection, the costs of our clothing, the food, the rent.

Many ah ku have the disease. I'm not alone. Our private parts burn with pain and itching, they swell and weep with pus! Not everyone dies from it. If Heaven allows, fortune will take a turn. I refuse to go to those clubs. Lying in a hospital bed with barely a curtain separating the living from the dead. There's gossip that whoever goes never comes back. Their medicine is too strong and kills. Poor victims, becoming restless ghosts who return to trouble the rest of us. I go to the temple, beg the goddesses Quan Yin and Pan Chan Leung to protect me.

Ah, but on a sunny and noisy day like today, how stupid of me to worry. Ghosts like to catch the living unawares, coming out only when people are asleep. They won't trouble me. Not in such heat, when the drains are filled with filth and sewage, waiting for the rains to flush the stench away!

I'm lucky I can walk distances. As the eldest, I was spared from bound feet because they needed me to plant and harvest in the fields. In those days, right after dawn, I waded out into the cool, watery fields in my bare feet, lotus boats I call them, feeling slightly ashamed of their largeness. While Ah Fong had to walk every day on those stubs of hers. Totter around the compound. The older women from the neighbouring farms would come by to snoop, see how her stumps were faring. People had heard of my father's decision to have Ah Fong's feet bound. Some showed disapproval, even disgust. They said, why should a poor man have such aspirations for his daughter? Waste of a good labourer. Others were in awe of my father's bold move. They came to our hut to congratulate him for his enterprising nature. A pretty face combined with tiny feet would greatly increase the chance of a favourable marriage, meaning a larger dowry.

I envied her getting all that attention, for having delicate blossoms instead of boats. But then she was the one who swayed so easily and fell when our two brothers pushed her. She was the one who retched when I helped Mother unwind the long cloth at night, to clean the pus and blood off her distorted lotuses. Oh, prized lotuses! Poor Ah Fong, tossing and turning in our shared bed where there wasn't enough room to start with. I would feel her sweaty hands on my arm, digging into my clothes, my skin. Until I would turn to her in exasperation, grab her by the hair or by her shivering shoulders and shake her until she stopped. Her hot tears rained down on my arms. *Shut up, shut up*, I wanted to say, even though I did feel a little sorry for her. She was only four and I was ten.

I reach my brothel and look up. Lan Ho's window is open, and she's leaning over, looking down at the rest of us in the street. She looks so confident up there, smoking her cigarette. Wait, just wait. Some day I'll inherit her cubicle and that window. All to myself.

Poor Ah Fong. She might have the beautiful feet and the rich husband, but I have a much nicer face. Sweet and full of good-luck features. Ah Fong's life probably revolves around the whims of her husband. Having to fry the pork fat to just the right crispness. To bring him tea and slippers the moment he enters the house. Mincing about with excessively dainty steps. Aiyah! If only my sister can see me now, walking the streets with the surety of unbound feet.

Chow Chat Mui

Funny, that beggar. He gets his money from others, but doesn't seem to see us move around him as he sits there, a tin can placed beside his stump, his crutch of bamboo poles tucked behind him. He alternates his gaze between Heaven and the pavement. Is his neck too stiff to look around him, at the rest of humanity?

Fool, if he expects to make money from the kinds of twisted stories he tells . . . like the one about Washing Silk Woman, who killed herself by jumping into the river, just because a young soldier stopped by to ask for some food and directions. To lose chastity just because a man speaks to you, and to surrender life for that disgrace. Then I'm unchaste a thousand times over.

Then there's his other favourite tale, for the locals. The one about hantu tek-tek, a ghost with pendulous breasts, who forces her milk on men until they choke from drinking too much and too fast. Does he want to scare the business away from us? He can't expect to win our favour!

My grandfather's stories were either about bravery in war or in love. He liked to give a speech between any two stories, always the same one, reminding his audience to live peacefully with others. I never understood how he could do that and then go on to tell a story about war, encouraging people to fight honourably, respecting the power of the enemy. A man who acted kindly yet spoke out of two different mouths. Sometimes he would surprise us with a tidbit or two about singing girls and courtesans renowned for their beauty as well as intelligence. They sang and wrote poetry and were skilled in the art of sexual pleasures. They certainly used all their mouths very well indeed!

If I were a storyteller, would I dare tell about my love for Ah Choi? What kinds of words could I use? She who is only a few houses away, her youthfulness, worry rarely disrupting her smooth surface. I could hold her close and closer still if only we could meet more often, if only others' bodies were not wedges between us.

That a kiss from her is such pleasure, while the hot pressure of another's mouth on mine is distasteful labour. Can lips truly kiss without possessing? I crave her. Heaven breathes its favour on my skin each time we meet. Moist and cool, like the air just before dawn. When I'm alone, the memory is a fresh, clean smell, dispelling the mustiness of my cubicle.

Yes, I crave her. I crave the rare feel of her skin under her clothes. Sweet scent as I search her with my tongue. If my father knew, he would spit in my face and rain curses down on me. But I'm no longer living in his cage, bound by his desire. He bound my body, and then only for a time. But my imagination, how could anyone own that?

The actions might still be the same now, opening my body for others' desires, but something important has changed. This prison is no longer my father's. My name and my worthy attributes carved into the wooden frame of our common window. Once I was not so ugly! In a moment of generosity about six years ago, before the New Year, after a particularly bad monsoon season, Ah Sek decided he would compose some fancy lines for me. Maybe he felt guilty about not desiring me any more. Maybe he was being recklessly generous. Or more likely, he was following the fortuneteller's instructions to do it for better business in the brothel. He summoned a craftsman to the house to carve his creation onto the frame, so that people on the street, if they cared to look up and strain their eyes, could learn a few flattering things about me.

But those lines on the window frame are lies now. Take a good look at me. How the years of change have distanced me from those words. *Chat Mui, a willow of supple limbs bending to the wind.* Ha, nothing stays the same. Did I say little has changed? Now I say, both must be true.

I remind myself to expect only uncertainty from others. Not to trust. But stories are different. Reliable companions. Keep telling them, and they live on, changeless.

How to speak the unspeakable? This desire for her. Without

language to name it, it is not fixed like the window frame. Free like the wind, not a willow rooted to the ground, dependent on earth for its fate.

This is my secret and my power.

* * *

I myself have experienced three incidents since his death. The first time he was merely a shadow, a shape that smelled of formaldehyde and, oddly enough, chili sauce. I suppose in that other world the usual conventions don't apply. It happened the third night after I arrived back in Singapore. I thought, how odd that death, chemical preservation and chili sauce could all belong together, if only for this brief duration of a trance. The second time, only a month ago, he brushed past me lightly as he picked his way between the aisles at Safeway. Dressed in a short-sleeved batik shirt and his too-loose beige trousers over his matchstick legs. I trailed him from a distance as he pulled cans of food from the shelves. Cornflakes instead of Weetabix, Cream of Mushroom over Chicken Noodle, no vegetables except a small package of frozen corn and a few heads of broccoli, and a half-litre of homogenized milk. Typical of him to crave the fatty foods, with his bottomless pit of an appetite, yet without any visible consequences. The heat all that food generated must have gone somewhere, but where? That was the great mystery. I was caught up in my puzzlement, and then realized too late that I had lost sight of him. He was gone as quickly as when he first caught my attention. I felt frantic, even though some part of me was arguing against such an irrational, outrageous presumption that it was Father in the flesh. Buying groceries like the rest of us, with a hunger that still needed satiating.

The third time I encountered him, I didn't see him at all. On the #10 heading west, when the bus neared the stoplight in front of the Big & Tall building, his baritone voice was humming a Duke Ellington blues tune.

I wasn't completely convinced, since I had never heard Father sing the blues while he was alive. But it was his voice travelling the melody line lazily, as if melancholy was natural, innocuous. He sang from the back of the bus, hidden behind standing passengers.

What does Father want to tell me? What he didn't get to say before he died? I feel some kind of urgency has infected me as never before, and I keep thinking of eggs, of blood, of the water in our bodies, and the fragility of boundaries.

* * *

LEE AH CHOI

I haven't forgotten my first family, their reliance on me. I should keep sending money. Can't blame my father. After all, they need-ed rice, and why keep me when the fields were flooded? Every month I take my packet to the remittance man, watch as he trans-lates my words into neat, black strokes and dots. I recognize a few characters, the ones for numbers, days, and, of course, my own name Choi, meaning prosperity, reminding me of my parents' wish.

Every time there's an important family event, a letter arrives care of the remittance man. My father travels to the nearest town for a letter-writer. A bit of hardship for him. The important news was Ah Fong's marriage last year. How ironic, that her husband is Liong Soon Fatt's third son. My sister married off at fifteen. No mention of how my brothers are. Then news early this year of another sister born. Wonder if she looks like me or Ah Fong? My father sends pleas for more money. Every time the man reads my father's desperate words out to me, in his monotone voice, I see my father's dark shadow deep in the hut while my mother stands resolutely shielding him and my brothers and Ah Fong from me. Why doesn't he beg from his rich son-in-law? No, they can't have all my earnings. The money I've hidden under the mat is extra, earned from secret tips and gambling. Each moment my hand unleashes chance.

CHOW CHAT MUI

Her feet. She insults them. She believes the lies, that they're ugly, and she can take comfort only in their ease. What is beautiful in a woman? Only what men want? Such beauty brings pain. But I've a secret. That first time I cupped her feet in my hands, I knew I wanted to feed on them. It was the anticipation of tasting what others consider ugly. I've licked each toe's separate thought into memory. I see how my tongue trails pleasure through her body as it moves along the length of a foot, slowed down by the roughened areas, the signs of those early days in the fields.

There is a labour that doesn't mark us. Seething within, a turmoil that churns, muddy in the intestines, film of vomit at the throat, the language of secret desires.

Do men want her feet as I do? I dare not ask. The pleasure of hidden beauty, raw and rugged.

LEE AH CHOI

This afternoon, she comes to pleasure me. When I try to take her breast into my mouth, she stops me and presses her lips against my throat. Presses until I feel the mark of her passion enter, become the next words I will speak. As quickly as she steals into my brothel, she disappears, flees into the fast-fading light. Soon the evening begins with its parade of hunger.

When will I get used to this work? A man can groan and sweat all he wants, then be finally overcome with his momentary release. But I lie below him, wooden until I fuse with my straw mat, becoming like it, rasping thin and insubstantial.

That's why I sometimes scream. As if something inside me needs to make a sound, to prove I'm still alive. This satisfies some of my clients, because they think I've reached my height of pleasure. Some fools enjoy having such an effect on an ah ku. The more soiled the woman, the sweeter the victory. These are not the men who relish virgins, or who have the money to afford such fantasies. So they settle for the paltry satisfactions. Most of them don't talk much, except to tell me their names, what they would like. But there are exceptions. The happy drunks who insist on their songs of lust and loneliness. I try to sing along with them, or look sympathetic. The least I can do. Most aren't good singers, getting their lines all confused, straying out of tune. Then there are the clients who come to bemoan their wives. The ones who drool on my clothes and suck at my nipples like anxious babies. Blubbering idiots, thinking they can convince me they're victims of their wives! What did I say about infant mouths and ugly husbands? I curse them under my breath for staining my garments. A man who ruins silk will not make a good husband.

Chow Chat Mui

Almost time for work to begin. I mark time by the colours of the sky. Soon night will arrive with its own seductions. Today, daylight leaves with a brazen gesture. The sky is tinged rose red, the colour of a woman's blush. That smooth face of hers betrayed the body's heat. She pretended to be unaffected, but I felt the shiver of her body against me, her growing pleasure travelling the sweet silence between us. She welcomed the urgent passion of my hand, the slow delight of my tongue. The sky speaks, but who sees? I see, and I remember.

* * *

It's a rare sunny Tuesday, the sky so clear when I walk out of the apartment in the afternoon it would be easy today to forget the usual bleakness of a Vancouver winter. To forget the cold, dismal rain that was outside my apartment when I fell asleep last night. The sense of urgency hasn't left me, the nagging feeling that I can't quite put my finger on.

I set out on foot towards Chinatown, occasionally stopping to scan the mountains, their indigo blue bodies insinuating their calming presence underneath a shimmer of white.

The Buddhist temple is a few metres ahead. Its brass urn is full of joss-sticks smouldering their requests into the air. I've passed by countless times, mildly curious, yet never bold enough to enter. But the mountains encourage me today, *Go ahead, don't let Father stop you.* I pull firmly on the brass door handle and step in.

The place is practically empty. One other person faces an altar at the far end crowded with deities. A small man, probably in his forties, judging from his salt-and-pepper hair. He's wearing a dark green corduroy shirt and khaki pants and is kneeling at the altar, joss-sticks clasped firmly between his palms while he makes several quick bows. Long red banners drift down from the ceiling on either side of the large room. Mah-Mah used to go to temples to pray for the family. Sometimes she brought me along and showed me how to hold the joss-sticks, how many times to bow before placing the sticks into the prayer urn. But Mahmee decided against praying to gods. *Too many, give me a headache.*

Why is my name, Wu, written in large black strokes on one of the banners? Along with characters that I don't recognize. The man gets up and plants the joss-sticks in an urn. Maybe he can answer my question. I walk up to him.

"Excuse me, uh—" I'm thrown off because when he turns around, I realize it's a woman.

"—madam." How foolish of me.

"Ahhh," she exhales the vowel slowly, as if it's her way of greeting me. Smiles kindly at me, exposing not one, but two gold front teeth.

"I wonder . . . do you have any books . . . reading materials?"

She motions for me to follow. We walk up a flight of stairs, down a narrow corridor, and enter a room dimly lit by sunlight sneaking through half-shuttered blinds. Oak shelves along the walls are packed with books, and a long table sits in the middle of the room. On the walls above the bookcases are silkscreen depictions of various deities. She walks up to one of the windows and twists the rod that opens the blinds. Light floods in. I squint from the sudden change.

"My name is Tze Cheng. Means Poetic Greeting."

"Mmm, how nice. My name is Wu Lan."

I use my left index finger to write it out on my right palm. Ghost-writing, ghost-word. How many times I'd written my own names out in school, and not really known.

"Show me again," she prompts.

This time I do it more slowly, careful to start the horizontal strokes on the left, move to the right, not the other way as I had been more inclined to do as a child: 巫 蘭 .

"I know Lan means Orchid. But Wu . . . it was a name my grand-mother gave me. It was never clearly explained. I hoped you might be able to help me. It's that character on the banner downstairs."

Tze Cheng frowns, deep in thought. "Hmm, of course. . . ." She writes it out with her finger on her own palm.

"Yes, that's right." I nod my head in hopeful anticipation.

She raises one eyebrow. "Unusual. But you are lucky, I can help."

She pulls out a large, forest-green book from a top shelf, places it on the table, and begins flipping through it.

"You speak a Chinese dialect?" she asks me without looking up from the book.

"Our family spoke mostly Hokien at home, with a few Malay phrases. I learned Mandarin as a second language at school. I know a bit of Cantonese. Champoh-champoh." The Malay phrase slips out, familiar yet dislocated. I shrug my shoulders apologetically, "I mean, a mix."

"You from Singapore or Malaysia?"

"Singapore," I mumble, feeling suddenly uncomfortable about the attention.

She opens the book to two pages of reproductions of ancient paintings. On the left, a man with half-glazed eyes and dishevelled long hair lies on a rattan couch. Standing around him, a handful of men and women point their fingers, swords or wands at him. Their mouths are open. Scowling, I think. On the right page, another painting, the same scene except a woman is cutting the sick man's palm with a small knife. She has incised a word. I recognize it:　火　　Fire.

"What's happening?"

"This is a wu shi chasing demons out from the sick man."

All these years, I never knew. Mahmee said that Wu meant Someone Who Helps Others. Now I learn that my name is connected to the casting out of demons. Oh yes, Father would have loved this. His written Chinese was below average, so he had relied on Mahmee and Mah-Mah to find a good name for me. It must have been Mahmee's wish that I help others. While it may be true, as Michael puts it, that I like to "separate from the herd," here is evidence that I have been an obedient daughter: going into psychology, becoming a therapist. Ben, my supervisor, and my other colleagues would laugh if I tell them what my name really means.

Tze Cheng turns the page. Photographs of charcoal rubbings. In one of them, five dragons with wings are joined tip to tip in the heavens above swirling clouds, while gnomes occupy the middle section of the sky. Below them on the ground are some dignitaries and their attendants with mouths agape.

She points to the mound where some of the winged creatures

have landed. "Heaven and Earth are joined here, where humans and gods commune."

I blink at her several times. Is this her attempt to engage me in some metaphysical discussion about our place in the cosmos? I turn the page back. "Why are the others so ... they look accusing. I mean, as if it's the man's fault he's possessed."

"Oh no, no. They have to do that to make the exorcism work. You know, scare the illness out of him. They must show they don't approve of his condition."

"Tell me some more about these wu shi."

"Oh yes! That refers to people who have a certain gift." She pauses, sweeping her hand dramatically upwards as if conjuring up some presence.

She continues, "The wu shi can see things, they are visited by spirits from other worlds. They make kwei, the demonic spirits, leave people alone. You see how this woman here is cutting a character into the sick man's hand?"

I nod, feeling queasy. She stares at my eyes, and rubs her smooth chin as if stroking a beard. "What is your full name?"

"Lim Wu Lan. Why?"

"You ... not someone famous?"

I laugh, embarrassed by the question. "No, of course not."

"Do you know what dragon eyes are?" she asks.

"No. What are they?"

"Very complicated, too much explanation." She shakes her head vigorously.

I stare down at the pictures again. When I was eleven, Mahmee took me aside one cool December evening just when the air outside was thick with an impending storm. We'd just finished dinner. Michael was lying on the sofa, playing with his Lego set. I remember that I'd begun menstruating the previous month, and this second time, I was not as nervous about it. Mahmee led me to the balcony, and we sat down on the small rattan loveseat. This was a familiar ritual, when Mahmee decided there was something important to tell me, either a story from the past, or some revelation about what was crowding her mind at that time. She told me that when she was pregnant with me, Mah-Mah had an important dream. She didn't go into the details. Just that the dream included drawing a baby out of a deep well in the earth, a well glowing with a bright orange fire around its mouth. She said it was a good time to tell me, now that I'd become a woman. "Your name, Mah-Mah picked for you. Don't forget." She delivered her speech as if announcing the next day's dinner, and then disappeared into their bedroom. I didn't know what to make of it. For some reason, through the years, I decided not to ask Mahmee any more about it.

So it was Mah-Mah who picked my name. But it was Mahmee who told me its meaning. Why did she omit the original meaning and substitute something far more innocuous?

Tze Cheng pulls out another book, a smaller one, its pages yellowed to a deep saffron, bound with a muddy brown cover. I look down at her hair: centre part, very neat and precise. Looks as if the grey hairs are beginning to overtake the black. Wonder how old she is, when it was she started to go grey, if her parents are still alive, and if she has family in Canada. I noticed my first grey hair a very long time ago, just before I left the country, but who knows how much longer before my grey predominates.

"Here," she offers, "you may sit here and read. This is in English. But we close at four. Come back another time if you wish."

"Uh. Will you be here? Are you here often?"

"Oh! Many times, many times." She bows to me, and leaves me feeling disappointed.

The book opens up to a shih, "The rain is not controlled":

> Vast and mighty Heaven,
> Why withold thy goodness,
> Sending down death and famine,
> Ravaging the four quarters of the land?
> Great Heaven, in thy majesty,

Why no concern, why no plan?
Regarding not the guilty
Who have suffered for their crimes,
Why are the guiltless
Swallowed up in wide calamities?
Why, mighty Heaven,
Does the king not hearken to righteous words,
Like one wandering afar
Unknowing of his goal?
Let all those in authority
Attend to their proper conduct.
If they fear not other men
Have they no fear for Heaven?

There they were, out in the fields, their bodies and clothes beaten wet and cold by the slanting rain. The peasants sang this appeal to Heaven, a way to complain about injustices suffered at the hands of feudal lords. Perhaps it was a wu shi who composed this song for them, and that's why Tze Cheng showed this to me. If the rain could not be controlled, if the appeal was made to Heaven, what did the people do to help themselves out of their own misery? Did they believe themselves to be totally at the mercy of outside forces?

I look down at the shih again. *Why are the guiltless swallowed up in wide calamities?* Father, after a long workday, his pallor heightened by the crimson cave of his armchair. Maybe he desperately needed a wu shi, someone to provide a scowl formidable enough to scare the illness out of him.

I admit that I've judged Father's suicide as an act of cowardice. Does that count as a scowl? He wasn't brave enough to fight off his despair. I can't help but think the demon that had to be expelled from Father was Grandmother Neo herself. Or rather, his grief over her absence. Why is it the absent ones sometimes have a greater grip on us than the living? When I was quite young, I already sensed that Grandmother Neo's absence grew larger than life for her son, so large that his pain about it filtered through to me. All those "what if's" Father indulged in, all that grief that came quickly to him if he watched a sad movie. The emotion became more available when he was drinking.

I continue reading about the shih. The poem was probably written around 600 BC, when the Chou Dynasty was losing its power, and the country was entering a period of political upheaval. Yet it was also a time when creative thinking in language and philosophy thrived through the "Hundred Schools." Maybe this shih was not merely about people expressing their powerlessness as victims. It could have been a way people spoke to each other in code, to spur themselves and others towards rebellion. *Let all those in authority attend to their proper conduct.* A warning to their oppressors?

When I leave the temple, I notice rain clouds low on the horizon. The air has turned noticeably cooler. When I reach the edge of Chinatown, I'm struck by the visibility of people's breath as they crowd around the fruits and vegetables. Coils travel in the shapes of snakes or clouds or feathers. My own is a wisp of a maiden's hair. A flick of a magic horsetail wand. There is a heat to all sensations. Pungent smells of garlic and black bean, honeyed smokiness of barbequed ducks, and the swirling textures of fabrics and faces.

Today must be a special occasion, because the stores on Keefer have heads of lettuce hung over their entrances, waiting for the lion. A few naked light bulbs glow brashly. Farther down the street, a crowd forms around the lion prancing to the reverberating gong and drums and clashing cymbals. A performer wearing a lolling Happy Buddha head teases the lion with a fan. The animal rears up, bows down, rolls its eyes, snaps its hinged jaws, and charges in mock rage at the Buddha. It finally snaps up the red packet of money. I watch the agile limbs of the dancers extend and retract deftly under the lion's body.

If there are any demons or ghosts around, this loud ritual will certainly chase them out. Prosperity can't thrive while a place is haunted. I remember the sick man's face, and that queasy feeling returns. The lion moves away from the meat shop where sides of roast pork hang on hooks, edges past the tubs of fish and prawns at the fish store, to the row of grocery stores. A man in white cap and apron pushes a fat green bunch of kai lan at me, "Yu pheng, yu leng! Yu pheng, yu leng!" Cheap and beautiful. Sunshine breaks through the clouds for a few moments, and the water in which some rainbow trout are dying flashes with needles of light.

At the New Town bakery, three elderly men are seated at the counter. Instead of my habit of claiming a booth, I join them. The waitress with the lusciously full lips and cherubic face recognizes me, but she's startled that I've chosen to sit with the men.

"What you want today?" She smiles politely and scribbles on her order pad as I ask for food in a smattering of English and clumsy Cantonese. I'm having a brief fantasy about other ways her question could be interpreted, when a large, steamy deluxe bun and coffee arrive inches from my clasped hands.

After the snack, I walk out to a clearer sky. The rain has come and gone as quickly as a temper tantrum. Twists of aquamarine clouds reassure, *we are swimming gracefully into the dusk.* I stroll through Chinatown looking at window displays, feeling myself part of the larger animal, how I am yet am not like the bodies shuffling for space on the sidewalk. How many of these people are on the verge of utter despair? How many of them have tried to kill themselves, and which ones will eventually succeed?

* * *

MAHMEE

Nonsense. Of course I know her. Of course I not abandon her. Who know her better than me? Lan-Lan, my own flesh and blood! Out of my own body. How many times does she need to see the afterbirth wrapped in the piece of muslin? How many days and nights pass without anyone in the flat now he gone and she so far away?

I told her Mah-Mah's dream long ago. Now she grown, why suddenly she want to know so many things? She phoned me. I was in the middle of plucking the hairs from chicken, fresh from morning market. Planned to make stew with horse chestnuts and Chinese mushrooms and whole chicken chopped up. When I told Lan-Lan that, she joked, can I send her some?

Her name! I told her, when I was pregnant with her, her Mah-Mah picked the name, not my fault. Ah Mak insisted must name her with that Wu, because of the dream. Okay, okay, I said to my mother, you win.

I want my daughter not be selfish. I want her to be useful to others. That was my thinking when Ah Mak picked the name. Then I added the Lan part, because I think woman must be like flower. We have Chinese tradition, many people understand this about women being beautiful and delicate.

Lan-Lan, always her head stuffed full of questions, never happy with the way things are. What else did she want to know? Something about longans, dragon's eyes. Her Mah-Mah's eyes. Who can remember such things? Who ever bother to notice? Enough worries each day. Lan-Lan sometimes make up stories, tells me I told her. All these questions on the phone, just because she gone to temple a few days ago and saw her name.

* * *

LEE AH CHOI

Alone, in the last moments before sleep. I hear Loke Kum's screams. Why must she make sure we hear her suffering? She wants to disturb the rest of us, wants us to know she suffers the most under Sum Tok's hands. The sharp snap of our kwai po's punishing rattan cane. It must be painful. I'm lucky to have avoided Sum Tok's disfavour. She has great hopes for Lan Ho and me.

Rain. Every time the monsoon arrives, I remember the old scarcities. What if that woman had not come to ask for me? What if my father had refused to sell? The questions float above me, mixed in with the smoke, while outside the fast rain strikes the zinc roof noisily. This is my fate, what Heaven has wrought for me. All there is, this moment, the urgent staccato sound of rickshaw coolies' feet hitting the wet pavement stones.

CHOW CHAT MUI

Ah Choi keeps hoping for a promotion. She believes in the power of her beauty. Her skin is still smooth, her head swims with dreams of being rescued. As for me, I know I'm not beautiful. With these ugly marks all over my body. Red eyes with yellow centres that weep pus. They weep for me like no one else does. So I don't hope for the things she does. There's enough worry to fill my days and nights, what with fatigue, cramps, the need for opium. Women like Lan Ho or Ah Choi, or Sew Lan from my brothel, they can hope for a promotion, either to concubine or to a larger cubicle. A window of their own. I have my dreams, but at least I know they're fantasies. Like the tales of my grandfather, good for temporary escape.

Even the power of opium's first compelling caress is gone. But I won't increase the dose. I still make sure a packet of chandu lasts me four smokes. I wait until the tremors and the stabbing pains in my gut are unbearable before I smoke again.

Did I say, not too long ago, little has changed? The pain plucks at my insides, some invisible hand stripping the skin off this chicken body of mine. I think it's late. Time for opium to help me sleep.

* * *

Drinking coffee in the Java Cat café, I think back to my meeting with Ben, the president of our organization. I was tense, cautious. Ben sat across from me in his office, and asked me some general questions that I answered with as few details as possible. He told me the other psychologists had been talking about a staff retreat for next year. What did I think? Sure, I said, good idea. I knew he was trying to be kind, inviting me for coffee. He was also doing his job, checking in with me. Afterwards, I rushed out of the office, relieved I didn't bump into Daniel. The funny thing was—I recalled as I walked into the elevator—in the past three years my colleagues haven't said a thing about what happened with Kim and Daniel and me. I know they knew. But just because they've helped other people, their clients, doesn't mean they've known how to respond to me.

Once I got back down to street level, I walked around downtown and, after half an hour, turned down Hamilton. That was when I decided to try out the Java Cat and walked in. I was surprised to find, among several popular magazines and the usual newspapers, the current issue of the *Southeast Asia Post*.

I look up again at the woman behind the counter. She's tall with a solid, curvaceous body that could have stepped out of a Renoir painting. Except she's not a blonde. She's wearing a burgundy cotton knit top, its scoop neckline exposing the olive smoothness of her chest. Her dark brown hair is elegantly restrained in a French braid, reddish highlights gleaming under the halogen lighting. She stands there, hands on her hips. Her lips are slightly parted as she stares at me.

"Would you like a refill?"

"Yes. But can I have it decaf this time?"

"Sure."

She brings the pitcher over, pours into my cup. I watch her large, square hands move. The colour of her nail polish almost matches her top. I glance down at her black skirt, long and clingy. The soft, dark fabric flatters her ample hips.

I turn my body at a slight angle away from her as I settle down to the coffee. I grope in my pockets. I'd forgotten, I ran out of cigarettes. A blond man in a snug lime green turtleneck and black jeans is seated at the next table. His lean and sinewy body is almost off the chair as he leans forward, sorting out what looks like a collection of hockey cards. He might have cigarettes, but I don't feel inclined to ask.

I return to my paper. In Kuala Lumpur, there's a woman who dances with scorpions, in a cage suspended from the ceiling. More than seven hundred people came to see her at a shopping mall. She says that if a person likes such creatures, it automatically means she can handle them without fear. She makes it sound easy. For the person who can do it, it's never a question of difficulty. Two years into this act, she has expanded her menagerie to include venomous spiders, giant centipedes and millipedes. She now dances with such exotica as an Indian Ornamental tarantula, twenty centimetres long, and the Goliath Eater spider, which spans twenty-five centimetres.

Early on in university I understood that one could learn more from the exceptions than from the rule. How does this woman do it? There she is, travelling the cities in Malaysia, making money in a venture that would either frighten the life out of most of us or kill us.

My hand strokes the red velvet upholstery of the chair seat, thinking about her body crawling with those creatures. If she dies from this work, it will not be an ordinary death. It will be witnessed by a titillated, horrified crowd. Sort of like the woman who jumped from Block 16. Except the crowd watching the

Scorpion Lady will get to witness her actual crossing from life into death—if they watch closely enough. But I would like to see her survive her performance, bringing me along with her, past my own fears.

The cappuccino machine makes its rude farting sounds, disrupting my concentration. I fold up the newspaper.

"Hey . . . it's you again." Stephanie stumbles towards me, a pile of books in her arms, her yellow canvas satchel slung across her shoulder with more stuff inside. She plops herself down on the other chair.

"What are you up to?" I ask, not bothering to hide the mild irritation in my voice.

"Doing research for a course I'm taking at Vancouver Community College."

She looks different. Not the cheeky persona who picked me up at the library, but someone more subdued. Or perhaps daunted by the pressure of homework. I'm annoyed because she's caught me by surprise yet again. I glance at her books on the table between us. *The Emperor's New Mind, The Selfish Gene, River Out of Eden.*

"What sort of project?"

"On Darwinian theory."

"Oh? Tell me more."

"Like for instance," she explains as she opens up one of the books to the beginning, "I've just started reading, so I can't say much yet, but listen to this: 'Ancestors are rare, descendants are common.' Isn't that cool?"

I pause to think over this statement and glance sideways at the book spine: Richard Dawkins. Don't know what he's getting at, but in my imagination, I still see a woman dancing with scorpions. A woman who dares. A woman who's not going to shrink away from danger.

On an impulse, I grab Stephanie's hand and say, "Hey, why don't we take a walk?"

She's startled but smiles, and gathers up her books. I take a quick last look at the Renoir contradiction as we go out the door.

"Where are we going?"

"How about to my apartment?"

"Oh!"

"I mean, if you'd like to."

"Sure. But . . . I can't stay very long. I have to be home by ten tonight, otherwise Dale will be upset."

"What is he, your keeper?"

"No . . . but he is my brother."

"Your brother? I thought—"

"You didn't ask, but you assumed, didn't you?" She raises a disapproving eyebrow at me. But why hadn't she said something that first day? She knew I had been confused.

"But the bed . . . ," I begin, weakly.

"We just moved to BC three months ago. One bedroom and one bed were the best we could do."

"Sorry."

"Listen." She pauses and scans me from head to toe. "I don't know about you baby-boomer types. It's tough making it in the city. Lotusland indeed. Tight-assed hypocrisies of corporate culture. Just how narrow-minded can a person get, anyway?"

I clench and unclench my jaw a few times, feeling heat spread across my chest, up my neck to my face. "Look, don't generalize. This is only the second time. We've hardly had fifty words between us. How would you feel if I made sweeping statements about your generation?"

She narrows her eyes, hunches her shoulders slightly forward, and pushes her tongue against the side of her cheek. Remains quiet for a few minutes, then, in a softer tone, asks, "Where do you live anyway?"

"Off Commercial Drive, close to Victoria Park. Know where that is?"

"Oh yeah. Where the old Italian guys play bocce ball all the time."

"Right."

"Okay, okay."

Neither of us says much more. I don't care if she's angry. My own anger doesn't seem to matter to her either. She's walking home with me, and that's what counts. That's the nice thing about a fling, you don't have a point to prove. Whereas in a so-called committed relationship, losing was a problem. I let Kim win, because I didn't want to play, just as I never wanted to be part of my family's drama scenes. I don't care, I don't want to care. I look at Stephanie's neck, at the way the fine light red hairs are like a gentle grassy slope down to her back, and all I want is to stroke and be stroked into a pleasurable distraction. The character Brando played was right. Anonymity is crucial for sustaining a certain kind of passion.

Along the way, she tells me more about theories of evolution. Like the controversial one about psychological complexity being selected in human beings as a favourable characteristic.

"Oh yeah, what does that mean?" I retort back. Does it mean that abilities to read social situations and the harsh realities of life lead one to survive better? But some research suggests that depressive people have a stronger tendency not to distort reality. Our debate dies down. I mull over some questions privately. Wasn't Father depressed? Yes, of course. Was he realistic? I think not. He was in fact depressed because life didn't fit his romantic or idealistic expectations.

In my apartment, I switch on the nightlight in the hallway outside my bedroom. There's no need for more light. I prefer partial or total darkness, that way I can let my imagination run unhampered. I want the pure sensations of touch. She must have known this, because she too is silent.

* * *

LEE AH CHOI

Chat Mui and I met last night in the alley. The rain stopped at about half-past one, soon after I finished with my last client. I sneaked out through the courtyard at the back. Old Fong was asleep so he couldn't stop me. Bodies deep in the shadows, holed up in different corners, whispering. Kept company by the narrow belt of visible night sky above, and the rats scavenging at our feet.

"Ah Choi!" came her low voice from the other end.

A hot ache spread through me, my body quickly drenched in sweat. Her thin lips rough with desire, devouring mine. To be consumed, drawn into her mouth's pleasures.

What if someone discovers our secret?

I'm sneaking an hour this afternoon under the shade at People's Park. Thinking about last night. That was a dangerous thing to do, meeting out there. Should stop worrying so much. Worry, like too much yang, is bad for the complexion. That's why I come here to my favourite bench to cool off. When I look up, I'm under the largest flame-of-the-forest tree in the park. Its brilliant red canopy dazzles me. There weren't such grand trees where I came from. On a hot, humid day like today, its shade is merciful. The delicate yet luscious petals land on me like a gentle blessing from Heaven. Chat Mui is like this tree, she envelops me. When I'm in her arms, I forget my anxieties.

The dear birds. I like all of them, but sunbirds are my favourites, charming me with their bright feathers of purples and reds and blues. Yellow suns on their bellies race before my eyes, while the birds insert their slender, curved beaks into flowers for nectar. It doesn't take them long to fill themselves! I laugh to see them flit between blossoms, the messy fliers. Watch out, over here. Be careful. I chide them, the way a mother should scold her reckless young.

But the real mothers parade their precious babies in cloth slings on their backs. I give these lucky ones my best smiles. I'm envious of these young wives. They need only open themselves to one man, and suddenly, they're taken care of. Magic. I smile steadily at them with the hope one might be kind enough to let me play with her bundle of delight, let me caress the cheek of a little one, feel the soft but sure closing of fingers around my one finger. I wouldn't like to have a herd of children screaming their needs at me, but one sweet little angel would do. My smiles aren't working today. They never do. It's like being in Mr. Ong's jewellery store, surrounded by wealth, and being ignored, not allowed to finger the merchandise. Worse than that. Fine gold or jewels can be bought, but how is a woman to have a child, unless a man grant her the honour? Heaven's decisions remain mysterious to me. I don't understand why some women are blessed, and others like me, saddled with the infant needs of men.

I hear that some men become kinder when they make an ah ku pregnant. Some can even afford to make the women their concubines. Yes, if I get pregnant, I'll protect my precious treasure and convince the man to take me away from the clutches of Chan and Sum Tok.

While I'm here in the park, I never smile at the men who pass by. I cast my eyes into the far distance, or upwards at the canopy of leaves. I never present myself as available outside the brothel, lest people think I'm cheap. And I would get into trouble with Chan. If only some decent man would look at me without the cheapness of lust, would consider me as a woman he could marry.

Now and then, a woman of class and prestige passes by: a Chinese woman, the wife or daughter of a towkay, in well-tailored silk cheongsam and shoes, or a British wife in her fashionable dress, with tight-fitting bodice, leaking like an oily pig in the humidity. Leaking the smell of rancid butter. Such women will almost invariably lower their eyes down to the ground when passing in front of me. How do they know? I'm in my plain samfu after all, not my showy red one. Don't any of them know we share common sorrows? Just because I'm an ah ku, just because I smoke opium, doesn't mean I'm lesser than them. Some of us have to work.

I don't care what Chat Mui says. I hope a man will take me away from this dirt-ridden labour someday. Either a man who adores me, or a man who makes me pregnant and will maintain his honour to me and his child.

CHOW CHAT MUI

I had a special friend when I was nine. Siew Fan lived in the nearby village. Her father was the innkeeper, her mother baked buns for the inn. Our mothers were friends. Siew Fan was an only child. I used to be puzzled by this even as a young girl—where did her parents hide the others? She wore her long hair in two pigtails rolled up on either side of her face. I laughed to see her because she looked as if she was wearing two of her mother's homemade buns! She was beautiful, her skin not quite as dark as mine—whether because she didn't have to work in the fields as I did, or because her skin was naturally fairer, I don't know. I liked the way her white teeth sparkled, even under the shade of a tree.

Her mother brought Siew Fan to visit us. While our mothers talked, we would sit just outside the door and play our pebble games. We threw pebbles into the air and scooped up others on the ground before the first ones returned. We always felt better if the visit happened while Father was away in the village. Otherwise, he and Mother would argue after the visit, about letting me take time away from work.

My sisters didn't want to join us. They knew I didn't want to play with them. Siew Fan and I liked going to the back of the house to seek out the puddles and the odd twists of tree roots, and to see if we could catch any grasshoppers or toads. Whenever one of us found something, we asked the other to close her eyes, then placed the creature into the other's cupped hands. The small urgent life throbbed against our containing fingers.

Who knows where Siew Fan is now? We stopped playing together after our mothers had a fight. I was never told what it was about. We heard their raised voices, the heat of their arguing, something about reputation. Her mother rushed out to where we were sitting and grabbed Siew Fan's arm and dragged her away. I never saw her again.

But I still think of her. I remembered Siew Fan because of what happened earlier today. I was in a merchandise store looking at the jewellery, not for myself, but wishing I could buy something for Ah Choi, when I spied a small picture-locket around the neck of a young and wealthy Chinese woman. She'd either forgotten to close it, or it'd come open. It bore the photo of a small child. It reminded me of Siew Fan. She noticed I was staring, looked down, blushed, then closed the locket. For a few seconds, our eyes met. "My sister, as a child," she said to me.

"She's beautiful," I replied.

Siew Fan was my true sister. Unlike the ones my parents produced after me, the ones I've never felt close to. I used to watch them doing chores or playing, and wonder, did Father also visit them? I don't think so, I would have known. They were lucky, those two sisters of mine. I resented them for their innocence. Sometimes I catch myself wondering if our father started to pick on them after I left. But I can't think too much about that.

Perhaps Siew Fan has a happier life than mine. How quickly people or fortunes can be lost! Heaven didn't return to earth what we flung into the air, those pebbles of affection.

I'm glad to have Ah Choi now. How sweet to bend to the soft ways of her body. The danger of our meetings in the alley mixes with the thrill. The rats and the sky are our witnesses.

* * *

The luminous face of my clock glares back, 9:12.

"Have to go soon," she says, handing me the end of her bidi, and starts to root around in the dark for her clothes. I pinch the short brown cigarette gingerly with thumb and forefinger and bring it to my lips. The taste of cloves is a pleasant change from my usual pack of Players.

I switch on the light. Unlike her pleasant amber lamp, mine is a cheap Consumers Distributing fluorescent type. There's a split second between the time I depress the button and the full glaring light. I've always liked that split second, reassuring for its lack of commitment.

Her breasts have that enviable firmness. But I can tell they are cold, the goose pimples like a fine-grained veneer over her skin. It's odd to see her body for the first time after experiencing it. Two Stephanies, one after the other. She pulls on her white undershirt quickly, then her panties, but seems completely untroubled by my stares.

"Will you make it home on time? Maybe I could call you a cab."

Her foot is halfway into its sock. She looks up at me with her mouth turned down. "Hey, it's okay. I'll figure it out."

"I was trying to be helpful."

"Look, I don't have the money for a cab. I wish I could, but...."

"How about if I paid your cab fare, or at least part of it?"

"Oh." She's buttoning up her purple cardigan, starting from the bottom, thinking through this offer slowly, one button at a time. "Okay. Why not."

The Yellow Cab arrives too soon for my liking. I hurriedly press a crumpled ten-dollar note into her hand. She's out the door even before I've figured out what I want to do. Too late. I don't even have her last name or phone number.

After I lock the door, the darkness in the apartment becomes markedly oppressive. As if I've shut myself out from the rest of the world, and crawled back into the womb. I hear a few footsteps from upstairs, retreating from the kitchen into the living room. They usually go to bed early, so these must be the final movements before sleep. In my own kitchen, the silver streak on a half-empty bag of crinkle-cut potato chips gleams for a few seconds from the light of the motion detector outside the window. In the bedroom, I stumble over the books in a pile by the bed. Ouch, the corners of hardcover books are bad news for naked ankles. In her rush to get home, she'd forgotten. How will I return them to her?

With the light on, I pick up the one she'd read from. It's not hard to find the quote at the beginning of the book. *Ancestors are rare, descendants are common.* But it's the last line of a whole paragraph: *Of all organisms born, the majority die before they come of age. Of the minority that survive and breed, an even smaller minority will have a descendant alive a thousand generations hence. This tiny minority of a minority, this progenitorial elite, is all that future generations will be able to call ancestral.*

I imagine a Mendelian generational diagram. Tiny plastic figures, like the kind Michael played with, generic green farmers and soldiers, lined up in a row, and above them the handful of ancestors, whom I've embellished to look more colourful, minia-ture versions of Chinese opera figures. A fat magistrate here and there, a noble lady. Somewhere in that mass, even strangers like Stephanie and me might be distantly related if we trace it back far enough. Is that possible? I laugh at the idea. She does have Father's slim legs. This comparison makes me uncomfortable, yet the notion is compelling.

Father survived long enough to breed, and now here we are, Michael and I, in two different parts of the world. Any day now, he and his wife will start a family. But I am childless, and unin-terested in breeding. I will not have a direct descendant to survive me. Can I honestly say that I don't care? Even though I've made the decision not to have children, something in me feels the absence that goes with such a choice. Feels it, even though my mind is made up. I place my finger on the lamp button. There's that liminal dimming again, just before the complete darkness.

* * *

MAHMEE

Peranakan, yes, that's what we are, doesn't mean we not pure Chinese. Funny child. So Ah Mak wore sarong kebaya, sanggol siput on her head. She even chewed betel nut, ugly! But she not Malay. She do that only because she come from Java, and they got some bad habits there. But we are pure, we belong here, come from China, Ah Bak was singkeh, he followed my grandfather here. Lucky and smart he went into his father's business, selling shoes, selling Chinese medicine. So good, take care of people's feet, and people's insides too.

Ah Bak never let us go hungry. Very scary during the war. Singapore fell February 1942. I was only seven. We heard bombs exploding far away, and sometimes, planes swooping down. Very loud! The cries of everyone scared and confused. We hid in the house while Ah Bak made servants go out get supplies. I saw newspaper photos of some people kept in Changi prison by the Japanese. The faces of the prisoners like dried-up longans, squeezed of all moisture, not too lively. Worse than the old ones. Good thing my Ah Bak never let us go hungry! He welcomed the conquerors into our home, fed them fancy dinners on our expensive blue and white porcelain. Very pandai of him, because we got extra coupons for rice. I so excited, went with our amah to get food.

Yen's family didn't have such luck. His older brother Samuel arrested just because he talked too much at the factory where he worked. Taken to some room in their headquarters and tortured. Force-fed water until his belly swelled larger than a balloon, then they laid him down on the cold concrete floor and took turns, youngsters all, jumping down on his belly with their full weight. Poor Samuel! He was lucky it didn't kill him.

I think of those war times a lot. Now that Yen's gone, what bad luck! Start to think, didn't do all right things as mother. That's why Lan-Lan went away. How to know? My own mother treated me so poorly. All she really cared about was Ah Heen, my older brother and her only son. Spoiled him silly. She knew how much I loved school. Yet, every day after I got home, she kept me from my homework, forced me to do chores with our servants. She said a girl had to learn how to clean, to cook, that's how she learn to be good wife. I never forgave her. To think she loved Lan-Lan so much, spared her nothing.

But I was Ah Bak's favourite even though Ah Heen was first-born. My father paid me ten cents every time I found mosquito and killed it. He liked me very much.

When I think of my own children, Lan-Lan and Michael, no favourites. She the first child, Michael the boy, balance out, I say.

* * *

LEE AH CHOI

I leave the park with its beautiful young mothers and their children. Taking New Bridge Road back, I pass by Pagoda Street and my ears are disturbed! The tinsmith's clanging rhythms as he shapes pails, basins and other vessels with his tools. What a noise! I match the rhythm of my footsteps with his banging. March, *bang*, march, *bang, bang!*

This time of the afternoon, the goldsmiths in their stores are also hard at work. Their apprentices watch from a slight distance, learning through observation, also making sure their masters' teacups are never empty for long. I see the rapt attention of the younger ones, the jaded looks on those tired from more than a few years of it. First watch, then try, then get scolded. The masters peer over their apprentices' shoulders with hawk eyes. Soon their work will be done for the day and they can return to their families.

When I near the brothel, an impulse pulls my feet towards the river. I walk past the brothel to South Bridge Road. Tempted to try the tramcar as always, but I remind myself it's new, and new things need time to become reliable. The screech of the wheels terrifies me, a sharp sound like the scream of a wounded animal just before death. The shouts of hawkers, the brisk-moving smells of bodies, the rambling tramcar competing with rickety bullock carts and speedy rickshaws, all these sensations propel my restlessness. I want to watch the boats ply the river, laden with goods from the junks.

Even from a distance, the sleek tongkangs resemble giant versions of the river rats. How marvellous to move along water, what magic! I catch a whiff of the river as I lean over the bridge. The smells of life and the many ways of dying. What suffering exists below the surface? I shudder to think what strange turns of fate occur underneath, enough of them to create such a stench. While no one's watching, I whisper my confessions into it. My deepest hopes, my strongest passions. Red silk, a life of ease, beautiful clothes! I look up to see coolies on the wharves and those who run the boats straining themselves. Muscles moving over bones, bones jutting out from their sickened, opium-poisoned bodies. They have their own confessions, pouring what they can't speak into the river. Their bodies' waste, their bodies' half-hearted lusts.

If the river could speak, what would it say? What kinds of stories? To receive so much and remain silent. Except for its dreadful smell.

CHOW CHAT MUI

Ah Loong and I discovered each other only a year after we landed in Singapore and got separated. Sometime in June. I remember that because it was just after the start of the southwest monsoon. It was almost evening, there had been a sudden downpour. The wind was so strong that it whipped the rain against the trees and the houses, causing a terrible din. It didn't last very long, but long enough that, in the midst of it, a person forgot that silence ever existed. When the noise ended and it was quiet again, some of us went to the common window and looked out. We were stunned to see the rainbow. I wanted to get a better view, so I walked out to the street corner with my cigarette rolled and ready, and lit it.

The rainbow. As my eyes followed its shimmering arc back down to the horizon, I caught sight of Ah Loong as he ran with his empty rickshaw down South Bridge Road. He passed me without noticing, his bare feet covered with mud up to his ankles, his clothes dripping with sweat and rain, the smell of his exertion signalling the expulsion of a hundred demons. I shouted his name several times before he heard me and turned around. I couldn't believe the sight. My cousin, barely twenty, looking as haggard as a stray dog. How thin he'd become! His face many shades darker from sun. His tongue hanging out of his mouth.

"Mui-Mui." He dropped the handles of his rickshaw to the ground. One, two loud thuds. His eyes took in my clothes, paused at the cigarette in my hand, and then travelled back to my face. "Where do you work?" he continued, this time his voice assuming a certain sternness.

I took a long drag at my cigarette and blew a thick smoke trail out the side of my mouth. "Up the street, at Number 64."

He was silent for a long time, then he whispered tentatively, "Do you smoke opium too?"

"Yes, don't you?"

"What have we come to? Surely your parents will blame me." His voice was tight, as if there were creatures struggling to escape from his throat. He lowered his eyes to the road.

"We both wanted to escape. Why would they blame you? Besides," I took a final drag of my cigarette and extinguished it with a stomp of my wooden clog, "one less mouth to feed."

That was how Ah Loong and I found each other again. He took me for a short ride in his rickshaw, around the Hokien district, past their temple on Telok Ayer Street, circled the Scotts

Hill cemetery, then back to my brothel. Along the way, he yelled out comments about good places to eat, the kind of wages he made, the problems with his aches and pains. I marvelled at how he could do that while his body heaved and trembled with each desperate breath.

Today being the last Sunday of the month, Ah Loong is coming to visit. He'll bring his usual gifts, a bag of oranges and several packets of cigarettes. My predictable cousin. Now that he's newly married, he tries to stay away from the opium and gambling. And the ah ku. Except me, of course, seeing we've no other family here. Sometimes I think, why couldn't we have married each other? The prohibitions against cousins mixing our blood....

What would I have done if I was a man arriving in this country? I suppose I would have decided to be a rickshaw coolie too, and risked my life on the streets with angry customers and drunken types. Beast of burden. But Ah Loong is lucky. He has paid off his debt. Maybe soon he'll find some other work before this kind of labour kills him.

Did I say he looked haggard back then? Now, years later, he looks like an ancient, half his remaining teeth blackened, his back dramatically curved, his legs resplendent with veins. But I'm glad he's alive. My strong cousin. When there was that dreadful epidemic of cholera two years ago, we were all terrified. Especially the coolies who are worse off than the rats, passing diseases to each other in their cramped lodgings, drinking from polluted wells. How quickly a man could shrink in the space of a few hours from losing water from his body, eventually turning into a pale black and blue carcass! The others in the same lodgings would scatter like rats, terrified of catching the disease. Or some would dump the infected body elsewhere, in a drain, a field, even the verandah of a stranger's house!

Our labours are so different, yet Ah Loong and I both sweat with similar needs and hungers. While he pounds the pavement, bruised with the weight of his passengers, roaming the streets with his magic vehicle, I'm holed up in my box transporting men to some heavenly release. Heaven knows if it's truly divine, or if it's merely a brief detour from Hell. As for me, who can say? I've been opening my legs for so many years, it's as automatic as peeing.

Ah Loong has never invited me to his lodgings down on Smith Street. I think he's ashamed of me. I think his new wife doesn't approve. But we escaped together, and the whispering of stories as we journeyed past the ominous towers into that first town in 1900 has bound us irrevocably to each other. At least, we're not like that beggar at the corner of Nankin Street and South Bridge Road with the one stump for a leg. We still manage to hold ourselves up.

* * *

The old Italian guys stand around, waiting their turn. My spot on a bench nearby gives me a decent view, yet it's far enough to avoid their scrutiny. I hunch forward, folding my hands tightly under my armpits, inside my denim jacket. Cool but sunny for February, so I shouldn't complain. Mustn't forget the university years in snow-ridden southern Ontario. Some of the men betray in their paunchiness the years of indulgence, while other bodies are lean with sinewy ease. Many wear baseball caps, navy blue, black, neon green, red, as if it's the dress code for a game of bocce ball. From this distance I can afford to feel envious, wishing that I could join in and be able to lose myself with such abandon.

I wonder what it would have been like for Father to hang out with men like these, ones who discuss practically every issue as if it was a question of life or death.

Father had his outbursts, but he lacked a certain kind of fearlessness. Only the family witnessed his alternations between cool distance and hot tantrums. His public persona was one of consistent, polite respectfulness.

Two old men are cheering on a third. His bowling hand shoots out of his green corduroy jacket, pale but marked with purple veins. The smile as he releases his hand in a well-aimed throw shows up the lines on his face. Document of a life rich with laughter. I look over the men's heads to the small building just behind them. Trimmed with bright blue along the top and bottom is a mural depicting underwater life. Colourful fishes with striped bodies and pointy mouths blowing bubbles, an oyster with open shell revealing a very large pearl, and sea eels mimicking seaweed.

A few days after Stephanie's visit to my apartment, I tried to find her building. The most sensible thing would have been to take the books to the library, make up a plausible story to tell a staff person, and let them contact her. Instead, I wandered down her street with the library books only to discover three identical buildings. I clearly wasn't paying attention that first time. I went to each building and stared at the board of names, hoping to find their first names displayed together, but there were no Ds and Ss placed together. I gave up and returned to the library and did the sensible thing. In addition, I paperclipped a note between the pages of one of the books: "Stephanie, I'm in the phone book under Lim," and initialled it W.L., hoping she would take out the book again.

"Senora, good morning!" He chews on a fat cigar, while strolling confidently towards me. His friends are watching. He takes the cigar out and purses his lips, "You have beautiful eyes."

I find my best cynical smile, and reply, "You're leaving your friends behind."

"Oh, but I wanted to pay you a compliment. Women must be appreciated by men, always, always."

I find it difficult to judge whether a man is going to leave me alone after a brief chat. Or whether I should be entirely standoffish.

"Have a good game," I encourage him.

"Hey, can I buy you a cappuccino?"

"No thanks, my mother might get upset," I reply, with a deadpan expression.

He shrugs his shoulders and looks puzzled.

"She forbids me to go out with men. I'm waiting to be married off. Arranged marriage, you know what I mean?"

He doesn't get that I'm joking, but he goes away, mumbling something in Italian and politely nodding his head.

Back at the apartment, I notice the flashing light on my answering machine.

"Hey, I got your note. Call me." Click.

It's her. That was fast, it took her only a few days. But she doesn't leave a number.

I press *69, but the BC TEL computerized voice comes on and tells me that the number I'm trying to reach is unavailable.

Frustrating. It's beginning to feel like a cat-and-mouse game. I stuff my swimsuit and goggles into my gym bag before heading out the door.

* * *

LEE AH CHOI

That first time I met Mr. Wu, it was at Chat Mui's brothel. He paid Sum Tok extra to have me visit him there, in Sew Lan's cubicle. He had seen me stepping back into my brothel one evening. Money will buy anything, and a man with money is powerful. But I don't know what he sees in Sew Lan, with that squeaky high-pitched giggle. To have to live with that day and night. If I were her husband, I would go crazy.

Mr. Wu, a man of regular habits and consistent preferences. As a young girl, I couldn't imagine being a man's slave. But then

I was imagining some ugly old one like Liong Soon Fatt. Mr. Wu, still young and very kind, is nothing like Liong. Fair-skinned and wealthy, he has money and the charm to play around with a few ah ku. Wouldn't it be nice to be taken out of this confining life, to eat and laugh and go to sleep with clear mind and strong body? My family would be proud of me. How do I make him like me enough so that he might marry me? It's more likely to happen than winning at the gambling dens!

* * *

At the pool, I dive into the rude, cold water, feel my muscles momentarily tense from the shock. I do my version of the breast-stroke, feeling this rare amphibious self propel me forward. Up for a breath every fourth stroke. In the chlorine blue, eerie and surreal, I enter a world of muted vowels and consonants. A trail of bubbles exits from the mouth of a swimmer heading towards me in the next lane. Here we are, strangers bubbling the common ocean with our breaths, our bodies creating turbulence together. Here we are, generic green descendants. Limbs and torsos, Speedos, distorted body shapes, colourful fishes or eels in disguise.

Swimming from the shallow to the deep end, I panic when-ever my eyes catch sight of the broad blue mark on the bottom of the pool. No matter how many times I do this, it still happens. *Can you make it? It's very dangerous now.*

Lap eight. I touch the end of the pool and turn around. Time elongates, and I feel myself travelling backwards through centuries, wondering whether it's true that certain psychological traits are selected over others. Optimism over depression. Courage over fear.

The PA blasts gospel rock, "... hold on, change is coming ... hold on, you can make it ... just lift your head up. ..." A lifeguard instructs seniors in an aquatic aerobics class. "Move your arms clockwise, clockwise . . . now switch directions . . . switch again . . . switch. . . ."

Switch consciousness. On land, my body forgets this buoyancy, forgets the feeling of being supported by the whole environment around it. Now I slice through, become as smooth and sharp as a steel blade. Exhilarating at first, but halfway through lap twelve, someone's arm strays into my lane and slaps against my right leg. There's no time for apology. The interruption somehow makes me more aware how tired the muscles in my arms and legs have suddenly become.

The remaining laps are unbearably long. Until lap twenty. This is it. I look ahead. A pair of short, bony legs cuts quickly in front of me. Too late. I collide into her, and splutter upwards into the air. I'm breathing hard, feeling my whole body heave with each breath. I remove my goggles, turn around, and look back along the length of the pool. Heads dance up and down. The surface of the water breaks out in waves of froth.

"Sorry, sorry! See, my niece and nephew!" She grins as she points to two lively kids, perhaps eight and twelve, at the other end of the pool, playing at the slide. She must mean to say that her attention was on them at the expense of swimmers like me. I force a grin, but the lie doesn't work and I end up choking. She wades over to me and pats me too firmly on the back three, four times. I try to be calm getting out of the pool, but my legs are embarrassingly like rubber.

After showering and dressing, I walk out to a sky fast approaching darkness. It depresses me still, this climate. Twenty years, and you would think I've gotten used to it. But no, it seems I'll always feel the darkness as coming on too soon and too strongly. It's a constant reminder of loss, of that even balance of day and night, a certain kind of innocence.

* * *

CHOW CHAT MUI

Her dreams are foolish. How many of our customers would want to marry an ah ku? Not Mr. Wu. The ones who rescue ah ku are those who are insanely obsessed with their women, must keep them all to themselves. The ones diseased by jealousy. Can't she see Mr. Wu isn't like that? Her greed blinds her.

Maybe because I'm much older, been longer in this business than she has, I'm sceptical. Careful, I warn her. She wants to get pregnant with a rich man's child, wants him to take her as wife or concubine. She trusts in a man's loyalty to his seed. How could she, after her father betrayed her like that? She believes in filial piety, as if we are lesser beings if we turn away from our families! I ask her, what is the use of piety towards those who betray us?

Women risk their livelihoods when they get pregnant. Then they risk their lives if they try to expel their accidents. Dreadful, how mean some kwai pos can be, sticking needles into the women, making them drink special medicines. Careful, Ah Choi.

What does our love mean to her? She craves being rescued by a man. Wish I could take us away. Her face is like that of a child, looking out at the corrupt world with eyes of longing. How is it that suffering doesn't erase that optimism in her?

I confess I've my own fantasies. Good for passing the time, for helping with the pain. At night, I become a many-headed monster with large, paper-thin wings that move with a great strength. With enough power to propel me towards some mountain, some place I've never been to before, perhaps Europe. I've seen picture of such mountains. In the calendar downstairs, in Ah Sek's room. I sneak in to look at them when he's not around. Photos of castles and elaborate gardens with several fountains. Entering a new month, he tears off the previous sheet and throws it away. But I rescue each picture, and now I've saved up many. Keep them wrapped in newspaper underneath my bed.

What if my eyes could penetrate walls? Surely such an intense glare could melt at least a few obstacles. One long gaze, and I'll break through the hateful confinement to reach her.

I desire a place for Ah Choi and me. Po Leung Kuk, we could go there. Office for the protection of our virtue! But then the place can give us soiled women only temporary refuge. The men who can't afford a dowry go there for a cheap wife, someone who has been taught sewing and domestic service. Yes, Ah Choi would be quickly taken, but what about me?

How much longer? I'm tap tang, and surely . . . Wong Ah Yee keeps telling me I still owe money for the clothes, the protection.

Ah Choi loves me, I'm sure. All her talk about being married, I mustn't forget it's plain foolishness. There's purity in a feeling. The ugliness falls away when she touches me. She draws out the fiery brightness that lives within. I look into her face and something in me remembers . . . how simple to want beauty itself, to long for what pleases.

She has made me wish for a different life. After eight years, my heart stirs with a kind of longing I'd felt only fleetingly that first year, when I thought Ah Sek would take care of me. If only Ah Choi and I could run away together. There's a rumour that some women have started their own private brothel in another part of town. . . . What if we went there, start saving the money we make, instead of this continual pawning of our bodies.

Oh, my imagination! As bad as hers. I'm a different kind of fool. Wishful thinking . . . how easily it slips my mind that they would send samseng after us.

* * *

I lie back on the sofa, and light a cigarette. I'm exhausted from the swim. Dom and Gerry are having a pre-Valentine's Day potluck later this evening. I'm all set with my agar-agar jelly dessert in the refrigerator. There's time for some relaxation and another smoke.

I feel funny about Valentine's Day. Should I call Mahmee? Probably not. It would upset her.

Why did Father kill himself?

The first possibility that comes to mind: he went to the doctor for his annual check-up and found out he had some serious medical condition. Cancer. Or more likely, cirrhosis of the liver. I imagine the doctor looking wide-eyed at him, "Mr. Lim, didn't know you drank!" Father couldn't forget the horror he suffered when he watched his mother die of cancer. He didn't want us to experience that. Noble of him, except didn't he realize his suicide would be just as upsetting, or worse?

Second possibility: Father realized he was living a lie. He was essentially dead all these years. His vitality sacrificed to a mundane reality, responsibility to family, a boring job. All those bottles of booze emptied into his system. Hadn't he been full of spark and passion as a young man?

Third: it was an accident of the subconscious. Deep down he felt a desire to annihilate himself, to erase his suffering. But since his conscious self found that completely reprehensible, he had to allow some slip to happen.

I've talked Dom and Gerry's ears off with these endless variations. But broach the topic with family? I'm terrified. Yet I want to, I must. Perhaps Michael can tell me things none of my friends can. I want to find out what he knows. Why not now? Seven-thirty AM their time. He would be just up and getting ready for work. I dial Michael's number. Susan picks up the phone.

"Hey, it's you! Aiyah, why so long you don't phone? How come you didn't come back for Christmas?" Her voice is controlled, seemingly friendly. But as usual, I'm not convinced.

"Is Michael awake?"

"Oh yeah! I let him tell you the news."

"What news?"

"You wait, wait huh? Michael!" Her voice is raised to a shout, then I hear the muffling of a hand over the receiver.

"Hallo, Lan? Hey, guess what? Susan is pregnant!"

"Oh? Do you both . . . want this?"

"Of course, lah! Where's the congrats?"

"Congratulations, you two. When is it due?"

"Late October. We got pregnant just before Chinese New Year's." His voice announces this news with childish glee.

I sigh with my mouth slightly away from the phone. Not a good time to talk about Father's suicide.

"So, any special reason why you call?"

"No, no, just thought I'll say hi."

"Oh?" He doesn't hide his surprise. "Hey, Sis, not one to lecture you, but—"

"What?"

"You should go back to work soon, huh?"

I'm quiet for a while. It's that wonderful Singaporean industriousness again. After all, everyone works six days a week other than the teachers. Working five days is considered slacking off, and the idea of a leave of absence still has my family reeling in shock and disapproval. Even though they haven't confronted me with it until now.

"Yes. Soon. Well, talk to you again some other time."

I hang up. Wow, what a filial son. His wife finally gets pregnant, not long after the requisite hundred days of mourning. The phone rings. Michael having second thoughts about our conversation? I let the answering machine take it.

"Hey . . . it's your library friend, what do you say about meeting again? Call me, 681-0844."

So now she decides to leave me a number and sounds so confident. I lift up the receiver, listen to the dial tone for a few seconds. Place the receiver back down.

In *Last Tango in Paris*, Maria Schneider doesn't know his name until the very end. This revelation follows the scene in which Brando cries over his wife's dead body. I was sceptical. After all that earlier dogged devotion to anonymity with Maria, then a cathartic weep over his wife's extremely well-preserved body, he's suddenly ready to shed his secrecy and launch into a fully intimate relationship with dear Maria. The one who doesn't show attachment to sentimentality, to an emotional intimacy built on history and knowledge, suddenly reveals his name and proposes love.

Who betrays whom? Brando betrays Maria by the abandonment of anonymity, and so Maria has to kill the man to protect the myth. I liked the ending. It made a certain kind of sense. It said to me, *Watch out for confessions of love.*

I get up and replay the message from Stephanie, copy down the phone number. Slip it under a pile of papers.

* * *

MAHMEE

Me! A little grandchild. Yen, you got no chance to show off with baby! Selfish, not want to pay attention to me, so fierce and everything. Now maybe this grandchild will have some good qualities of mine, and others of yours, from the time you younger and carefree. Don't know why you ever went into selling cars. Show upholstery, engine, paint. Aiyah, boring. But you bring the money home, why I complain? Funny, you sell expensive cars and you drive that old Morris Minor. I give your brother Samuel. Now I think he give one of your nephews to drive around.

That job. Something so tired about you all the time. You no longer the lively man with the bright eyes. In the beginning you asked me to join you for a drink. But my parents teach me it's very chor lore for a woman to do such a thing. People will think I'm low class and cheap. But you replied, no one but us will know. Yeah yeah, I know, and my parents turn in their graves if I ever joined you. But now too late. Before you lonely for companion, and I too careful, too busy with housework, to want to do such things. Forgive me, please stop coming back to bother me.

* * *

LEE AH CHOI

She too dreams of escape, yet accuses me of foolishness. Leave me to my dreams then. Some man who has pity on me. Can't hope for better. The way my luck is these days, it'll take many years to pay off my debts. I think about using the money I've hidden away under the straw mat, but it's too little to make a difference. It's only money to risk with at the gambling dens, money to throw at Heaven, in the hopes that good luck will visit me.

Chat Mui is a fool. This love between us is worthless in the eyes of the world. Too melodramatic, she and her stories. My dream is more possible than hers.

I'm afraid. The deaths. The sisters who've taken their own lives. I'm afraid of their ghosts returning. Now that it's evening, the shadows plague me. No sunshine to distract demons. First, the woman in the Tan Quee Lan brothel in May. Then Sin Chow at 4 Trengganu Street. Opium overdose. I'm sure they killed themselves. All of us at the brothel were shaken up, even though only a few of us had known them. Rumour has it that Sin Chow died with her eyes open . . . oh, what a bad omen.

What if it's true, that the ghosts of ah ku who killed themselves will come back to torture those still living? If Sin Chow returns as a ghost to haunt the rest of us . . . horrid! I pray for protection. I go to the temple across the street almost every day now. As I chant the prayers, fear is a gripping pain in my gut. Quan Yin with her calm face understands. And P'an Chin-lien too, goddess of all brothels. She knows what it's like to live at the mercy of many unknowns. She has suffered enough to deserve our homage. I prostrate myself in front of the altar and let the words flow out of me. There are all kinds of people who go, the rich and the poor, the infirm, the healthy. Everyone seeks some compassion, some relief from suffering. The mumbling voices, weaving in and out of each other, highs and lows, echoing in the large, generous room. How my tears flow in the sanctity of that temple, in the presence of those goddesses.

I keep telling Chat Mui she must visit the temple. Even a moment's peace is surely precious. Heaven hears us, if we're passionate enough, if we're desperate enough. I believe it. If Heaven has the power to wreak chaos, it also alone has the power to save us. The smell of incense smoke soothes me, in a darkness neither dangerous nor rife with the heaviness of other bodies. A darkness of disembodied voices, companions in this invisible journey. A darkness that is a kind of light, inseparable from all the hundreds of lit candles burning within it.

CHOW CHAT MUI

The beggar! After all these weeks of absence, I see him when I pass by Dr. Lim's private hospital. The open door invites the unhealthy to enter. There he is, lying on a bed. It was his stump that caught my eye. The only part of him that's visible from the outside. Now it's crawling with creamy worms in the hundreds, their mouths tearing into a gash on one side. The bloody, yellow pus dripping onto the bed sheet, the odour so foul it rivals the worst garbage pile.

I feel sick, yet I'm curious. I want to see his face, want to know what this man's suffering has done to him. So I walk through the entrance, into the room. From the other side of the wall comes the faint voice of some authority, giving instructions to a nurse to clean wounds.

He's asleep. The flies are madly buzzing with interest. I clamp my hand over my nose and mouth. I feel my insides heave with disgust. He stirs, his eyes open slowly and stare at me.

"Shame. You've come to witness my suffering."

I say nothing. I have no words to comfort him. I'm guilty for being unable to help. I turn around and run out. Stop at a drain and feel the bile and food rise up my throat and pour out of me.

People walk by and avoid me. I wipe my mouth as clean as I can with leaves from the nearest tree, and continue towards the brothel.

* * *

I don't like that queasy feeling. It arrives now along with that cliché about hindsight being perfect.

Michael's announcement about the pregnancy has upset me. He's made a baby in the time I've been away from work and cut back on my social life. When Father killed himself, I'd thought that grief was the only reason I needed a year's leave of absence. Now I know I'd lost confidence in my ability to help people find a way past their powerlessness. Something more. Something I never had dared to acknowledge before. Father's death has served as a kind of earthquake that has exposed a part of me I don't relish seeing: a raw and ugly sore that reeks of an increasing resentment, an intolerance for the suffering of others. Some people at Father's funeral were terrified, not only rudely reminded of their mortality, but also aware of their capacity for self-destruction. They wanted me to help them forget, to soothe them with words, a gesture of kindness.

How angry and envious I became at others' ability to express their needs. I sat in that cold funeral parlour, smelling the heat and the wetness of their upset. All I could think of was that phone message, the few words he left repeating in my mind.

Back in Vancouver, it occurred to me that I've become used to being just a listener, a repository for others' stories. I've learned to set aside my feelings and my needs in order to do my job responsibly. Wasn't that also what Father had expected of me? He expected me to listen whenever he turned on the sadness late at night. How selfish of him to leave that message on my answering machine! Didn't he think about the impact it might have on me later? Later and too late.

The first few weeks after the funeral, every time I expressed empathy for my clients, an inside bitterness spread through me. I felt nauseated after a day's work. How could I help others when I couldn't confess my own inner turmoil?

I was an impostor. My clients spoke in my place. They confessed while I hid, unable to face myself. Their sharp insights scored my raw wound.

Where are they all on this dark February evening? Do they have spouses or families to celebrate with them on Valentine's Day? Those ordinary yet brilliant people who came to me for solace, for advice. M., whose line was "I'm so angry, I can't let anyone get too close to me."

T., who believed, "I don't deserve, I can't believe, it's impossible."

And F.: "I'm lonely, but no one suspects because I look so cool and live so cool."

Their comments reverberate still somewhere deep inside my gut. This evening, I'm regaining some appreciation of their collective wisdoms, fleeting yet obviously memorable to me. What was Stephanie's line that first afternoon? "We believe in being ourselves." That too startled me with its fresh honesty. Someone who's no longer anonymous to herself can say that, someone who's no longer besieged.

* * *

LEE AH CHOI

Mr. Wu and his friends and three of us ah ku. A horse-drawn carriage sent from the stable nearby. Their money buys us a night out. Ha, if only Chat Mui could see me here. A rare sight.

I was pleased to receive Mr. Wu's wang choy, a protection against the hungry ghosts. So pleased that I insisted on hanging the red banner immediately outside our common window before we left for Lai Chun Yuen. Surely this is a good omen.

The British architect who designed Lai Chun Yuen is the same one who did the Raffles Hotel. That's why their exteriors look similar. The hypocrites won't let an ah ku like me into the Raffles. But I've seen some European prostitutes from Phan Tsai Mei get in with their clients. What do they know? At least I can enter the opera house. Class, I insist, I have it.

The carriage dropped us off right at the entrance. There were swarms of people outside in the night market, jostling against each other to buy food, squatting on the sidewalks to eat, buying joss-sticks, and special red-tipped buns as offerings for the ghosts. Couldn't the swarms see me stand out blushingly sweet and waiting to be eaten?

Of course they could. Those with greed in their eyes were probably staring at my jewellery. Mr. Wu insisted I wear his pieces for the night. I will have to be careful.

Just inside the entrance, at the top of the stairs, we were met with an enormous altar. Laden with offerings, dishes of delicious meats and green vegetables gleaming with garlic and oil. Mandarin oranges, piled up in two pyramids. How generous. We mortals must restrain ourselves from stealing. Must remember to respect the ghosts. We do, we respect out of fear, but how everything dazzled me with its seductions!

For the whole of this seventh lunar month, ghosts, swarms of them, are released from Hell. They must be fed. They can't go hungry very long before disaster strikes. Must be fed on the dramas of live flesh. The man who built Lai Chun Yuen must have known this.

The first floor of the opera house was already packed by the time we arrived, but no matter, because Mr. Wu and his friends had secured the more expensive tickets for the balcony.

How grand a place this is, with lights from the ceiling and the walls, and tall shadows reaching up almost to the second floor. I'm dizzy from looking down on the bobbing heads of men, women and children. I trace their restless, fidgety movements. Is it the opium I took that makes them appear like bursts of light darting about? The sounds of coughing, of lips smacking as food is eaten, of throats being cleared. Too loud, too large, stop it!

When the lamps are turned down in the house and only the stage is lit, I take a few more puffs of the pipe. How graceful these women-men. I like them. See how they appease the ghosts. Brave. Their fluid shadows on the wall draw me into the world of invisibles.

Give me those two-foot-long water sleeves. I'll do justice to that language, I'll show them my watery hands of innocence. Dipped in my own blood and sweat. Ha, the labour of love. Transport me into another's life, another's body. I will be a virtuous chan yee, tragic heroine. I know enough tragedy to play the part. I'm less than merchandise, I'm too cheap for fame. Sorrow looms over me, a nasty shadow, even though my eyes are trained on the stage. I feel its weight descend onto my shoulders.

Lai Chun Yuen, already twenty years old! Stories of heroism that overcomes obstacles, of justice that rights imbalances. Poor people's house of hope, always full, even with two performances every day. We hunger for this, I say, we hunger. We the common ones, who must be silent, who must obey. We're the ones who want what we don't have. Hunger makes us ghosts in our lonely lives.

Tinge of sweetness, smoky sweet dirt. And I'm on the stage telling everyone my story, all eyes transfixed by my presence....

Chow Chat Mui

Opium, don't fail, don't leave me. Precious moments in the early morning, this floating sensation. My body drifts quietly, spared from pain. The lake is untroubled by turbulence, no wind disturbs it. This moment is forever.

My sisters are out there in the back alley, gossiping about this and that, anything their minds can feed on. About me, about how despicable I am. Why was I born so unloved? O Heaven! Do they know I hear their every whisper amplified a thousand times? Their cruel whispers prompt my tears to flow.

Gossip, we live and die by it. Who would tell our stories if not us? Who else would bother to spend the early hours smoking cheap cigarettes and trading pieces of cheap lives? "Psst, psst. This client, you know what he did?"

Can't they be a little kinder? They don't know what my father did. Can't they see past my ugliness and dirt, the way Ah Choi can, the way fear doesn't stop her from touching my body, with its glaring sores? If they only knew what Ah Choi and I dare to do. Maybe they already do. People must see the way we turn towards each other. Careful, they'll name our desire sick and despicable, crush it under the hateful weight of their gossip. Or maybe they think nothing of this love, and only laugh secretly to themselves. Make it as trivial as a passing cloud, a raindrop disappearing into the vast ocean. If my tears are as petty as raindrops, then why cry, but I don't want to stop. My eyes will wear heavier shadows, but no matter, even a torrent of tears can't topple this mountain.

I hear their shrill voices, the coarse sounds expelled by their mouths, their clucking tongues . . . like rude explosions in my head. The air is dirty, the thunder keeps sounding. Stop it!

* * *

I don't understand Mahmee. Why would she send me a pair of old brocade slippers? No letter, no explanation. Except a book on sightseeing in Singapore. The reason I know for sure it's her is the return address in her familiar scribble on the large brown bubble-envelope. The stamp bears the date 18/2/95. The parcel can't have been sitting here in my postal box very long then. I've never seen Mahmee wear such slippers. They were probably Mah-Mah's. Ancient with use, the edges already fraying. The velvet inside the heel is worn away to expose the network of threads. The embroidery on the front is ornate, with an unusual pattern of two entwined phoenixes. The scales on the dorsal sides of their bodies are azure-blue, edged with a thin border of pale green. Feathers of yellow, red and purple adorn their necks. Their crimson heads sprout wisps of blue from the top. Beads had been sewn in for the eyes. They stare at me, undaunted by the history and distance that separate me from them.

I stuff the gift back into the parcel, leave the post office, and walk down Hamilton. The Java Cat sign up ahead reminds me that I haven't phoned Stephanie. At the café, I'm disappointed: instead of the dark beauty, a man with a mop of hair dyed excessively black hovers behind the counter, poring over a fashion magazine.

"Uh, where is . . . the other—"

He looks blankly at me, then: "Oh, she doesn't work here all the time."

Do I dare ask him? I study his eyebrows and eyelashes. They are a light blond. Guess he couldn't be bothered to match them. "Coffee, please."

I retrieve a fashion magazine from the shelf under the counter, and turn to the horoscope section. "Pisces: You're prone to get yourself in too deep romantically in the early months of 1995. Planetary influences unsettle you in both personal and professional spheres. Stay close to your intuitive sensibilities." I chuckle to myself. Yeah, sure, Ms. or Mr. Stargazer.

A familiar voice enters the café, offers a greeting. Fake Black raises his head and nods. I turn to look. It's the woman. She doesn't smile at me, but walks right around to the other side of the counter, and starts to whisper to the man. Looks slightly worried. I wonder what's going on. I move closer under the pretence of searching for another magazine, trying to eavesdrop. My elbow knocks against something hard. Hot coffee covers my left hand with a strong, sudden pain.

"Aargh!"

"Oh God. Quick, over here. Under the tap."

Her arm guides me firmly to the sink. I stare numbly at my hand, reddening under the jet of water.

"You should keep it under for at least twenty minutes," Fake Black says, in a very cool voice. In contrast, the woman is quite upset, her eyebrows furrowed in concern.

White and yellow spots start appearing in front of my eyes. "Dizzy . . . I need to lie down."

She finds a bucket, fills it with water, and I plunge my throbbing hand into it. Then we move me, hand in bucket, to the sofa on the other side of the room. "Close your eyes, relax. Don't worry about rushing off."

Feet off the ground, body reclining, I feel some relief pass over me, even though my hand still stings. It all happened so quickly. How careless of me.

The swimming pool. That wonderful feeling of being underwater. I would like to be there right now. I let my mind drift, while people's movements around me are rustling the air with crisp, sharp noises.

* * *

MAHMEE

For Lan-Lan's forty-second birthday I sent her Ah Mak's slippers. Maybe they make her homesick. I sent her book I got free from Tourist Promotion Board. Who knows? She misses the food. The pictures might make her think twice. Nothing as important as hunger. I know.

How could I tell Ah Mak her precious granddaughter gone so far away? After Ah Bak died, my mother very lonely. She sent servants away. Lived in big house with only Ah Heen. I was very sad about my father. But then things between Ah Mak and me seemed to improve, very slowly. She very different person when husband not around any more. More kind, more easygoing. Not so fussy about what she eat.

One day in April 1984, she fell down the stairs, and died soon after. Brain aneurysm. I didn't even have a chance to wish her farewell. When we got to hospital she was already unconscious. Stupid staff, asked us if we were really family, and Yen and I had to pull out our identity cards before they let us in to see her.

I remember, it was a cool day. My head full with noise and worry. We went fast on Nicholl Highway. Couldn't believe it, my mother was going to die. And where was Ah Heen? Out somewhere spending Ah Mak's money, up to no good. He has no heart.

Lan-Lan angry. She wants something from me, I know it, except I don't know what. Why she don't ask? That's why I give her those slippers. Found them in a sandalwood trunk in the house. Her Mah-Mah's kasut manik, such beautiful nonya handiwork, you don't see such slippers around any more. When Ah Mak died, I was the only person who could take care of things since Ah Heen was usually too drunk or drugged with something. This is the son my mother spent all her love on? What a waste! The government wants the property, but how much will they pay for it? I still have to take care of this business. Find Ah Heen a home he can't gamble away.

Never mind, I say. If I think too much, it make me even more khek sim, my heart upset. Those slippers. She used to wear them a lot before the Japanese came. And then she stopped. How come? She used to put them on in the evenings after dinner. When everyone finished eating, and the plates washed and food put away in the cupboards. Then she went to the open-air tap at the back of the long kitchen, filled the bucket with water and put her feet in it for a long time. Every night no fail. We knew must not disturb her. I still remember, sound of water rushing into the bucket. *Slosh, slosh, slosh.* Then sweet, sweet silence. When her feet went in, the water made slapping sounds.

I was shocked to find the kasut manik. Wrapped in a piece of batik, one of her sarong kebayas actually. Why she stopped wearing those lovely slippers? I never know what to think any more. But at least I brought them back and placed them on Lan-Lan's bed. I glimpsed them sitting there every morning on my way between bedroom and kitchen. It's almost eleven years now since Mah-Mah's death. Why not, I thought, why not. Send her something precious of her Mah-Mah's.

* * *

LEE AH CHOI

The gambling is not going well. Fever, o fever of my need! Why doesn't my name bring luck? As a name should. The two hundred I saved, dwindled down now to a hundred. Heaven is merciless! The value of our money plummeting, with all the troubles in the city. The riots among the samseng, what a mess. Go where there's scarcity, and you'll find the grasping hands of greed.

Who deserves our outward loyalty, who deserves our trust?

We must choose, but we must be careful. How foul-tempered the samseng are. I see the dark anger seething in their eyes, even as they collect protection money from us. They're full of hate. Who will protect us from the samseng?

Oh, the ache in my bones when I pull myself away from the gambling tables and hail a rickshaw home.

CHOW CHAT MUI

I woke up this morning to air heavy with anticipation, my fantasies of a different life lingering above me. I got out of bed, walked down the hallway to the window, flung open the shutters and looked out into the far horizon. On some clear days, I can make out fragments of the ocean and the ships that depend on its wild mercy and strength. But today the vision was limited by striped layers of ash-grey clouds stretching across the sky. I began to will an illusion, so much so that I tasted the ocean at my lips, beckoning me outside.

Now I'm on the streets, in plain, unflattering clothes, wandering, restless, still not knowing what it is I'm looking for. I think about Ah Choi's admonition to go to the temple. She is so impassioned about her visits there. Perhaps it will soothe me just to be in a large, quiet room with many lit candles. I head towards South Bridge Road and cross over to the Ning Yeung Hui Guan. Worshippers with their hands full—joss-sticks, oranges, pomelos—flock into the temple. But what's this? Outside the entrance, at a table covered with saffron yellow cloth, a pair of bony hands, the veins pronounced yet the skin still alabaster smooth. One hand gracefully moves an ink brush over a section of rice paper. A beautiful picture forms in front of me. My eyes slowly travel up the sleeves, noting the faded blue cotton, up to the shoulders, finally resting on the face. Fine, delicate eyebrows and lips, then I see a distinct Adam's apple. A man, but with long hair rolled up into a sanggol sipot. A thin face with large eyes that rise like moons above pronounced cheekbones, and his skin is as liquid-smooth as coconut oil. His slender, dark eyebrows are like swallows' wings, tuned for graceful flight. I am mesmerized by their beauty.

He must have sensed my stare, because he soon raises his eyes to meet mine.

"Yes, can I help you?" he asks me in Hokien.

Since I know only a few words, I answer back in Cantonese instead, "Ngei cho maht yeh?" pointing to his brush.

"Writing characters," he replies in his singsong Cantonese.

I blush, because my ignorance has been discovered. Still, I must ask, and the confession stumbles out of my mouth, awkward as a stone caught in the throat, "I don't read. Please, tell me what word you're making with your fine brushwork."

He smiles, perhaps because I've complimented him, although who in his right mind should take seriously the remarks of an illiterate? He tears off the section of paper, separating the picture he has drawn from the blankness.

"Here, take this." His smile widens into a charming warmth. "The word here 田 is made up of two meanings. This one is field, and the 心 one below is heart. Together they make up the word for contemplation."

Our fingers almost touch as my rough, dark hand receives the precious word. I pull out my purse, but he shakes his head. This moment is like a sharp light that has penetrated a dirt-infested room, changing it forever. No stranger has ever given me a true gift, something for which I needn't pay.

After managing a quivering thank you, I turn around to walk back, this gift clutched close to my body. I glance at it several times. The top part does remind me of a field, its boxy shape divided within by a pair of crossed lines. The lines so strong and clear that I can feel the movement of the brush as I follow the strokes from thin beginnings to thick completions. How beautiful. I watch my father's field from afar. My body is light despite the memory, because I am no longer there. My eyes shift to that other symbol below the field. He said it stood for the heart. It's true, the shape is much like the hearts I've seen torn out of animals in the marketplace. Small and fragile, tilted slightly as if at rest, its three thick dots signifying the inside chambers. Throbbing with secrets.

When I reach home, I rush up to my cubicle. Four PM. The urge for a smoke presses thickly into my temples. Sharp edge of pain cuts through my guts. I place the paper on the small crate next to my bed. I lay down with the pipe after lighting the pellet. The sweet smoke slowly permeates my cubicle, draws my body into a lazy warmth. The character for thought has become mine, without even education or money. I too can enjoy a word, feel its beauty and peace calm me. I know what a field is, and I know what my heart yearns for! A word after all is a thing I touch and see . . . I let its shape enter me, while I'm carried on the waves of this exquisite poisoning.

* * *

She bends over me with a wet towel, wiping my forehead. I watch her doing this from underneath a watery barrier. Somehow I had slipped back along the evolutionary process, back into the ocean, my limbs lost to human function. Soft blur of the underworld. Where fear-ridden eyes had peered into mine, warning me of dangers. What dangers? How long has she been wiping my forehead? Her hair falls freely over her shoulders. I would like to reach up and stroke it, but my arms feel like lead.

Her lips are pursed. I make out a fuzzy outline of her breasts just above the low neckline of her top. Lovely dream. The coldness of the towel finally reaches me. I come up for air, shudder into full consciousness.

"Are you all right?"

An arm frees up, and I slowly reach up to my mouth, pull one of my hairs out of the way. Speak, I urge myself. Speak.

"Wasn't sure if you fainted." Her fingers caress my cheek.

"I'm fine, really. Just drifted off."

I blink quickly several times. I was mistaken. Her hair is still neatly in a braid. She gently lowers my head back down to the sofa. I turn my head slightly to the left and notice that the package is on the coffee table.

I close my eyes and murmur, struggling against sinking into the watery depths again. "Guess I should get up. Your customers."

"Oh, don't worry. The big wave doesn't arrive for an hour."

The three seated at the far end seem not to be bothered by my reclining presence. I place my hand on her arm. It is smooth in a different way from mine, covered with soft down.

"Thanks," I offer weakly. She returns to the counter. I sit up awkwardly, not feeling as if all of me has returned. The burn on the back of my left hand is bright red. I reach for the package with my other hand. I take a few deep breaths, stand up shakily, and walk towards the door.

"Hey, hope the accident doesn't stop you from coming back?" She winks at me. I blush and flash her a smile.

I amble down Hamilton, the package under one arm, both hands stuffed into the pockets of my coat. The burnt hand feels raw, the skin alive with prickly pain. IS IT NOTHING TO YOU? the inscription on the Victory Park stone memorial asks yet again. At the bus stop an elderly man with a red, bulbous nose and flabby cheeks leans against the bus shelter, a Safeway plastic bag filled with Kraft Dinners at his feet. He seems untroubled by the lack of a warm coat, wearing only a blue and white checkered cotton shirt underneath a beige cardigan. A baseball cap sits squarely on his bald head. I notice its neon pink words staring at me: "Don't Panic, Eat Salmon."

We file into the bus when it arrives. I sit behind Mr. Salmon, contemplating his advice. A salmon steak, pink and succulent, baked in foil, with slices of fresh ginger, green onions, lemon juice, and a dash of salt and pepper. The heat on my hand is made slightly more tolerable at this thought. I close my eyes, sink into the seat, and try to recall how that woman's arm felt when I touched it. The softness of another creature. The bus turns onto the Drive. I get off at Kitchener, and head off to Antonia's Fish Store.

* * *

LEE AH CHOI

Many coolies need much more than me. What with their bodies racked with pain. Coming in at one or two AM, shaking in cold sweat, muscles weak from pulling rickshaws and from the drain of disease. If it's not some sex disease, it's that awful TB in the lungs. Somehow the body must shout some kind of protest: red sores, yellow pus, blood from the lungs. I swear coolies spend half their wages on temporary relief. What a sorry sight, heaps of bones and flesh lying on my straw mat, eyes glazed, breathing going from shallow to deep, their pain gradually subsiding if only for the next few hours. Barely bodies, barely alive, yet craving the momentary release of orgasm. Wretched creatures.

CHOW CHAT MUI

When I think of it, far better a half-limp client than a crazed one. A few nights ago, I heard muffled noises, then Sew Lan's voice cursing, "Tsuei chai, kum tsuei!" Shouts, hurried footsteps down the stairs, then Ah Yee and Ah Sek screaming at the man, ordering him to leave. I'd finished with a client only moments before, so I lay on my bed listening to the rise and fall of voices from downstairs. Ah Yee screamed a warning that the man never would be allowed to return to the brothel. I got up and lifted the curtain to look. From my cubicle, I could see past the stairs to the front entrance. The man's face was twisted with rage. Flames of heat burned in his eyes. There was a gash of blood across the top of his forehead, his hair was in disarray. Sew Lan! With one eye swollen and bloodied, she was leaning against our kwai po. Then I saw the piece of broken glass in the man's right hand. He was unsteady on his feet, and Ah Sek and the others quickly pounced on him, and brought him down to the ground. Ah Sek stepped on his wrist, and the man let go of the glass with a yelp. They pummelled him with their fists. His body caved inwards, his spirit diminished with every blow. Then they opened the door, and kicked him down the steps.

* * *

A gigantic boa constrictor curls around her naked body. The Java Cat woman dances on a small stage covered with red velvet, and the music is a souped-up version of "Ain't I a Woman," replete with too much brass and violins. I'm in the audience sucking on my burnt hand, suitably impressed, wondering where she trained to dance like that.

The bed gives way. I'm falling down a hole. Fast, slow, fast. A voice repeats intermittently, *Hell isn't always below.* The falling changes, becomes a different sensation, more like being pulled downwards. I'm moving fast, wind whips my hair, long and thick, against my face. What's wind, what's hair, soon indistinguishable. My cheeks burn with the stinging speed.

I wake up, my heart pounding in my ears. Four-thirty AM. I touch my chest and neck. My skin is chilled with a thin layer of sweat. My burn feels slightly itchy. I try to stay awake, not wanting to go back into the dream.

I don't see anything at first. Total darkness, then a low, droning sound. When the light comes on, I see that I'm in a plane. From my vantage point at the cockpit, I look down the aisle at the passengers. Everyone from the office, plus a few others I don't recognize. All dressed in clown outfits. Large balloons of many colours float above their heads. Balloons with slogans on them: "Fly me" and "Happy holidays" and "Send me." I don't know what the occasion is. Daniel waves at me from the back, alternatively pulling and pointing at his balloon. In the cockpit, Ben is seated in the pilot seat. He shouts at me to get back into my seat. But which is my seat? I stare at his face, which becomes increasingly distorted, his mouth stretched out like a gigantic elastic band, his eyes hanging lopsided. It's so upsettingly deformed that I have to laugh to cope, but my body is quivering with fear. The woman from the Java Cat appears with a cold towel and says urgently, "Let me wipe your forehead. You're very sweaty." "No, no," I tell her, "I have to leave now," as I place my hand on the exit door.

Five-fifty. A breeze from the minute gap in the window licks at the sweat on my chest. I try to go back to sleep, but my eyes are peeled awake, a fast pulse throbbing in my ears. It might be more peaceful to go outside than lie like this. When I finally walk out of the apartment, the sun is a luscious blood-orange barely showing above the horizon.

The streets are deserted, revealing no trace of last night's dreams. The world temporarily absent of others. I survey the gardens, imagine strangers asleep in their beds, falling into their own dreams. Crocuses are just nudging their purple and white heads above ground, their bright orange centres a touch of sun. I inhale deeply. Cool air, cleaner in the morning before the day gains its full blast of exhaust fumes. My cells crave oxygen. I must quit smoking. I wander the back streets and alleys, taking a wide loop around the neighbourhood. Finally I reach the running track at Britannia. No one else here.

The houses around the track move like snails past me. Then the mural, with its cheery representations of the East End: clean, renovated façades of houses. Bright blue sky. Emerald green grass.

No signs of used needles and condoms discarded on the streets. No hookers on the corners. No beggars. No people period. Just the happy faces of houses. The gravel crunches underneath my walking shoes. After a few rounds, I stop at one of the large boulders near the track and slump down on it, resting my head in my hands.

When I raise my head and look around, I catch sight of the profile of a woman who passes by on the other side of the street. It's a client whom I saw for only one or two sessions, just before my leave of absence. She doesn't see me but I feel quite self-conscious in my old grey sweatpants and faded denim jacket. I notice myself caving in, trying to hide.

I still remember her story because it was quite unusual. She wanted her husband to change, to stop being the loud, uncouth party performer. He was the heavy drinker who told too many bad jokes and expected people to laugh at them. The one who burped and farted in the company of strangers without apologizing.

I had asked her, "Is there something you would secretly love to do, but haven't dared believe is possible?"

She flinched and then snarled, "What do you mean?"

I tried again. "I mean, what would you dream of doing if nobody was watching, including you?"

I remember she lowered her eyes in response to the question.

She gazed down at the carpet. Her hands clutched her handbag while her shoulders twitched slightly. After a long time, she looked back up at me, with the same distant look she had when she entered my office.

What would I do, if nobody was watching?

I make a snap decision to walk to Chinatown. Have a bowl of preserved egg and pork congee, and a rice roll laced with sweet brown sauce and sesame seeds. The thought cheers me up a bit.

I cut through a back alley next to a dumping lot filled with old tires and the half-rusted bodies of cars. Pass by Kiku Fisheries, rank with the sharp smells of brine and fish bodies.

A squirrel darts out from behind a bush and hesitates. Then I notice a dark brown Pontiac that's just turning in from Clark. The animal rushes forward, turns its body sideways as the front wheels miss it. For a split second, my intense relief. But the squirrel fails. The back wheels run over it in one lightning slap-thud. The car disappears down another side street. The animal flails once, twice, three times. Then is finally still.

Breakfast does nothing to remove the slight tremor that's travelling through my body. I walk along Main, not very crowded at this time of morning. A white man takes up the corner in front of the CIBC building begging. In the cool spring weather, he's shirtless, exposing the numerous tattoos on his body, his arms, all the way down to his wrists. A cookie tin for donations lies at his feet. The people pass by, unsympathetic.

I enter one of the pharmacies. I would like to buy some Hazeline Snow. I remember Mahmee applying it on my skin whenever I had a sore from a mosquito bite, or just because I liked the cooling sensation. I recognize the box and label, with its delicate ink rendering of a Chinese woman's face. Squatting down, looking at her face, I suddenly panic. The burn on my hand. The dead squirrel. Father. When I straighten up, I feel myself lose balance for a moment.

On a wall next to the shelves is a bright yellow bristol board with a Chinese newspaper clipping and a short English translation. Dr. Hom, Chinese Physician. A man in his thirties who graduated from the First Teaching Hospital in Tianjin, then worked for a while in Hong Kong before emigrating to Canada. He speaks Cantonese, Mandarin and English.

Dr. Hom is in his small inner office tending to someone. A pink cotton curtain separates me from two muted voices. I sit down on one of two wooden chairs in the narrow corridor, the jar of Hazeline Snow in my lap. No harm trying.

The woman behind the counter speaks up in Cantonese, "Nei siong tye yi sun?"

"Yes."

"Ah, not wait very long, okay?"

The shelves behind the counter hold large glass jars with dead things, herbs and parts of animals, like antlers or hooves. Seahorses, their yellowed skeletons visibly fragile. The rings of bones along their necks easily snapped. I enter that jar, into the crush of that cramped space. Male seahorses carry the young in their pouches. Seahorses mate for life. Claustrophobic.

I remember my maternal grandfather Kong-Kong's store. Dark wooden drawers with semicircular brass-pulls, with the names of substances they contained written in gold letters on each drawer. Opening them released a range of magical smells. Some sweet as licorice, strong and direct, while others were lightly fragrant with the juicy past lives of flowers and grasses. But some drawers harboured intense, dark smells. Whenever I caught a scent of these, I saw a pitch-black murkiness, a deep well from which no human could possibly emerge.

Kong-Kong's large fingers piled herbs on the plate of his daching, working deftly yet calmly to balance the amount on the plate with the weight placed at a certain distance from the fulcrum of his instrument. Balancing amount and need. The small bronze weight, suspended by a piece of twine, would rest along one of the red markings on the ivory stem of the daching. The red mark that was like a wound. A gash.

When it's my turn, I'm like an awkward teenager called into the principal's office. I meet his gaze briefly then cast my eyes down to the desk.

"Oh hi, how are you?" I say, giving Dr. Hom the instant clue that we'll need to use English.

"Sit down, sit down," his cheery voice invites. I look up. The doctor has a very shiny bald head, and wide, deep-set eyes full of curiosity. He opens the cover of his spiral-bound notebook in preparation.

"Last name please."

"Lim."

"Chinese name?"

I write out my full name in Chinese characters on a slip of paper.

"Tell me why you come here," he begins. I notice traces of a British accent.

"I've been having lots of dreams, sometimes nightmares. Then I wake up covered in cold sweat. Actually I . . . I feel quite shaky right now."

"Stick out your tongue." Then he also peers at my eyes. Questions about eating and bowel movements. Do I smoke? Yes. Take any medication? No. Boyfriend? No.

"Put your hand here."

"Which one?"

"Doesn't matter."

I place my right hand on the tiny satin cushion on his desk. The cushion is exactly the same shade of pink as the curtain. His three fingers press points on my wrist, first as lightly as a feather, then with slightly more pressure.

Dr. Hom closes his eyes, tilts his head slightly down and away from me, as if concentrating on some barely audible music.

There's a pliable strand of faith running through me still. A belief in foul-tasting brews and poultices the colour of mud which took away the fevers and aches of childhood illnesses.

A few minutes later, "Miss Lim, do you sigh a lot?"

The question takes me by surprise. "Yes. What is it? Is there something serious?"

"Oh no, nothing serious." He gestures to me to place my other hand on the cushion. "You have been . . . unhappy?"

"Yes. How did you know?"

"There is heat in your heart and your liver. Your shen, your spirit is trapped and needs to be freed. You feel dizzy sometimes?"

"Yes, I fainted recently. A few weeks ago, after an accident. Burned my hand. See?" I turn my hand up to show him the dark maroon scar.

"Don't worry," he says, as his pen materializes words onto the page: a watery script, vertical curves and horizontal lines flowing into each other. He's creating a prescription for me, that much I know. I'm relieved he doesn't ask me for any details about my unhappiness.

"Take this for five days. Try not to smoke. It blocks your shen. And oh . . ." His eyes meet mine then scan upwards across my forehead, ". . . don't think so much. Come back if you have to."

Don't think so much? Mahmee used to say that to me too. Out in the corridor again, I wait while the assistant measures out the herbs and divides each amount equally among five large, square sheets of newsprint. She runs her finger down the columns of the prescription, checking that she has measured out all the herbs in the right proportions. Then she wraps up the five packets. She tells me how to brew the herbs, and draws five bowls on one of the packets, to remind me how much water to add each time. She places the packets into a plastic bag, and adds five boxes of red haw flakes. A childhood favourite.

"Why, is it going to be bitter?" I make a face. She smiles tolerantly at me.

"You will get better quickly," encourages Dr. Hom as I leave the store.

Construction workers at the southeast corner of Main and Keefer are mixing cement, and laying bricks. A new branch of the Hong Kong Bank. I pass in front of the loud, thudding piler. Progress is deafening sometimes. The men are in orange coveralls, with mud and cement splattered on them. Their faces are bright red with exertion. The cement mixer churns away with its uneven rhythms of slapping and sloshing.

In the silences between phrases or a word or two, Dr. Hom with three fingers on my wrist was listening as if he was hearing some kind of music. What was the music like, those sighs of my body? Like the wind whispering through trees?

I will add Possibility Four to my list of hypotheses: Father's vitality was trapped inside him. He could feel a loss, but didn't know what to do about it. The more he didn't change, to allow his vitality to be expressed creatively, the more he felt powerless. Loss bred more loss. Eventually, this was why he did what he did. Quickly, anonymously. The wheels of the car. The squirrel. He was perpetrator and victim. Without witnesses.

As I turn the corner at Keefer, heading towards Union, I glance up at the bright saffron flags flapping furiously on the roof of the temple. Fire. That was what the wu shi had used. Fire as cure. Some people believe it's impossible to walk through fire and still emerge alive. When Einstein discovered his remarkable equation, that only a small amount of matter is needed to release a tremendous energy, what would he have thought if someone asked him to apply his ideas to psychological or spiritual malaise? And if that tremendous energy trapped inside is not released, what would eventually happen to that body?

* * *

MAHMEE

My grandfather, Ah Bak's father, so rich. Made a lot of money from shoe stores and then the Chinese medicine store. He such a smart man, always knew what people needed. So people went to him. Taught Ah Bak to be like that too. Ah Bak got rich not really because he worked as hard as Grandfather but he very good with people. He took over medicine store and became sinseh. He made medicine to heal people's bodies, but he also made jokes to cheer people up. So everybody who went see him for Chinese medicine all go away very hopeful.

That's why I say to Lan-Lan, help others and they will like you. They grateful and never forget you and your family. They will tell their friends and family, and your good name will continue. That is what most important about my daughter's name. I say to her, never mind about Mah-Mah's ideas. Mah-Mah said some people can see demons and even cast them out of sick person. She also had too much wind in the head.

Okay. People say, must forgive and forget. I try. I try not to be angry at Yen for suicide. My blood pressure a bit high. Not get enough sleep. I also go see sinseh and get bitter medicine to cook up. I tell Lan-Lan, good you take Chinese medicine to help you, you can go far, far away to Canada, but you still your Kong-Kong's granddaughter, still must do it our old way, brew with herbs, drink, good for you. Swallow, don't spit out, swallow bitterness, and you will be cured.

* * *

LEE AH CHOI

My face, so ghostly pale this morning. Where's my mask? Getting difficult to wake up, the line between dream and life refusing to stay firm, and instead dissolves into the atmosphere, like steam from wet cobblestones drying in the sun. Was it only a dream last night when I heard myself screaming, gasping for breath, groping for the kerosene lamp, the packet of chandu, with my fiercely trembling hands? Was it a dream, Lan Ho and Ah Loong, Chat Mui's cousin, arguing in the hallway just outside my cubicle?

My face. What will it look like in five years' time? Will it bear witness to all the sorrows? I have no heavy makeup like the opera singers do to submerge my fears under a bold façade. I wish this seventh lunar month would end soon. Hungry ghosts are wandering hallways and alleys, the gaps between bodies, the dreadful silences. Shadows warn us. I'm superstitious, can't concentrate. Fearful....

Month of ghosts. Mustn't show disrespect. I regret I was so frivolous that night at Lai Chun Yuen. For the past week since then, I've been afraid. There I was, intoxicated with opium, talking as if there was no difference between humans and ghosts. Of course, there is. We're still alive and suffering, they're dead. And still suffering! What if some ghost overhears me and takes offence?

CHOW CHAT MUI

They call them John Chinamen. The ones cheap enough to clean up cesspools. The lives that can be risked to infections from the sewage. The government is tight-fisted, won't spend the money to clean up the drains and the sewers. But at least now that the rainy season has begun, the filth is being washed away down the drains, and the smell is not as awful.

But what of the beggar? Not an able-bodied Chinaman at the beck and call of the British boss, his life is seen as far more worthless! I wonder if Dr. Lim at the hospital could save his life. I haven't seen him back on the street, I hear no news of him, not even through the sisters. The ugly sight of his infested stump comes to haunt me in my opium stupor. I'd been angry at him for telling those stories. Making us out to be tragic heroines, or mad, insatiable ghosts! No imagination. But I fear I've cursed him. Showing my disgust, surely that has brought him bad luck. But I wanted to see for myself what the look in his eyes was. What are the words to describe it? Lost. Someone whose body had been taken over, whose soul no longer lived peacefully in his eyes.

It is a bad omen.

* * *

I go past it then change my mind. The inside is only vaguely familiar because it's been about three months since I first came in here to look. At the altar, there are about forty different statues of Buddha. I hadn't paid them much attention that first visit. The upper tier holds five Buddhas in lotus position, painted with a fake golden sheen. The tiers below hold smaller figures, some seated, others upright. A fierce black one, with eyes popping out of his head, and such a scowling mouth! His eyebrows are red and curve out and away from his face. Looks like he too has excess heat in the heart and liver, and a spirit that yearns to be freed. The most predominant Buddha in Southeast Asia when I was young was Tua Pek Kong, popular among the Hokien. Very different from this image of warring energy. Tua Pek Kong, the fat, happy one, laughing in the face of everything. Sometimes he was sitting, and other times he stood to stretch his arms up in a gesture of playfulness. I used to think he was laughing because he was pleased with himself but somewhat oblivious to the suffering of others. But lately, I've wondered if Tua Pek Kong was actually more like someone's uncle, handing out gifts and lollipops to the kids because he knew that hardships were ahead.

I drop a loonie into the donation box and light a couple of joss-sticks at the small oil lamp. Then I plant the sticks in the urn at the front of the entrance. I've never been religious, but I do like the smell of the incense. An elderly Chinese couple walk past and glance approvingly at me.

"Choe sun!" the man greets me.

Back inside, I ask a young woman seated at the reception table if she knows Tze Cheng. No, comes the shaking head reply. Perhaps Tze Cheng doesn't come here every day, or it's too early in the morning still. I was hoping to see her again, to learn more about the wu shi. Upstairs, I pause for a moment in the hallway to peer into the room next to the library. A group of about twenty people are chanting. The sound is pleasant even though I don't understand the words. Something in Cantonese. Many voices meeting, sounding paradoxically like harmony. A spacious sound.

The library is empty, the blinds lowered. I let in some light and scan the bookshelves. Where was that book? I find it quite easily as it's the only large book with a dark green cover. The picture of the wu shi healing the sick man floats up to me, like a dream from long ago. That first time I had focussed on the picture on the opposite page: the sick man's fearful face and the expressions of disdain on the faces of the onlookers. But now I see the wu shi's face in the second picture. She looks remarkably calm as she cuts into the man's palm. It is the face of someone who knows what she's doing, and who has no doubts about her power. I put the book down and close my eyes. If I were a wu shi, what kind of a spell would I have to cast to heal myself? What character would I have to etch into my skin? I let myself be carried along by the fluid movements of voices from the next room. Soothing. When I was frightened by nightmares as a child, Mahmee came to me and rubbed my back in long, calming strokes, pulling the distress away from me, out of me. That was her way of exorcising. I always fell asleep easily after that. Perhaps I still need some soothing of my spirit, someone to help me with the fear.

Where did Dr. Hom say my spirit had gone? Proud of my escape from Singapore, I convinced myself that leaving the country was the solution—a flight into exile which resulted in internal fissures in the psyche, the cleaving of memory from memory. Here I've been in this country two decades, with the unsaid and the unsayable still swirling inside of me. Once I had been Lan-Lan, my mother's precious orchid. Lan-Lan stayed close to home, homing in on her parents' needs. But who is Wu Lan?

In Mandarin, a sound can have many meanings, depending on its tone. In first tone, "Wu" can be a medium or shaman. In second tone, it can mean "without." The third tone can refer to dancing, and in the fourth tone, it can mean "mistake."

Four dimensions. And the fifth? The silence in which the word falls, the echo of meaning resounding somewhere in space. Music matters. The falling of rocks into the abyss. How would my life have changed if my name was sounded differently, if the tone of it could draw on a different realm in the universe for significance? If only I could ingest my own name the way I consume food, swallow its various possibilities, assimilate their meanings into my blood.

* * *

MAHMEE

One day—was it just last Monday? Or last month? All the days are the same now that Yen is gone, my memory is failing me—anyway, I dreamed I called her in one of my fits, I was so scared! *Come home,* I pleaded. My voice shake down to my toes, even my hair touched by electricity. Why I work myself up so badly, I've no idea, but I tell you, I can't stop. I'm like that. Even in a dream!

I could have told her I knew from the very beginning she was different. I saw it in her eyes. How could she hide from me? Blessing or curse, don't know any more. Sometimes I get excited, see? My own daughter do better than me, have more money. Be happier. But sometimes I scared by her. So strange, she is. Of course I'll never say that. But I try to encourage, no need to push yourself so much. What for? She has these ideas, going to Uni too many years. So now she on leave, maybe good for her. We women have a delicacy men don't have. Men don't have menses like us. Bleeding every month and we're still around!

After all that hard work, she rest. Maybe her life these days bring her some happiness. Not like me suffer so much. Used to think if I was good person, I get the fortune I deserve. But I waited. And waited. For him to retire, as if suddenly then we can be free. We can do all kinds of things, go travel. But then he died. Stupid man. Why he cut his life short before he could enjoy?

I didn't really know. Now he gone but he still mean and want to upset me. Why take it all out on me? After all, I loved him. I was a good wife. Ah Mak taught me well how to serve husband. I always knew he was unhappy, but I don't want to think too much about it now. Must be happy, especially about the baby.

* * *

LEE AH CHOI

I get up at ten, after another long night, with a different skin. A film of dirt sealed in by sweat. Some of the other ah ku don't bother to bathe much any more. Filthy. But I always do. A hot bath first thing in the morning. While I scrub my body, soaking in the wooden tub in the open-air courtyard, the bulbuls are boldly making their music in the tree overhead. Old Man Fong's in the kitchen, juggling pots and knives and food. To think I had been shy in front of him that first day.

I can still taste traces of last night. Smoking and sex in my mouth. How good to have a few hours in the morning, untroubled by cramps or difficult breathing. Temporarily free of that desperate need that runs my days and nights, that twists me around with its magic promise. I scrub myself with my white washcloth and watch as the water gets murkier and murkier. Goodbye to yet another skin. How dirty I used to be, working in the fields. The memory makes me scrub even harder. What a pleasant feeling to see the water turn cloudy with that layer of dirt. Ugly presence, I chase you out from my body. Ah, precious cleanliness. It won't be until three or four PM when I need to soil my fingers with my first ball of opium. And not until much later do I open myself again to my clients.

I'm the last to sit down at the eating table, having taken my time to dry myself and change. I'm polite as usual, greeting everyone. Ghostly fingers of steam swirl up from the bowls of congee. Preserved eggs, slivers of pork, and the smoky softness of dried oysters. In the middle of the table, a large plate of deep-fried pastry rolls. Our trusty cook. Here in this colonial house, we don't eat the foreigners' food. Chan wouldn't have it. Nobody complains. Who wants to smell of butter and bacon? Ha, to think I used to live on melon gruel. My family would be so envious of how well I eat here.

I start to scoop the congee into my eager mouth. Several mouthfuls later, I realize that Sum Tok is staring at me. I put my spoon back into the congee, and it slides down the bowl, drowning in the semi-liquid. She picks up her chopsticks, and stabs the air forcefully with them as she speaks.

"Ah Choi, you're ah ku two years now. You know we've treated you well here. In fact, Chan and I had been thinking of letting you have the front room. You see, Lan Ho might be leaving us. A client is buying her as his concubine."

Lan Ho smiles a very broad smile. Loke Kum giggles. Sui Peng and Sui Leng glance at each other anxiously. Ah Leen eats her congee quietly, with a blank look. My sisters are acting strangely this morning. Lan Ho's leaving is good news, means I have a chance to take over the front room. But then why is Sum Tok's expression so severe? Her face is collapsing into itself like a sour plum. She aims her chopsticks downwards and jabs the wooden table suddenly.

"But hope no more. Not after this!"

I'm breathless with shock, my eyes captured by her look of rage.

"You take any tips you don't tell me about?"

My heart begins to thump rapidly. I clear my throat, feel the heat of the congee burn a slow trail down my gut.

"No, of course not." I cast my eyes down at my bowl briefly then back up at her. How did she find out?

She makes a slow, deliberate movement with her mouth, her lower jaw moving from side to side while her cheeks collapse inwards then puff out again. A ball of spit splatters against the right side of my face.

"Filthy cunt, don't you know the price of betrayal? Do you want to be out on the streets, never able to work in any other brothel again?" She fishes out a wad of money from inside her samfu, and waves it violently in front of me.

"You think you can get away with this?" She stands up, reaches over the table with her free hand, and spills the bowl of congee onto my lap. I scream from the pain, but what's worse is the sight of my precious money in her hand! I rush out of the room crying, up to my cubicle, tearing the clothes off me. The skin on my thighs is red. As if stinging from the bites of a thousand rats.

CHOW CHAT MUI

A girl played games with her friend under the shade of a tree. Innocent love. No questions troubled her happy heart. Open and waiting, like that symbol for contemplation. The heart underneath the field . The scholar's gift. Must a heart be tilted? Three dots were the pebbles I threw up to Heaven. One falling behind, one landing too far ahead to grasp, and then . . . this last one . . . maybe, I can catch this last one.

Too long ago, the heart's rhythms were clear. But then it became sullied with the intents of others. I turn towards a dream . . . a thought. A story swirling rainbows in the mouth. Round and round, spinning past into present into future. Dizzying.

* * *

"Michael, it's me."

"Hey, what's up, Lan?"

"I got some stuff from Mahmee recently. Mah-Mah's slippers...."

"Uh-huh." He's waiting.

"You remember Father's *Daily Bread* booklets? You know the ones."

"Oh, yeah, the mad collection."

Why can't he help me out? "So, how's life?"

"Business going very well. And the pregnancy, no problem. We have the baby coming one month after you go back to work, huh?"

"I mean, how do you feel about Father's death?" I blurt it out, unable to bear it any longer. But I can't bring myself to say the other word.

Long pause. I can hear his breathing, suddenly quicker and more audible. "Well, what's there to say? It stinks."

I didn't expect this.

He continues, "Father was a wimp. No backbone, know what I mean? I hated the way he took out his frustration on me. Just because I'm the son? Anyway, I'm going to treat my children very differently." His voice is tight, almost muscular.

"I didn't know. We've never really talked...."

Michael, the well-mannered, pleasant guy, can express emotions like joy and appreciation and even sadness. But anger?

"What about you?" he asks.

"Me? I've been obsessed with why he did it. Hate not knowing. Guess we'll never know."

"Don't you think it's because he got too tired?"

"Of what?"

"The world was not up to his standards. Not as wonderful as he would have liked it. Nothing was as great as his mad collection: full of helpful hints, power strategies, power tools. Whatever."

"I see. Doesn't Mahmee wonder? What does she think?"

"Mahmee deals with it by complaining he visits her at night."

Michael doesn't believe Mahmee. That's because Father doesn't bother him with night visits.

"I wish she would take those pills to help her calm down at night," he says, sounding annoyed.

I'm silent. His remark sounds familiar. I've said the same to Mahmee.

"I . . . uh . . . I. . . ."

"Yeah? What is it, Sis?"

"He comes . . . he bothers me too."

"Hey, really?"

"Yes . . . and I. . . ." Should I tell him? The tension in my throat is almost unbearable. "I haven't told anyone . . . don't tell Mahmee, okay? He phoned me two nights before. . . ."

"Huh? What did he say?"

"Nothing. He left me a message, only said . . . let's talk." I break down into sobbing, drawing in quick breaths, relieved and ashamed at the same time. Finally, I've said it. "What did he want? If only I had been home, if I tried . . . I didn't know. . . ."

"Sis, hey, hey . . . not your fault . . . come on!" Then he continues, "Why doesn't he bother me? Only you and Mahmee."

"Maybe . . . ," I feel myself calm down and breathe more easily, "he knows he's bothered you enough?"

He laughs loudly at this. "Oh sure."

Our conversation ends in a familiar way, with me wishing him well and sending my love to Susan, half-heartedly expressed, while he abstains from asking about my personal life. It's always left to me to offer information. But there's been a slight change. He seems more relaxed with me, more willing to be candid, no longer the shy little brother. He even sounded protective.

I'm brewing my third packet of Dr. Hom's Chinese medicine when the phone rings.

"Hey, remember me?"

It's Stephanie.

"Yes, of course. How are you?"

"So-so. Thought I'd call and see what's new with you."

"You remember the garden? At the back? I pointed it out to you when you were here, but the sky was getting dark. . . ."

"Uh-huh."

I offer some mundane details about the vegetable plot outside my apartment. Now that the weather's warming up, I've taken the opportunity to prepare the bed, and will soon put in some seeds. Beets, carrots, beans. Can't think of what else to say.

"What I mean is, how come you haven't answered my calls?"

"Oh . . . I . . . I've been preoccupied with other things."

"Someone else?"

"No, no, it's personal. Family. . . ."

"You don't want to explain, do you?"

"It's difficult to talk about it."

"Well. That's fine. I would have appreciated a phone call."

"Sorry."

"Never mind. I still think you're cute. Call me if you feel more than a few moments of interest, okay?" Then the sound of a kiss before she hangs up.

So much for that adventure. I let a long sigh escape from me. I envy Stephanie her forthrightness. It's attractive and inhibiting at the same time. What else is there to figure out? I know I'm not as bold as she is. I return to my chat with Michael, his unsparing words: *Father was a wimp.* We would never have dared say such words while he was alive. And now he's dead, we accuse him of having succumbed to his fear of living.

As Visible As the Moon

ں

The concourse in the new library is packed. Balloons extend out from people's wrists or backpacks like extra limbs. It seems as if everyone in the Lower Mainland is here. The CBC has set up a platform just inside the north entrance, and a jazz ensemble is finishing off the final notes of "Squeeze Me." The male host has on a tight polo shirt, showing off his impressive chest span and biceps, while the female host boasts clunky gold earrings. These remind me of the kind of jewellery I used to wear to work—that slight extra weight on the ears that one gets used to and never questions.

The hosts persuade volunteers from the audience to answer some questions: Who designed the library? How much does each of the special chairs cost?

I tilt my head back to gaze up along the height of the building, tracing the edges of the glass walls, a seemingly fragile, transparent honeycomb. Facts about the library are being belted out by the male host: thirty million dollars, forty-eight toilets, twelve hundred seats, seven million kilograms of steel.... I drift towards the entrance of the library, following the will of the larger body. I take the escalators up to Level Seven, Special Collections, hoping for the distinct, musty smell of old books, but no, the books are sealed under glass cases, too precious to be exposed to the elements. At the window facing the side of the building away from the main activity, I look down at the passageway below. Occasionally someone appears and disappears from view, like a bleep on an otherwise desolate radar screen. Dizzying to be at the edge of such spaciousness, as if there isn't anything separating me from free fall.

Before long I back away and sink into the solace of a chair. Curvaceous buff-coloured arms and ink-blue seat. Quiet here on this floor. Down one level, in the History section, it's a completely different story. I wait several minutes in line for a turn at the glowing green and black face of a computer terminal. The old library was never this crowded, but then again I wasn't there at its opening. The young man next to me has a half-open mouth that wants to catch something, but hasn't yet. He's swimming in some kind of a fish trance. It's the same look I see when I walk into the Pacific Centre, where shoppers are swept along by an ocean of longing for what they don't have. Yet. I look up the call number of the book on the ah ku. That time I took it out in November last year, it belonged in the old library on Burrard. It's been six and a half months. I find the right aisle, and scan the rows. Locating the book is easy, almost purely based on the sensation of colours. Its untarnished vermillion red spine contrasts loudly with its more rundown neighbours on the top shelf. I clutch the book close to my chest and make my way down the escalators to the check-out line.

The concourse is quieter, the CBC no longer broadcasting live. I head out the doors on the north side. On the outdoor stage, the Uzume Taiko drum troupe has just begun their performance. The tale of Amaterasu Omikami, the Numina, bringer of light and consciousness. The Japanese goddess has been coaxed out of her cave. The frenzied climax would give the score of any Hollywood movie a run for its money. Amaterasu is thrashing it out with her brother, the Thunder God. The people's fate in the grasp of these deities. He stomps around in a foul mood while she takes time to contemplate her plan of action. Time slows down in this moment of suspense. How different they are, brother and sister. One charges around, ego as large as the skies, while the other retreats from the world. My eyes flit away from the action on stage, down to the audience. In the centre of the crowd, at the very back, I see the familiar profiles of a woman and a man. Kim and Daniel, his arm around her waist, drawing her firmly against him. She, petite with short, black spiky hair, and he, slightly balding, with salt-and-pepper hair and beard.

I mustn't be seen. It would be awful. I move briskly away, cross at the lights and walk down Hamilton. My face feels hot. All the old anger returns. At Dunsmuir, I sit down on a bench in front of the BC Hydro building, and feel myself pulled back into another time.

* * *

Lee Ah Choi

My mind plays tricks, I catch myself going to check for the money under my straw mat. Can't believe it. I'm ill again, my thighs shuddering with the horrible memory of the burn from the congee that Sum Tok spilled on me. Her heart is truly sickened with poison. How did Sum Tok know? Someone betrayed me. I thought my sisters were kind and well meaning. Haven't we lived together as family? I've always clung to the belief that Heaven rewards the virtuous. If life doesn't satisfy me, I'll return as a ghost. I'll make bowls of congee topple onto the laps of my dear sisters. And Sum Tok? What revenge shall I exact on that false mother of mine? Torture her slowly with some disease that eats up her insides. I'll become a demon that crouches in the seat of her bowels and stabs in all directions with giant chopsticks.

I'm tired of the cramps and vomiting. This morning I forced myself to go see a nearby Western doctor, despite my terror. The brews don't seem to help these days. The white man poked his fingers clumsily around inside me, and pursed his lips before he announced, "No children for you. Gonorrhea has spoiled you."

Just like that. Without any kindness or sadness in his voice. Must I pay extra to see emotion, the way a person pays to watch an opera? His coldness cut cleanly into me like a cleaver. I said nothing. I couldn't cry, since my shame would have been doubled had I shown my sorrow to him, a white man. He wrote me one of those fancy prescriptions. But I couldn't even utter a thank you as I left his office. He must have thought I was rude. Doesn't matter.

I walked home along my beloved streets. Once I had been stunned by their foreignness, everything about them, including the red dust stirred up in dry weather. But it's all familiar now.

My mother, I remember the quiet forbearance of the one who sheltered me in her body. The hole that I left in her when I emerged into the world, how quickly it was filled with other pains, other babies. I can't blame her, she couldn't have stopped my father anyway. I haven't forgotten the life I shared with my family before the journey, but if you ask me to recall now, I can't do it as well as the day I was snatched from her hands. Today her face returns to me as hazy and elusive as the horizon on a humid day. Is it disease or opium that muddies up the once-clear pools of memory?

How could my mother have borne all her children? I can't imagine her sorrow. But if her blood courses through me, then I must still know her in a mysterious way. Does her blood thicken mine, does mine echo with her silences?

My mother's blood must end here. And my father's, his blood disappeared from my body when he sold me. It's enough that their other children will bear that need. I was hoping . . . I was dreaming. That trail of red silk.

I don't want to think too much, must lie down quietly, enjoy the moments I have. The money gone. And now, what man would want me as his wife if I cannot bear him children?

CHOW CHAT MUI

In her absence I'm filled with memories of her. A shadow, a scent. Her smooth breast caresses my dry lips. Her hands float me above the weight of pain. Lighter than breath. The contours of her body are like small animals stalking through my solitude.

Another fantasy: I'll win enough money gambling to buy our freedom someday. Why not believe? Hold onto a fantasy and it will become true, as real and precious as the songs of magpie robins while they search the grounds and bushes for insects.

She is a fire razing through me. A cool wind awakening my skin to pleasure. Water for thirsty lips. Earth that meets my falling body.

* * *

It happened in September 1991. I'd temporarily lost my sense of direction. One moment I was totally myself, in control, lucid, calm. The next moment, I'd forgotten where I was. Looking down at my hands on the steering wheel, I noticed that my knuckles were bone-white from gripping too tightly. Gripping still the memory of what Kim had just tried to tell me. The changing shapes of her mouth, the way the words came out like slowed-down distortions. She was telling me that she was leaving. She said his name. I didn't make the connection at first, a common enough name. She told me they'd been aware of the attraction for a long time, but had talked to each other about it only in the past six months. No point telling me until now, since she hadn't been sure. She said emphatically, "Daniel and I are madly in love with each other." Then that remark about wanting a normal life with husband and family. Why wasn't Daniel there? He'd left it up to Kim to break the news. Coward.

In our kitchen, I was already losing my sense of direction. I glanced around at the kitchen we'd created when we first bought the house and moved in. Red and yellow cabinets, black tiled floor, lime green ceiling. Bold and confident, like our relationship. A model lesbian couple. Perhaps *Metropolitan Home* might have eventually considered featuring us? After all, they were already doing the gay couples.

Kim said to me as I left the house, "Sex is fragile, Wu Lan. Very fragile."

I drove around for a long time in a heavy daze, not paying attention to the street names. When I finally looked at the clock on my dashboard, it flashed 10:03. It was pitch-black outside. I'd taken myself all the way to UBC, to the edge of the Endowment Lands. I drove off the main road onto a shoulder, switched the engine off and partially rolled down my window. It was raining outside, a quiet, gentle rain.

She'd fallen in love with someone else. Did it matter that it was a man and not a woman? Did it matter that it was my friend and colleague Daniel? Sitting in my car, I answered myself, *Of course. Everything matters.* Listening to the soft fall of rain around me, I remembered Father's admonishment to us as children, *Never trust strangers*, and I laughed at the irony.

I'd had no idea. I thought she was as happy as I had been. I hadn't seen the signs. Maybe I didn't want to.

* * *

LEE AH CHOI

Sum Tok comes into my cubicle. "What did the Western doctor say?" Her eyes narrow down suspiciously at me. I hear the sounds of some whispering in the hallway.

"Nothing. I'm fine." I try to keep my voice free of any signs of distress.

"You will work extra hours. And now you must be punished for the way you tried to cheat me."

I say nothing. Isn't working extra enough punishment? I dig my fingers into the mat. Sum Tok retreats into the hallway, and I hear some more mumbling. Then she reappears with the rattan cane.

"Take your samfu top off." She points the weapon at me.

I feel light-headed with fear. I've never been caned before, not even with my original family. Pinched and slapped, yes, but not caned.

"I said, take your top off!" She draws closer, her mouth in that menacing scowl I detest.

I turn my back to her, unbutton my top and lift it up over my head. I feel her body move behind me, and when the cane reaches me, the sound of it striking my body and the sting of my skin are one and the same wound. I make no sound, but bite into my lower lip. My skin is alive with pain! One, two, three, four . . . hard to count. My body, once beautiful . . . seven . . . eight. . . . Silently I plead to Heaven, stop, it is unbearable.

* * *

Sunlight glints sharply off the glass windows of the BC Hydro building, at the corner of Dunsmuir and Hamilton. I return from the painful recollection. Kim and Daniel must be still at the library, checking it out. I wonder if they had turned around and caught sight of me escaping.

I get up from the bench and continue down the street with the book wedged between my right arm and body. Squeeze history until it aches, until nothing separates me from it. I glance up at the Del Mar Inn. UNLIMITED GROWTH INCREASES THE DIVIDE. Farther down the street is the Java Cat café.

"Hello there."

It's her. Her hair falls loosely around her face, framing her shoulders and her chest. She's wearing a cream cotton tank top and black and white checkered shorts. A strap of her aquamarine blue bra is showing. This time no nail polish, but lipstick, a different shade from last time: very dark, very brown. I catch a whiff of her scent, perfume and body scent intermingled. I'm convinced I remember it. She stubs out her cigarette under her black platform sandals.

"Coming in for a coffee?"

"Sure, why not."

"How's your hand?"

She glances down at my left hand. I smile back calmly and lift it up to show. A light brown shape, flat and faint enough to be missed.

"What have you been up to lately?" Her lips curve slightly upwards with a hint of mischief.

"I was at the new library."

"When was it you were last here? Your hair—"her hand reaches up, almost touching my shoulder. "Grown a bit, hasn't it?"

"It's been almost three months."

Two men get up from the sofa and leave. No one else is in the café.

"What can I get you?"

"Mmm, cappuccino, please." I sit attentively on the high stool at the counter and watch her operate the coffee machine.

"What's this?" Her fingers lightly brush against the book.

"A book about sex-trade workers. Prostitutes. Turn of the century. Singapore."

"Oh? Why?"

I raise a spoonful of froth up to my lips. "There's something compelling about their anonymity."

She rests her hands on her hips, looking as if she wants to say something but isn't sure. "Uh-huh. Mystery draws you?"

"No, anonymity does." I don't feel like explaining. I squirm on the stool when I notice the mole on her chest halfway between her neck and her left breast.

"What have you learned from reading the book?" She sounds confident, curious. She leans slightly forward, exposing more of her blue bra. I skim its outlines casually with my eyes. Elaborate lacy design. She looks at me again to remind me of her question.

"Oh, lots about turn-of-the-century Singapore. Effects of mass migration, cheap labour, colonial expansion. But especially about the social blight of opium. But it's not just facts I'm learning, it's like watching a movie in my mind. Going back to another time and place." Going back? I hear myself questioning silently.

"The power of imagination." She laughs lightly as she wipes her hands on a towel. "What do you do, anyway?"

"I'm a psychologist." I brace myself for some reaction. Perhaps a comment about my ability to read minds. I dread the inevitable quip when I'm at parties.

"Listen, I'm closing in ten minutes. Business was very brisk earlier, but it's been fairly quiet the last hour. I was across the street having a smoke, watching the café. Then I saw you." She pauses, and a deep blush covers her neck and face. "I'm glad you came by."

I curl my left index finger cautiously around the handle of the cup. Take a deep breath. I'm going to be brave now.

"What are you doing after you close up?" My hand starts to tremble slightly. I quickly put the cup back down on the counter. I forget. Desire can disrupt even the most ordinary gesture.

She smiles at me. "I'm walking home. I live just beyond Chinatown." She grabs her red denim jacket from inside the closet and lifts her backpack up from the floor.

"Can I walk with you?"

We take Pender. Past grocery stores that are already packing up their wares. Workers sweep stray pieces of fruits and vegetables into their large, roomy dustpans. Bleach solution is scoured across the pavement with fierce sweeps of wide, black-bristled brooms. The smell seizes my lungs. A chorus of objects being emptied. Boxes of vegetables, tubs of water. Wooden crates are stacked up along the sides of stores, wound with chains, and padlocked for the night. Sounds of withdrawal, of shutting down.

The sun is still warm behind me. I curl into myself, clasping the precious dying light to my chest. We turn down Gore.

"My name is Francisca, but I like to be called Francis, with an i."

"Oh?"

"It's the Spanish spelling, not Italian. My father's Spanish and my mom is French."

"My name is Wu Lan."

On Union, we pass a small park where seagulls are gathered, like an air squadron awaiting their next mission.

"I moved from San Francisco to Vancouver two years ago."

"I've been in Vancouver over nine years."

It's slightly uncomfortable as well as exciting to be unable to rely on a shared pool of memory. The woman of my dreams, I joke to myself, recalling the nightclub dream with the exotic boa constrictor wound around her lovely body.

Here and there, a newly painted or re-stuccoed house makes an optimistic statement in the midst of rundown buildings. A fleeting image of Kim and Daniel at the library returns. But the warm wind soon chases away the memory, and sways lemon-yellow tulips and white canterbury bells along the front borders of a garden in a shy, tentative dance. We pass "Lucky Rooms," freshly painted in dusty pink, three storeys with a large sign in the ground-floor window advertising rooms for rent. Above the third-floor balcony, the Pa Kua hangs with its mirrored centre deflecting unwanted spirits. I steal glances at Francis. Wonder what kind of a spirit she is.

She says she came for the landscape. The relative lack of steep slopes, of stunning, dizzying vistas. She doesn't miss San Fran's frequent, minor earth tremors, warning of an impending and larger danger. For some reason, I'm not entirely convinced, but I don't probe further. I'm already being forward enough. I describe my early days in Toronto. The first place I lived in, a bachelor apartment in Cabbagetown. I shared the floor, mattress to mattress, with two other young women, one from Malaysia, the other from Vietnam. We were reeling from the shock of being far away from our homes and our countries. In fact, I think we were all quite depressed. We seldom cleaned the apartment, inhaling the accumulation of dust every night, listening to the quiet fluctuations of one another's breathing.

"I've come such a long way from living like that," I say, but my tone is flat, empty of emotion. Have I? "Do you work full time at the Java Cat?"

"Uh-mmm. Here, cross over."

She gestures at the boxy blue building with a Canadian flag flying from the top, fishes out her keys from inside her jacket pocket, pauses with key in lock, and half turns towards me so that I can see the question materialize across her face.

"Would you like to come up? For a drink?"

No question about it, it's too soon to say goodbye. The stairs are broad, with a dim light at the top barely giving us enough light. I'm developing a bad habit. Following women home after a visit to the library. I walk a comfortable distance behind her. The stairs creak far too loudly. We're swaying in the hold of a ship, and there's only a thin boundary of wood that separates us from the utter chaos of the ocean. What is the name of her lipstick? Chocolate. Clove. Or why not Mud? Each name amplifies my courage. She doesn't look back as we climb the long flight, but I can see the colour anyway. A rich brown, as luscious and inviting as moist earth.

* * *

CHOW CHAT MUI

The welts. She feels ashamed. She wouldn't take her top off to show me, and wouldn't let me touch her back. Her face is swollen from crying, and she keeps pushing me away every time I draw near to her. A vacant look in her eyes. It reminds me of how the beggar looked in the hospital. A tremor overtakes her body. What can I say to her that will give her comfort? I struggle through the desperate silence and say, "Go to the temple. Remember how it gives you peace."

To my surprise, this brings a halt to her crying. She stares at me and stammers, "You ... now your turn ... you go." For some reason I haven't told her about meeting that scholar, about his gift of the word, which I've kept hidden under my bed. I nod my head at her quietly. I beg her one more time to show me her welts but she shakes her head, says she has to return to her brothel, and runs out of my cubicle. I hear the door downstairs close very quietly. In the distance, the cock crows, so I know it's six AM. I lay back down on my bed and close my eyes for a few more hours of sleep.

* * *

The apartment is a single enormous room with a long stretch of windows along the south wall. Not much furniture. A solid oak table below the windows, a queen-sized futon against the adjacent wall, a collection of dried branches in a tall black raku vase: twisted coerulus, pussy willow and bamboo. Along the north wall, about thirty feet away, is a small kitchen with pine cabinets, a gas stove and sink delineated from the rest of the room by a dining counter with a couple of rattan bar stools. In front of the bed, on the wooden floor, are two large, red velvet cushions fringed with golden tassels. The recurrent velvet.

I can't help feeling slightly entranced. Picking up a stranger, being picked up, doesn't that conjure up a certain kind of romanticism? As in one of the first scenes in *Last Tango in Paris*. When he takes her in a fit of animal passion in the then-empty apartment.

How does Francis afford this place on her income? She notices the look of puzzlement on my face and offers, "It used to be a warehouse, a long time ago. Belonged to an importer of biscuits, tea and canned goods from England. The space had been larger, but was divided into two apartments in the sixties."

"This place must cost quite a bit to rent."

She blushes. "I inherited some money from a relative before I left San Fran. I'm going to fix myself a martini. Want one?"

"Martini?" It's been a long time since anyone offered me a martini.

"Made with Bombay Sapphire Gin. Ever had it?"

"No, but I'll try some."

"If you'd like some music, take your pick over there." She gestures to the stereo system next to her bed, then walks off into the kitchen.

Towers of stacked-up CDs rise precariously from the floor. Jazz, classical, rap, blues, pop. Practically everything. I press the Play button. Violin music, sad and full of longing. At the table by the windows, a hodgepodge of pastels, pencils and charcoal stubs lies about like a scattered rainbow. Newspaper clippings of cartoons, reviews of concerts at local clubs and venues. A heavy glass ashtray, a packet of Top tobacco and some cigarette papers.

She returns with the martinis. "Here. Try this."

A slim twist of lime sits at the bottom of each glass. The cold liquid teases my mouth with a mix of tastes. Licorice and cumin?

"Mmm, very nice. What's in it?"

She goes back into the kitchen, reads off the label, "Grains of paradise from the West Indies. . . ." As she returns her low voice relaxes into a mock-religious incantation, listing some nine or ten other ingredients. A phoenix flies down from the sky into a field of swaying tall grasses under a full moon. It begins to pick off grains from the stalks. With each grain it ingests, a gem appears on its body, sapphire blue, gold, a blackness more brilliant than light.

My eyes scan her walls, particularly the charcoal sketches above the bed. They're untitled and unsigned.

"Did you do these?"

"Yes." She answers tentatively.

Women of various ages sitting, standing, alone or in groups, some naked, some clothed. Women with their faces partially hidden behind others' bodies, or fully exposed, framed by white space. I keep returning to one drawing in particular. It's the only one with a single face on it. The face is bold, the teeth bared in a gesture of aggression. She seems more animal than human. I suppose people might consider it ugly. But it's not revulsion I feel. It's recognition. A raw, red sensation burns between my eyes.

"They . . . she is," I point to the face, "so blatantly . . . I can't find the words."

"She doesn't pretend, does she?"

I say nothing.

"Does she frighten you?" she continues.

"No . . . not that. . . ."

"Sometimes when I'm drawing, I lose track of the present. My mind doesn't work in the usual way. It becomes this move . . . and this . . . and so on." She moves her hand quickly in the air, demonstrating the definiteness of each stroke, while her eyes are drawn inward, seeing without sight.

"Like being possessed?"

She doesn't answer, looks at me as if not quite sure what to make of the question.

The only equivalent I can think of is the experience of being besieged by Father's suicide, the way I felt when I stared at that egg in the refrigerator, sensing its awful vulnerability. But Francis's kind of possession is far more creative than that. At least it allows her a way to make palpable some internal experience. At least it saves her from imploding.

"Why have these women come to you like this?"

"I'm not sure. I find it difficult to describe how it all happens." A slight hesitation in her voice. Perhaps I'm being too forward. She retrieves a book from underneath a pile of papers. Turns to some photographs of ancient sculptures. "Look at this. Priestesses of temples. Sacred prostitutes. I thought I would show you this, since you have that book." She casts a glance at the red book I'd dropped beside a cushion. "But those prostitutes of yours . . . I bet they weren't treated with respect, not like these ones."

"No, quite the contrary."

"Do you know that sacred prostitutes used their bodies to free themselves?"

"I'd read about it, don't remember where." I shrug my shoulders.

"The Athenian temple prostitutes included courtesan philosophers and political actors, the hetairae."

The edges of my scepticism slice uneasily through the silence, my mind struggling with the notion that women in any period of history would, in all strength and wisdom, prostitute themselves to free themselves. Seems a contradiction in terms.

"Why are you showing me these pictures?"

"I told you, since you have that book. . . ."

"What is it about these ancient prostitutes, sex-trade workers, that interests you?"

Francis is distracted. I follow her glance and notice a black face and a pair of small emerald green eyes peeking out from behind one of the speakers.

"Come here, Spooky. C'mon, sweetie," Francis coos to the creature who emerges softly on its four white paws, its body black and sleek. I reach down to stroke the cat, but it stays for only a few moments before scurrying away.

"That's why I named him Spooky. I found him last summer in the park, crouching by a garbage can, terrified."

I wander over to the cushions, move my book onto the floor, and sit down. Tension around my forehead and temples. My face feels as tight as that face above her bed. Odd confrontation. Even so, the music manages to snake its haunting appeal through to me, reaching me under the tautness.

"What's this playing?"

"Béla Bartók's *Violin Concerto No.1*. Beautiful, isn't it?"

She sits down beside me.

"The violin is like a woman who yearns to be taken beyond herself." Does she hear my confession?

She continues. "Béla Bartók wrote this concerto for a woman, but she rejected him because his views of the world didn't mesh with hers. Ironically, when he presented her with the concerto, he also attached a poem written by a contemporary of his, about how futile it is to rely on others for happiness. The idea of the poem was that two human souls were farther apart than two stars."

Yes, how futile. I fall into silence, its dark spaciousness. My parents in their room, backs turned toward each other in bed. I used to know this because in the morning, between the time they got up and the making of the bed, I would stand at the open door and stare at the deep imprints of their loneliness, aware of some subtle, inarticulatable absence.

"Are you okay?"

"What do you mean?"

"You seemed far away."

"Sorry. I was thinking how sad it is."

"But, don't you think, how true? If only we could accept it, I think we would all be a lot less devastated by so-called love."

She uncrosses her legs and her body extends in a slow, feline stretch.

"How come you know so much about this music?"

"Guess what. The notes that come with the CD."

Laughter moves easily through me, a welcome release. Francis gets up to light candles, walks over to the table and starts to roll a cigarette. Candle flame ignites cigarette in a flare near her half-parted lips. Her hands and face burnished by the momentary glow. She offers the cigarette to me when she returns, inching her cushion a little closer to mine. We've stopped talking. The music has taken over, carrying us into the second movement. The lyrical conquered by discordant chords. Bartók's inner chaos. The swirling confusion, the battle between cynicism and passionate attachment. The cigarette smoulders down, liminal and illusive.

And even when the music ends, the vibrations of absence linger. Death and desire.

What now? At the edge of another precipice. I sigh in surrender and remove my glasses. I draw my face into the wide curve along her shoulder up to her neck. She doesn't protest, but then whispers in my ear, "I barely know you."

Her hair rushes forward, and I dive in, without a thought for my life. A brief panic stuns me until her lips reveal themselves, two small fishes flashing welcome. I slide my hand through the water to reach her face.

"You smell of chocolate," I whisper.

"You smell of trouble."

The moist edges of our mouths, melting me into something familiar, a memory that's precious and painful.

"Wait, we've got to stop." She pulls away.

"Why?"

"This is crazy, we hardly know each other and—"

"So?" I raise my eyebrows at her.

"Could we just sleep together? For tonight."

"All right."

"You're not mad at me?"

"No," I say quietly, shifting so that my body separates from hers slightly. Why shouldn't a person be afraid? The final scene in

Last Tango in Paris. Poor Brando, shot by his lovely muse. Because he had revealed too much. He had betrayed his own anonymity.

I cradle her face with my hands. My fingers follow the slope of her prominent jawbone.

"I'd like to stay, but there's something I need."

"What?"

"I'm very hungry. Could you feed me?"

"Is that all?" She sighs in relief and drifts into the kitchen. A light comes on. I listen to the sounds of cutlery and pots and pans. The sound of metal against metal, of metal against wood. The refrigerator door opens and closes, with a familiar rattle of bottles. I lie down, using the cushion as a prop for my head and half of my body. With eyes closed, I enter again the inner world of moving spaces, the strange visual tricks of the eye turned in. A dream of stars. Dancing with danger, yet keeping the magical safe distance away from the instincts of others. Spooky approaches my shoulder cautiously, one paw then another, and soon he's walking all over me. I scratch his neck, and soon he purrs. Once an animal decides, instinct is clear and unapologetic. It doesn't waver. The smell of fried garlic. I inhale, grateful for the interruption.

"Here, eat this."

Asparagus tips sautéed with garlic and topped with almond slivers. Juicy pieces of roasted red pepper rim the circumference of the light blue plate. I forego the fork, using my fingers. As if sensing my need, Francis eats the red and green from my hand, and feeds me with her mouth. The caught food is a bridge disappearing between our mouths.

* * *

LEE AH CHOI

How could Chat Mui not understand how shameful it was that
I was punished by my kwai po? Not only exposed for keeping the
money to myself, but disgraced with caning. The less my sisters
heard of my suffering, the better. That was why I forced myself
to stifle my urge to scream. Who was in the hallway? Who
overheard?

CHOW CHAT MUI

Empty room. Dirt everywhere. Escape again, like that first day.
Chicken cage. Yes, escape.

Pain nags me. Don't bother me, leave! If only my body could
float upwards seeking Heaven, where the air is cleaner to breathe,
where there are enough shimmering rainbows to last one's life. I
could open my mouth to catch one. It will taste like coconut
candy, sweetness so thick you could cut your tongue on it.

That word. 忍 The field spilling out of its sides, melting
away right in front of me. Dripping . . . no! Blood
covers the heart. The blood of the Gaos and the Lius. All the way
across the ocean and the years, to this country.

Tricked again. Sweet relief turns nightmare. Pleasure surren-
ders to pain. Gifts of beauty turned bloody. Why does opium
betray me? I confess too much, keep forgetting I can't trust it.
Heaven spare me from ever seeing ugliness in Ah Choi. Leave her
untouched.

* * *

Wynton Marsalis's trumpet coaxes "Stardust" into the room. Cool
mastery, without any sentimental strains. What a relief after

Bartók. I sense outlines of objects in the room, of her body inches away from mine. Memory and imagination, like lovers losing boundaries with each other. We sink into the night, liquid with uncertainties.

Her breathing changes. She's fallen asleep. I stroke my own forehead several times, a slow, soothing rhythm. To sleep next to someone carries a risk separate from merely having sex. To sleep next to someone is to anticipate loss. The longer one hangs around, the greater the impact of ending. Mahmee waking up to Father the corpse. Fatal sleep. I wrap my legs around hers, larger and longer than mine. We're two trees entangling their roots. Or two commas cradling the sentence between them. I rest my cheek against her broad back, and slide my hand between her breasts.

Francis stirs. "How long has it been?" she whispers.

"Since what?"

"Uhh, since the last major relationship."

"Oh. More than three years."

"That's a long time."

"Yes."

"How about you?" I try to sound cool.

"Oh. In San Francisco."

I feel the muscles on her upper back stiffen, then relax slightly. "Maybe I'll tell you some other time. That is, if we decide to keep seeing each other."

"Okay." I pause, wondering how I should phrase the question I have in my mind. "The way you were . . . at the café . . . are you always so bold?"

She turns around, and touches my feet with hers.

"I wanted to touch you. Besides," she continues to stroke my feet slowly and steadily, "it takes two."

I reach up to find her face, tracing her features.

"Your fingers . . . chilly." She takes my hand and breathes into my palm. Once, twice, three long ones.

We lie together, facing each other, silent for a long time. The space between us is warm with our exhaled breaths. My eyes finally feel the weight of sleepiness. I curl myself into the cave of her voluptuous body, my face against her throat. Maybe I can let go. Just a little bit. Don't have to run away too quickly. We lie together, suspended in the final notes of "I'm Confessin'." I don't remember when I finally cross the boundary between wakefulness and sleep, descend into that other kind of awareness. Throughout the night, I partially surface, aware of her presence. Meeting at the mouth, at the thigh. Brush of the elbow against a breast. These small yet significant orbits in the language of desire. I hope for a passion that could shatter illusions.

* * *

MAHMEE

When I married Yen, I thought he a good man, upright and honest. Didn't matter he was poor, didn't matter Ah Bak and Ah Mak disapproved. Yen and I laughed a lot, silly in our young days. But I didn't guess he had this unhappiness inside. Why he not talk about it? Why did he sit there all those years like someone helpless? He could have gone to see doctor, he could have talked to friends. Well, he had only us and one or two friends at work. He kept to himself.

I make sure I won't be unhappy, now that the baby arrive soon. Children know when we are sad, we must keep up cheerful appearance for them always. Now I do some volunteer work, helps me keep my mind on other things. No point crying too much about such a tragedy. I have two children. Soon I will have my first grandchild, and more to come. Life can be simple.

* * *

LEE AH CHOI

Where is home? Its rice fields stretch out before my eyes, green with the promise of harvest. Its wind is a gentle lover caressing tender seedlings. Then the wind becomes fickle, ready to whip its cruel strength against me.

If there hadn't been floods, there wouldn't have been the famine. If only Heaven had been more merciful. Did we deserve such rage? Lightning casts arrows of shock down at me, thunder rattles my bones, threatening the walls, my bed. Away, unwelcome demons!

Isn't it enough I was already taken away once? Floods, why have you returned? And why is the river swollen with the stench of many deaths? Water threatens me from below, rises up to my bed. The money floats away from me, stop, come back! Water from the skies, breaking through the roof. Oh rage of Heaven!

His face appears now, with that blank resignation. He refused to see my fright that day as I was dragged away from the family. Father, how you betrayed me! Show some remorse. Can't you see, you have caused me great suffering?

CHOW CHAT MUI

A cubicle. Four walls of a box. Opium, sex, anger, fantasy. The last wall . . . Ah Choi . . . I can't reach you. In my half-sleep, past midnight, while outside, the stormy monsoon rains whip at the trees, rattling doors and windows, upsetting anything that isn't tightly secured. The violence of sounds, the violence of Nature. Weeping, weeping.

I press my hand into the bed. Deep within my imagination, her skin under my hand. Under my desire. If only I could reach her across the absence, touch with a gentleness that could reassure her, that could soothe those scars.

Her body lives in my cells, the unseen and unspoken wounds.

My lips open to air, gasp of longing for solidity. Where is she that I can't feel her under my hands any longer? That my mouth can't find hers?

Tonight, hovering between worlds, I clutch her body in my mind, breathing a window into another universe.

* * *

Francis reappears with the boa constrictor wrapped around her body. I'm in the audience again. Amazed that the huge snake hasn't squeezed the life out of her yet. She moves close to the edge of the platform, bends forward and gives me a long, firm kiss on the mouth. A mix of arousal and terror churn in my belly. I smell Bombay Sapphire Gin on her breath. Did Father drink that? The boa's cool, dry skin comes between us, running along the underside of my chin.

The alarm clock jangles us awake at eight. "Sorry, I forgot." She doesn't wait long before rolling out of bed and putting the kettle on. Sunlight streams into the room, casting small shadows in the crevices of the crumpled sheets.

The rich, robust smell of coffee. She hums "La vie en rose."

"I love that song," I offer lazily, from the bed.

"My mother's lullaby to my sisters and me, every night for many years."

"She could have substituted 'elle' for 'il'?" I get up and walk into the kitchen.

"True."

"Will you sing it?"

She blushes.

> Quand elle me prend dans ses bras,
> Elle me parle tout bas,
> Je vois la vie en rose.

Elle me dit des mots d'amour,
Des mots de tous les jours,
Et ça me fait quelque chose.

Francis pours us two steaming cups of coffee from the Bodum. Her face betrays the soft haziness of just having woken up, her neck and chest framed by the closing V of her bathrobe.

The woman from Francis's sketch reappears. The face that won't surrender. That refusal of despair.

"I'm afraid ... ," I begin.

"Of me?"

"No. I'm afraid of feeling too much. Last night ... you were right to stop us. Too much too quickly. ..."

"Feel too much? Or maybe, feel deeply?" She asks, resting her elbows on the counter. She leans forward and fixes a calm gaze on me.

"Okay, but feeling deeply has sometimes made me. ... It made it very difficult for me to continue working—in fact, I had to stop."

"Then maybe you need to make a change?"

She makes it sound so simple.

She continues. "I saw a nature program on TV a few months ago that showed a wild cat locked up in a cage. Once the effects of the tranquillizer dart wore off, it went berserk. Kept crashing its beautiful body against the bars of the cage, swiping at the spaces in between."

"What are you saying?"

"That some things we try to tame aren't meant to be tamed."

"And if we try ..."

"... violence is the consequence."

I take another sip of my coffee. Violence within the body. Where has the violence shown up in my life? I mean, I'm not the sort who acts out. Quite the contrary.

Francis resumes talking. "Let me tell you a story. I was six. My grandpa, my mother's father, took me out to the ice-cream parlour, and while we were eating our cones, he asked me what I wanted to be when I grew up. I thought about it for all of thirty seconds, slurping solemnly at my ice cream, then I said, 'An extra helping of myself, thank you.'"

How her eyes sparkle. Reminds me of some rare, tender moments in my own childhood. The times I watched the lives of clouds, entranced by their shifting, billowing shapes. I rose to join them, floating far away from my limited, ordinary life. I believed in my ability to fly.

She looks at her watch. "Feel like going for a walk? To Stanley Park."

"Sounds good."

"But first let's eat. I don't want you to faint on me again."

* * *

LEE AH CHOI

In this dreadful silence before dawn, before Chan's harsh shouts from his room downstairs, before the sounds of coolies heaving and sighing outside in their labour, this is a world between worlds, where most danger lies, where one's soul can be taken away by the last snatch of darkness.

All quiet now, the flood's gone. I'll make myself believe I can do the things she's dreamed of. I can float out my window to her brothel, to where she sleeps, her eyes closed determinedly against onslaught. Stroke her long black hair, smell her presence, lay my head alongside her shoulder.

Stay or go? Try harder. Why isn't it working? I want to fly. . . .

Eeeee, what's that sound? A woman singing out my name in the hallway, singing about washing blood out of garments. The opera singer! I recognize her voice. She has come to comfort me. My sister, my true sister. I must listen to her. Ah Fong, forgive me, I couldn't help you. Forgive me for feet that carried me far away from you. I see your garments, stained with the blood of your crushed bones.

What an entrancing voice. Yes, let me light this small red candle. Saved it for this, the eighth lunar month. So glad I survived last month's fearfulness. The ghosts have come and gone, nothing to be afraid of now. Their hunger has been satiated. This voice is a friend. And this candle, in a place where the sun doesn't shine, may this light protect me. Now a strong dose, to keep the flood away.

Opium, how I would be lost without you. Once I was helpless, watching as floods destroyed our lives, as I was dragged away in exchange for sacks of rice. But here's something for my own hunger, a power to remove all pain. Quickly, give me the wings I need! So that I can fly to her, totally painless, totally free.

* * *

The sun appears then disappears behind clouds. The path through the park is full of people. Francis and I hold hands. Twinges of panic pass through me, electrical bursts rattling my gut. Morbid images of women and men with their bodies bleeding, bruised, or marked by hate, flash through my mind. Daylight might not protect us. I turn away from observing people, and look at the ocean instead. I keep on holding her hand, even though part of me feels like fleeing.

How surreal it is to be two women lovers in a crowd of strangers. After all these years as a lesbian, I still feel strange being affectionate in public. I glance at the others. A sea of legs that move to discordant rhythms. Two gay men pass us by. Later on, three dykes together. They look at us with knowing smiles, openly showing their approval.

Ocean of many moods softly caresses pebbles, retreats, then rushes forward, threatening to reach over the edge of the wall and engulf us. Francis and I remain quiet while all around us chatter drifts in and out of earshot. The longer we walk in silence, the calmer I become.

My gaze sweeps upwards and startles momentarily at the Lions. Sometimes I forget, and expect that flat landscape of my childhood. Mountains seem immovable and stoic. Yet vision can make us forget the distant past, that these sentinels weren't always there, having originated from the depths of the earth, thrusting through the surface as molten or granite batholiths. Even now, there are invisible shifts occurring deep within them. Every earthquake that reaches this landscape, however minor or major, must register within their forms. The faults, the fissures, all the fragmenting consequences.

The stretch of beach just before we reach English Bay is crowded with rock sculptures, like UFOs that have arrived to colonize this area. I remember reading about them in *The Vancouver Sun*. They were made by some man who understands how to place rocks one on top of another such that they don't topple, but stay firmly tip to tip. That man's hands must be guided by a special kind of sensing, able to find the remarkable balance in nature. What compels him to do this?

At the foot of Denman, a crowd gathers around a juggler on his unicycle. Kids dart about in furious excitement. One fatally dislodges her chocolate ice cream onto the front of her pink Osh-Kosh overalls. Francis and I eat hot dogs and drink pop. We kiss. No one seems to notice. I feel like a kid again, not caring what's showing or who's looking.

We turn around and walk the same route back. Smell the sea.

The hours go by, unconsidered and irrelevant.

Back at her apartment, we undress each other to the slow, rhythmic drip of the kitchen tap. One button, another, then another. Peeling away time and hesitation. The unhurried conversation of gestures. The needs of my skin, to remember how to welcome another's touch, to shed resistance. Her crimson bra strap releases quietly in my hands. I cradle the weight of her breasts.

"Now your hands are warm," she observes, breathing into my ear.

The weight of sheer breath. Laden, audible. *Quand elle me prend dans ses bras.* The whisper, *elle me parle tout bas.* Long kiss of tongue diving for depth. Her bare, vulnerable neck, as the throat opens.

I hold up her left hand to my nose. Smells of coffee, hot dogs and ketchup. Soap and tobacco, and the complex, unanswered questions of the body. My mind caught in the palm of her hand. I lick the lines: heart, head, life, health. Her wrist with its pools of feeling, supple and complicated. I follow the passage of longing up her arm, until my mouth grazes the mole over her heart.

With my hand, I part her. Separate surface from depth where her thighs meet, where rivers of longing culminate. Sentiments, sediments. I taste her dense salt-drenched delta, and open her particular history with speech. The question of how, again and again. The sweat of seeking. *Alors je sens en moi, mon coeur qui bat.* I strain to reach her.

She draws me up, breathing close to my ear. Her fingers reach down to the base of my spine, a touch that sets off a spreading ache, upturning my body from within, earth when air enters it, solid becoming less solid. Pausing above me, breasts hovering, she's asking for surrender. Here where the soft, vulnerable indentation is, where throat meets clavicle. Her hair sweeps across my chest, awakening my skin with light, fast ripples.

Gathering into a single swirling ache. Everything is rushing at me, through me. I fall in, merging with the current.

* * *

CHOW CHAT MUI

How could it be? I wondered why she didn't come to the alley last night. Did she mean to leave like that? Without caring how her death would hurt me? I didn't know she wanted to die.

Who would have guessed that ah ku could love each other, meeting in-between men, in-between pain? Who would have guessed we shared a precious passion that no money paid for?

The sun bears down cruelly on the sweating bodies of coolies on this September day. But the winds are shifting. Bringing rains from the northeast. Then the red dust will settle, mix with the rain to become liquid mud.

Ah Sek is drinking and smoking opium downstairs. I hear him telling others the news. Laughing, he calls Ah Choi crude names, warns his women not to get carried away by gambling or opium. With the fervour of a white-man preacher, he warns against excess. Even tragedy doesn't make him treat her with respect.

Who killed her? Died by her own hands. Died by opening her too-hungry mouth to that sweet poison. Accident? How quickly a life is lost. Soon another woman will be taking over her cubicle. No trace left. Will they take her to Sago Lane and give her a proper funeral ceremony, pay for a few to mourn her? Her sisters in the brothel will act as if she never existed. They'll bury her memory even deeper into their bowels, where fear still churns.

I cry in my cubicle, crying for myself. I, the older sister, shouldn't survive her. What a fool I was to dream of escape together. I wronged her, I told her we could run away together. She didn't linger in her suffering as long as I have in mine. I don't want to rush to her brothel, to have her dead body as my final memory. Maybe they've already taken her away. I would rather think of her in her elegant red samfu. Wearing those shoes and carrying the lilac silk purse she dreamed of buying. In my fantasy her eyes light up with joy. Stay lit despite the world's attempts to dim them.

Will I find her still in the breeze that caresses my face?

* * *

MAHMEE

I'm tired. Scared of this living by myself. A person's fate can be so twisted, I never thought he die before me. I the one with aches and pains, he the one who didn't say much. Did Lan-Lan and Michael know he often cried to me about his mother, how during the war she left her sons with her oldest brother in Batu Pahat in Johore? Then she died of cancer, Yen only a young boy! Then both brothers sent back to father's house in Singapore.

Do Lan-Lan and Michael know he had all kinds of nightmares? He didn't sleep in the same bed with me sometimes because I complained too much of his snoring. Was there something I could have done that I didn't do? I think some people secretly blame me, say I not enough of a wife. But they would never say that to my face, they only whisper behind my back. Yes, let them talk. Do I care? No, a widow must never show need in case such people use it to insult her.

* * *

I roll out of the spooning position and turn towards her. Moonlight reveals fine beads of sweat on her forehead. We toss off the sheets, a film of moisture over our skins. We wear the humidity of this warm July night. I sit up and stare at the pillow. A long strand of hair, hers, framed by the shadow outlines of the window. In the distance, the sounds of a train clattering along the track, followed by a brief burst of voices from the pavement below. Sounds are so much sharper, more intense, in the warmer months of the year. A shiver reminds me of where I'd stopped in the conversation.

"My clients. Many of them are very resilient. I would even call some heroic. A kind of courage that isn't celebrated much. That's what I also think about the ah ku. They weren't rich or politically powerful so most history books tend to ignore them."

"They might have been brave, but how could any of us know what they had to endure?"

I gaze at Francis's cheekbones. They are cliff faces, treacherous and beautiful.

"I don't pretend to know. It's more that I've needed to imagine them so that I won't . . . can't be . . . defeated by their anonymity."

I lie back down. She strokes my arm in slow tempo, until her hand finds the inside crease of the elbow. Back and forth, two fingers travelling the sensitive slope.

Of course it's true. How do I know anything about anyone else's life? We're all strangers. And yet I've felt compelled to imagine them, Ah Choi and Chat Mui, together. I don't even know for sure if lesbianism existed among the ah ku of that time.

"Do you feel—if you're listening to people's problems all the time—you're getting a slice of life that's too heavy on the suffering, too much awfulness to stomach?"

Stomach. Why did she have to use that word? That queasiness I often feel when something disturbingly true confronts me.

"Yes, that's right. It has been overwhelming." I sigh and continue, "What time is it?"

"About one-thirty."

My fingers find her eyebrows, talking one to the next, as if my rhythmic gesture could bridge the worlds of left and right. She lifts my fingers away from her eyebrows, and kisses them lightly.

"I want to tell you something," Francis begins.

"Oh?"

"Do you want to hear?" A slight trembling in her voice.

"What is it?"

"It's about the relationship I left in San Francisco."

"Uh-huh."

"It's complicated."

I wait to hear. What could it be?

"The inheritance money I told you about?"

A tightness descends over her voice. "It was my uncle. He . . . molested me. No one in the family knew, although it went on through most of my adolescence. Then recently, I took him to civil court." She pauses, and tears form at the edges of her eyes. "I got a settlement. I wanted to tell you soon. Even though I'm afraid—"

"I might run away?"

She nods her head and says, "I suppose you still could."

I gaze at her reclining form, glowing with the bluish-white night. A sad light colours this bed. We are vulnerable, open to discovery. Or destruction. And then unbidden, surfacing from an ancient context, Kim's words return to haunt me, *Sex is fragile.*

I remain silent, wondering what's next. I close my eyes and breathe in and out deliberately slowly. It's not sex that's fragile, it's us. Human beings. The capacity to feel, to suffer. To be broken by pain or tragedy. Or the capacity to transcend suffering somehow.

"Crazy." My head feels light.

"What?"

She props herself up, and looks into my eyes. "Wu Lan, what's the matter?"

Can't breathe, can't think straight. Images flash before my eyes, a shifting collage of faces. Clients, Kim, Daniel. Mahmee. Father.

"Sorry. Can't make out what . . . I feel panicky." Again, that urge to run away. "A smoke. Will you roll me one of yours?"

"I thought that Chinese doctor told you to quit."

"Smoke's good for clearing the brain."

She gets up to retrieve her tobacco and papers. Returns to bed, nestling the open packet of tobacco between her legs. Her fingers dive in, while her other hand pulls out a piece of paper from the pack. A compact mound in the centre of creamy white paper. She raises the paper to her lips and licks slowly. With a finger, I carefully track the movement of her tongue along the finely textured material. This, too, like a veil of secrets between us, is inevitable. She begins to cry again, softly, as she inserts the cigarette between my lips and lights it. The smoke rises, a lazy presence, a prayer for the humid air. She begins to roll another. I taste her tears, licking them off her face. We smoke and kiss, swirling in the vortex.

"Freud said smoking is indispensable if there's no one to kiss."

I smile at her joke. Is that why we need it? "I'm going up to the roof. Just for a bit."

I slip on my t-shirt and jeans. At the back of the apartment, I move the bike aside, unlatch the door and push it open. The metal fire escape is shockingly cold on my bare feet.

But the air outside is pleasantly cool. It invites my body to relax. The moon is high overhead, its fullness bright and unimpeded by the cloud brows that frame it. Before the great white astronaut Neil Armstrong, there was Lady Chang-E, who downed a whole bottle of magic elixir and soared to the moon. She made the mistake of believing that a good thing still would be good in excess. The story goes that Hou Yi, her lover, finds a way to reach her every full moon.

I look down at the street. No one around. Must be at least sixty feet to the ground. Concrete pavement. A person stands a chance of surviving this fall. But what would be broken? The spine, crushed in several places, followed by the loss of sensations in different parts of the body. The skull with its fragile plates that could crack anywhere along its fissures. Or fracture of the limbs, internal trauma to the organs. Bruising of every kind.

Choosing not to die isn't the same as choosing to live. The smoke curls, dances around my nostrils. A tease, a temptation to forget.

* * *

CHOW CHAT MUI

Can't believe she's dead. In this week following her suicide, more news has arrived, through the whisperings that can't be stopped. This is how we separate truth from lies. Truth arrives from many directions, persisting. She had been taken to Dr. Lim's private hospital at 22 Nankin Street. Overdosed, but not yet dead. Placed on a hospital bed by one of his orderlies, propped up on pillows in her unconscious state. My poor Ah Choi. Left there, awaiting the doctor's attention. And then, so the gossip goes, Dr. Lim had her sent to the General Hospital, because her condition was too serious for him to manage. How long did it take before a doctor tended to her? When exactly did she die? I wonder if she could have been saved.

I stood at our window that night after hearing the news. Less than twenty-four hours after she left her cold corpse, she was already haunting the alleys with her unrest. Her pale face, her ghostly presence staring up at me from the alley below, among the rats, the garbage. Ah Choi, what you couldn't speak in life you soon expressed in death! Why did you flail your arms, why did your face wear such terror?

* * *

"Do you want to talk some more? About what happened to you?" I ask her, back in bed.

She shakes her head calmly at me, "No, I don't need to any more."

I gaze quietly at her torso. The length of her. If I make love to her, I would show her I'm unafraid of her pain. For those moments we could transcend death, what had been lost. But before I can act, she, the faster animal, turns me onto my tummy, her mouth gnawing at my neck, then her tongue pressing, insisting itself along my jaw, towards my ear.

We are waning with the moon. I roll into her, the ocean in me gathering its force, swift then slow, crashing against her body. She fixes my shoulder with her mouth. The wide kisses across my skin certain as footsteps deepening into sand. I stroke the lower curves of her belly, from her navel down to the curls of her mound. I want to purge the fear out of myself. This sweat, this smell of my own terror. In her eyes, I am captured, the double distorted self. Her hand fills my mouth, one finger at a time.

Under the weight of her body, there is release.

To surrender solidity itself.

Until I feel a pull inwards into darkness. A blue door. I open it.

In one corner, a girl of about eleven sits with knees drawn up to her chest, head down, breathing into her thighs. The hardness of the floor presses upwards against her hips.

The intermittent sound of creaking wood floors, footsteps that pause and resume with deliberate caution. Distant, very distant, then a light tumbling melody of voices. A man's voice, barely audible, in several staccato bursts, and a woman's pleasured laughter. Their voices echo down to me, through a hallway.

I want to believe. That they were happy when they made me.

Returning from that corner, I notice my toes dimly exposed by the moonlight, and feel my own sex enlarge. A hope, even if I don't know what was true. And the quiet tears of a girl who did not believe.

"Why are you crying?" She caresses the side of my cheek.

I shake my head. I don't want to answer. My body shivers. A breeze from the window brings this chill, not unpleasant, the sweat of fear slowly evaporating into the night. Had they known they were making a baby? Did they imagine how having children would change their lives? It's one thing to describe descendants as common, as that Darwinian has, but it's something entirely different to accept that a child depends on her rare ancestors, especially her parents. That she's entirely vulnerable to their intents and actions.

Francis draws me close to her and wraps her arms and legs around me. We're safe, for now. In this private temple of our own making. I want to believe this, yet there's that low, constant vibration again, spreading from my gut up through my chest, a sea of soft pin prickles. I was born, and I will be born again, as long as I remember. Memory is the elixir. If I speak the truth.

"My father killed himself. Almost a year ago." The words tumble out of me like water, fluid and careless.

She moves apart, studies my face, that furrow bridging her eyebrows yet again. Silence, and its familiar abyss. When she finally speaks, her voice carries a distinct quiver, "I'm very sorry, Wu Lan. That's awful."

Her softness is unbearable. I'm emerging from my own anonymity, like peeling off a thin, opaque membrane and meeting the air with my own raw life.

"Hold me. Don't let go until I say so." I push against her arms with an energy that erupts from within. To feel resistance, to feel my own body. All the words I couldn't speak. I am a writhing creature, I am the snake struggling against herself.

"What are you fighting for? You don't have to, any more."

Finally I let go, and collapse against the pillow, heavy with exhaustion. She bends down and kisses me lightly on the mouth. The fluttering flight of a butterfly, the awakening relief of a sudden breeze. I want her to cross into me, take me to a place somewhere on the other side of all I've seen and experienced so far.

"Make love to me. Don't be afraid."

"No, I'm not afraid. Tell me what you want."

I take her hand and bring it into me slowly, one finger at a time, until her hand is halfway in. Until I reach the edge of intolerable intensity. Here's the chance to escape. To break through some barrier of pain. Inside my mind, she has become an image, the arm with a disappearing hand. When I pull her out, and raise her hand to my face, I smell traces of the ocean, of lives that exist deeply, beyond capture.

* * *

CHOW CHAT MUI

Has it really been eight months since she died? Days emptied of her laughter, the stolen kisses. I swear, sometimes under the opium spell in the late afternoons, before my first client, I smell her skin approaching my face. I hear her voice echoing inside my head, a whisper at first, then amplifying until it is a thunder booming inside my head! She is crashing as loudly as the building outside.

They're tearing down one of the old buildings at the end of our street. The sound of bricks and mortar collapsing. Awful noise! Used to be the home of a Hokien kongsi, but then I heard that someone in government didn't like the way it was conducting its opium business. We're worried about riots starting up again. There were big fights here long before I arrived, especially between the Teochews and Hokiens. The Gaos and the Lius all over again.

Her loud voice accuses me of being a dreamer without action, of living a coward's life. *Why does a tap tang like you not leave for better things? I was a helpless kong chu, don't you know?* Her accusations surface, now that she's gone. I don't know how to answer her. I've taken to walking her favourite routes, especially down to where the river meets the ocean. Watching the boats come and go, come and go. And sometimes even staying as late as the sunset, that roundness travelling to unknown places below the horizon.

Does Ah Choi walk in that other world she inhabits? Does she sing? Perhaps this is what the wind is, the music of presences moving in that unknown world. As darkness overtakes the world of bright appearances, the music can be better heard.

I've taken to singing the ancient songs, the ones we sang as we toiled in the fields.

> At the end of the day, I am weary,
> too weary to tend to my hair;
> Things remain, but he is gone, and all is nothing.
> Try to speak, but the tears will flow
> Try to speak, but the tears will flow.

The words meant very little to me then. What did I know as a young girl? I enjoyed the tune, but I flung the words out of my mouth recklessly.

I've changed. I sing now with some understanding of that kind of sorrow. Meanings swirl through my insides, while I taste tears in my mouth. Singing is one way to tell a story, isn't it? A few lines hummed between clients. Or before sleep.

I've started looking into the mirror again. If I can no longer gaze at her beauty, can I find traces of her in my reflection? Let me wear her on my face. My brow is still unsettled from the memory of her touch. The radiance of her moon-face. I wish it would shine through me somehow, but no, I don't see that in me. Innocence lost is lost forever. How long before they tear me down too? Like a building that's far too old for anyone's use.

* * *

MAHMEE

Come soon, Hungry Ghosts Festival. What there to celebrate? Except a chance to feed Yen's hunger. Maybe this time, one year after, I make sure he get some of his favourites: steamed char siew bun, some whiskey, a few melon seeds. Maybe that's enough to feed him. Like people I know, they lose husbands, sometimes not very peaceful as well. Until Hungry Ghosts come next year. That's when everything change.

* * *

"Wu Lan." His voice awakens me from sleep. I open my eyes and there he is, holding a *Daily Bread* in his hand. He's standing at the foot of my bed. He never comes when Francis is here. His lips are pursed tightly, a look of determination permeating his face. He extends his arm out towards me. The cover is a grove of aspens glowing with golden light, the ground a mantle of its yellow autumn leaves. I recognize the cover: it's one of the booklets I brought back with me.

"What do you want?" I demand, unable to sound polite and respectful. He says nothing in reply. I pull up the duvet over me, as I sit staring at his apparition. His eyes are unblinking. The scar across the top of his forehead is visible, a thin line of dark red healed over, with the cross-stitches of the sutures still showing.

"Why are you doing this now?"

He nods twice, turns his back on me, and disappears into the air under the doorway. Is that all? After bothering to appear again after an absence of six months. I close my eyes and try to calm down. My heart races after him, after all the years of unexpressed feeling. He comes and goes, just like that. No wonder Mahmee is upset. I reach for the drawer of the night table, and rummage around. Pull out a few of the booklets and hurl them in the direction of his exit.

If only I didn't love him, and hadn't secretly longed for his love all those years while pretending not to mind his absence. Did he realize he wasn't simply leaving the world but was creating a hole in the universe, a black hole that sucked life into it? Hiding in our storeroom, reading those words of comfort. Hiding away from life. If he knew what it was like to lose Grandmother Neo, how could he not think of us and our suffering? A ghost is self-absorbed. A ghost doesn't care about others' suffering.

I flip on the light and retrieve the booklets. I pick out the one with the aspens. It falls open at the page headlined by a quote: "Come unto me all ye who are heavy laden and I will give you rest." The words that follow are full of reassurance about the peace God gives those who go to Him. I slap the booklet shut. Ironically, Father hasn't gained complete rest yet, and he certainly isn't contributing to mine.

He won't be coming back again tonight. I'm sure of it. With the lights off, I still see the aspens moving in their numinous world. What would it be like to stand under trembling leaves and hear their secret messages whispered in the gentle wind?

Maybe Father appeared with the booklet to remind me of something. Maybe he's still hungering for the soothing effect of words. Of course it was ironic that Michael and I called it his mad collection because the reality was that Father relied on it as if it could be his passport to sanity.

I pull out a cigarette and light it. Maybe that was it. He had phoned me for some words of reassurance. He wanted rest, a calming for his distressed spirit.

The next time Father visits, I could try to remember that he's a ghost now. No more, no less. What was Mahmee's advice about ghosts? Tell him you see, that you're not afraid.

* * *

CHOW CHAT MUI

I see that scholar person again. He still wears his hair the same way. He looks up and says, "Do you still have that word?"

I'm too stunned to reply at first. But I smile slightly. Then I try saying yes in Hokien: "Teo teo." I hope he understands. There are some other people crowding around him, two mothers with their children, three young men, their arms folded squarely across their chests. Oh, the arrogance of youth.

One of them asks, "Is this the way you make money?"

His friend points at a small banner, "What does this say?"

I listen intently to his answers. Yes, he earns a small wage by writing out poems and sayings, and no, he doesn't have expensive habits, so that is how he can survive.

"This character is 'prosperity,' this, 'peace.' This phrase means 'what the heart thinks will be completed in action.'"

I marvel at his calm. He isn't bothered by the questions, his brush continuing to make confident, luscious strokes as he answers. His hands are steady, left hand holding the paper, right hand holding the brush upright and poised in mid-air before its definite descent and movement across paper. There isn't any tell-tale smell of sweetness on him. Not an opium user. Unbelievable.

If only I had that skill to copy out words, make beautiful pictures. Maybe I can learn from a master like him, make some money the way he does. Then stop the opium smoking altogether.

I don't dare tell him I've been teaching myself to copy out that character. Many times over on the blank side of the calendar pictures. Copying multiplies the precious gift over and over! Every time my clumsy brush moved across the paper, leaving its trail of ink, I remembered that this special word means quiet, inner thought. The thinking of the heart. My brushwork might be poor, but the writing calms me. Even makes the pain retreat into the background for a few moments. I wish I'd told Ah Choi about this, I wish she could be here to see what I'm doing.

The scholar's simple elegance. Perhaps if I practise, something good will happen to me.

* * *

Can't sleep. He's gone but I keep replaying his visit in my mind, wondering if there was any detail, any subtle yet significant gesture of his I'd missed at the time. Something that will give me further clues.

I know what might help me. In the living room, I search in the bottom drawer of my filing cabinet. I finally find them in a large envelope under a pile of papers.

It's not true that he was always indifferent or sulky. He had been capable of tenderness once. I have the proof in my hands. The photo of him flinging a five- or six-month-old me into the air, while he lay on his back, a wide grin of delight on his face. The other photos. Family picnics at Katong Park. He and Mahmee on one of their wedding anniversaries. One of him doting on Michael. How long ago that was! There are several photos of him caught in unguarded moments at public functions. Probably office dinners and parties. In most of these photos he looked distracted, vacant. Where had he gone to? He was already a ghost so early on! The eyes of someone caught in another place and time.

The last photo at the bottom of the pile is of him and me together. We are both dressed up for some special occasion, although I don't remember what it was. He looks smart in a white suit, and I sit on his lap, in a light blue seersucker dress. I was probably about eight. Maybe it was my birthday. I stare at my child self, feeling a sense of disquieting recognition. My eyes were glazed, stunned. They're not much different from his.

It's too late for Father. But maybe not for me. Was that why he's been coming back? To remind me of what he had also been, vital and joyful. And is he warning me against going down the path he did? I look into the bathroom mirror, holding up the photo next to my face. Then and now. The resemblances are disturbing.

* * *

CHOW CHAT MUI

Once upon a time the wind was a willow. It loved a woman who rested underneath its supple limbs. The woman liked placing her head in the fork between roots, because that way she was close to the earth's smells, wafting up to her nostrils in the heat of day. She would look up to catch the colours of light filtering through the slender leaves. The willow wanted to tell the woman how much it loved her. It didn't have words, so it swayed its lovely limbs in the breeze instead, a plaintive song of longing. The woman visited the willow every day. But then a day came when she was nowhere to be seen. Weeks passed by. The willow stopped moving in the breeze. It became extremely still. People began to notice that it had lost its vigour and become shrivelled, so unlike the beautiful presence it once was. A few people from the village decided it was time to get rid of the ugly sight. At dusk they marched up to the willow with their axes. They hacked mercilessly at its body, sweating with effort and annoyance at the tedious task. The sky grew darker, choked with storm clouds. A strange howling sound escaped from the tree the moment they broke through the trunk. It was as if it came alive in its final anguish. The sky opened and welcomed the willow spirit, as it cried its entry into the wind.

The villagers then realized that something terrible had happened. Some knew they had misunderstood it, but couldn't guess at the truth. Many shrugged their shoulders and wiped their brows in a show of resignation. But there were a few who saw they had mistaken grief for ugliness, that immense loss wears the face of ugliness unless one knows how to see the beauty beneath it.

Now every evening, just before darkness completely covers the earth, the people can still hear that strange, howling echo through the village, a sound that is the wind itself.

* * *

I search below the kitchen sink, behind the cloth bag of rice, bottles of soy sauce, and can of olive oil. Two years ago, after a potluck, I tucked away a small bottle of Glenfiddich behind all my staples. A guest had brought it and left it behind. At my desk, I set out the photos in a shape of a circle with the bottle in the middle. Let the Scotch represent the power that stole his presence away from us and made him into a ghost. Let the photos document the gradual process of this theft. I peer through the bottle. Underwater distortions, the images behind the glass are long and wavy stretches of black and white shapes tinted green.

Did he do it unconsciously? Letting himself dive into the dangerous liquid, he surrendered to drowning. Soon it'll be Hungry Ghosts Festival back home, and they'll be offering incense and burning gold paper. Feed the Hungry Ghost with food and alcohol. I'll do my own version. I unscrew the cap and sniff. The distinctive smell registers an instant nausea in my belly.

The first gulp moves like a swirl of fire down my throat. So this was the beginning. I don't remember the first time I saw him take a drink. When was it that he crossed the boundary from the innocence of raw pain to the first act of denial? I never let him see how much his self-destructiveness bothered me.

The second gulp. The fierce heat that travelled through his guts must have seemed reassuring after a while. The more he drank, the faster the burning travelled, fire chasing fire until he lost the ability to distinguish between the fire that warms and the fire that razes in destruction.

Tyger tyger burning bright, in the forests of the night, what immortal hand or eye, could frame thy fearful symmetry? I pick up the photo where he shows delight playing with the infant me. The young parent who still knew how to meet joy with joy.

A few more gulps. Does a person learn to love this taste? He used to reek of it. The drowning, swirling nightmare. The deep end of the pool, and the failure to stay afloat. Who's crying? The son who could not, did not stand his mother's disappearance. That son's daughter who still keeps wishing. . . .

What's the alternative? The egg in the refrigerator. It lies in the dark, uneventful in its ordinariness. Like the pills in my cabinet, the knives in the kitchen. Everything desperately ordinary, until a person decides to invest such objects with a life-or-death significance.

What the hammer? what the chain? In what furnace was thy brain? What the anvil? what dread grasp, dare its deadly terrors clasp?

Enough. I've fed the ghost. Any more Scotch and I'll throw up. I screw the cap back on tightly.

* * *

CHOW CHAT MUI

Avoiding it all these months. Finally, I'm ready. Ten months since she died. I asked the sisters how to find her.

Too far to walk, so I hail a rickshaw. A few extra fen for his labour up the hill. This is the first time I'll enter the burial grounds. Passed by a few times but I never dared enter. I have with me two plain buns, dried spicy pork from this morning's breakfast, and a pair of joss-sticks. And one of my best copies of the character.

I'm surprised by the fast-moving rain clouds overhead. It was clear when I set out. The weather changes so drastically in a few hours! The cemetery is a sea of green interrupted by fingers pointing up to Heaven. Hundreds of narrow stone tablets stick out of the ground. Beseeching or accusing, they still all point to the ultimate power. I touch a few as I count my way up to the second large stone gate. My breathing is laboured, it's difficult to climb this slope! Her sisters told me, "Go up to the second one, then count fifty-seven to the right, then nine up, and it is the one with different coloured cloths tied around it."

I reach the place just when the first light drops of rain fall on my face. Five different pieces of fabric mark where she lies under this earth. A bright red, a white, a dark blue, and a flowery one, then a piece of black velvet with some embroidery work. What have they written on her tombstone? If not for the colourful cloths, she would be as unknown to me as the other fingers to the sky. I unwrap the bundle and place the food in front of the stone. I quickly light the joss-sticks and push them into the soft earth next to the food offering. I'm here, kneeling above her. Once, twice, three times, my body bends forward at the waist.

Ah Choi, have you heard my stories, and the songs I've been singing?

Here. This precious word 田. I got it first from a scholar in front of the Ning Yeung 心 Hui Guan. I've been practising, copying it out many times. This part here is a field. See how it resembles the ones we used to work in? And this is the heart. Deep below the field.

As I copied out the character, my own heart opened to all the stories I've saved up inside. A field of tears and memories. This word reminds me love doesn't erase suffering, but deepens it. Love and its secret danger. When a kiss touches a tear, doesn't it swell the tear with tenderness? Whatever Heaven chooses to do, there's something it can't take away from me—it can't claim my heart. Let the tombstones keep beseeching.

I wedge this gift between the food and the stone. Ah Choi, perhaps it will also feed you. May the smell of this incense perfume your thoughts tonight, may the fragrance bring to mind sweet moments. Remember me, Ah Choi. As long as we keep on remembering, our love will survive.

How fierce the thunder is! The chill of the wind creeps into my bones. I must leave now. My rickshaw is waiting. But I'll be back, I promise.

* * *

I'm walking on the Burrard Bridge in the middle of the night, dressed in a black t-shirt and green shorts. It's slightly chilly for a summer night. My skin's heat is soothed by the dip in temperature. There's no fear in me, as if it's the most ordinary thing to be doing. Down below, on the right, the green sign that marks Bridges Restaurant, its yellow presence lit by the floodlights. Near it, boats moored at the wharves. In the distance the outline of Granville Bridge. A taxi whizzes by, then slows down ahead. The driver must be wondering if I'm a potential fare. I ignore him, and he takes off. The bridge seems to go on forever, while the scenery over the water repeats itself. Tall condominium buildings, their glass bodies lit up like the insides of tapeworms. The water is darker than the sky, gleaming with moonlight one moment, receding into a blanket of darkness when clouds obscure the moon.

Finally I reach the end of the bridge near Pacific Boulevard. There's a crowd of people huddled together. As I get closer, I notice a few familiar faces. Clients whom I haven't seen for a while. I start to recall bits of information about each one of them. They're all dressed in cocktail party attire. Faces all giddily festive. Smoking and drinking faces. What's the occasion?

Then I see him as the others move away from the centre. He looks miserable, but it's as if the sadness is pasted on and exaggerated, the way it would be on a clown's face. A bottle of Glenfiddich is empty in his hand, his wedding ring clinking against it. He begins to sob when he realizes it's me. I push past the party people and face him. He's so much smaller than me. Shrunken. How did I get so tall?

We end up in a very large room. Completely empty except for a bed in one corner. A bed that matches the room's pallor, covered in a stark white sheet. Father is still crying, but softly now, as if his tears have all disappeared back into himself. The bottle is no longer in his hand. I feel very tired, my legs aching and sore from walking a great distance, all the way from the Burrard Bridge. We crossed a border when we entered this room. There are no windows, but light seems to filter through the walls. It is eerily silent.

I coax him towards the bed, lay him down, and lift the sheet up and over him, tucking him in carefully until he is a neat but quivering white form.

* * *

Chow Chat Mui

Betrayed! I'm dazed. Ah Loong broke down and told me a secret he has harboured for all these months. His face contorted with the torture of keeping quiet. Months and months of silence, how could he? He knows I was close to Ah Choi. Finally, his guilt must be eased through confession.

In the shadows of my cubicle, his face twitched with nervousness. His mouth stammered with uncertainty. The mouth that seemed alone in his face, because the light from the lamp cast its brightest focus on it.

"I . . . I . . . went to see Lan Ho. Uh . . . just after—" He paused, frozen in silence.

Fate had kept Lan Ho from becoming that other man's concubine. The man died only days before her scheduled departure from the brothel into the home he'd bought for her. How tragic. She had no choice but to stay put in her cubicle. Then Ah Loong began to resume his visits with her. None of my business.

"Lan Ho told me that it was Loke Kum who betrayed Ah Choi to their kwai po."

Why would Loke Kum do that? Maybe she was envious. Ah Choi would have inherited the front cubicle if Lan Ho became that man's concubine. Even I had been envious at first. Of a radiance that persists despite anxiety and illness.

Why didn't any of the sisters stop Loke Kum? If Sum Tok hadn't found out about the hidden money, if Ah Choi hadn't been so upset by it all, who's to say how different a turn fate would have taken. She might not have died, and now still be with me.

* * *

The sound of water against glass wakes me up. I gasp awake, feeling claustrophobic from the dream. Our next-door neighbour is watering his box hedge but as usual he's reckless with his aim, and the water hits my bedroom window with loud splattering sounds.

The heaviness in my head reminds me of what I had done. My tongue feels coated and swollen. I roll my face into the pillow, and press my hand against the bed. This is my bed. Not that other one in which I'd laid him to rest.

In my dream I had felt oddly free from anxiety, walking the Burrard Bridge. It was surprising to find Father, no longer hidden by my clients, smaller than the man he had been in my younger days. Then to lead him into a room that was completely white. The colour of grieving, of absence, the white square worn for a hundred days on the right sleeve. I covered him, bound him up as one would bind a corpse.

Poor Father. Poor Yen. A man I didn't, couldn't, completely know. And yet I've met him in a dream the way I never had in waking life.

A knock on the door startles me. I look at the clock. I've overslept, and Francis is right on time, saving me from further ruminations.

* * *

CHOW CHAT MUI

Don't know how long he's been standing in the doorway, watching me.

"What are you doing?"

"Nothing." I don't dare look up. I'm on the floor, hunched over the box where my calendar papers and ink bottle are. The hair on my neck stands on end. I grip the brush more tightly. Dangerous, dangerous.

"What are you doing?" he repeats, his voice louder this time.

I feel him move towards me. He bends down and snatches the papers up. His breath is hot and loud against the side of my face. Then he starts to scream right into my ear, says he wants me to stop copying out that word. He sweeps his hand across my face, and I fall back against the box, upsetting the ink bottle. It crashes down onto the floor, the ink splattering out black as night.

"You! These are my calendars. How dare you, stinky bitch!"

He rips up my efforts! The pieces of paper scatter in front of my eyes like drops of rain. His face is locked in a scowl, hatred churning in his eyes. Then he notices the paper on my bed, the original gift from the scholar. Too late! I try to save it, but he snatches it up and rips it apart with one quick movement. Is this the man I had trusted my new life to almost nine years ago? Is this the one who taught me the skills of pleasing men?

From deep in my belly a heat rises up and spreads to my neck and face. The brush makes a clean, hollow sound when it lands. I stand up slowly. Clench my hand in a fist. *You,* I thought. *You who once loved me. How could I have been fooled? I see you now.*

Had Ah Sek known about Loke Kum's betrayal of Ah Choi? Didn't he laugh the day she died? Callous man.

I bring my fist down on his face. Striking against that wrinkled side, where someone else had dared challenge him once, long before me. And now I dare bring my strength down on his ugliness again and again. The skin is like paper crinkling under my knuckles, soft and rough at the same time. Surprise and fear in his eyes. Owner, lover, keeper. Rat. Twisted cock-face. See what it's like to be terrified, to be collapsed under the fury of another. His cowering body crumbles under me. *I will push you deep into the earth. I will flatten you as Heaven flattens. No more.* No more money in my face, money on the ground. Promises of wealth, all lies!

* * *

The Jehovah's Witnesses are planted at their regular station in front of Carmelo's. They impress me with their clean-cut formality. No mess, no surrealistic leaps, unlike our dreams. They go to all that trouble for the Lord.

The men, one black and one white, don't appear deterred by Francis and me holding hands as we pass by.

"Would you like one?" The black guy dips into his briefcase and shoves a booklet in my face. It's a Chinese version of *The Watchtower*.

"Sorry, I don't read Chinese," I reply, with a touch of hostility.

The two men look surprised. When we are out of earshot, Francis speaks up, "But I thought you do."

"Not enough to read the whole bloody thing."

At the greasy spoon, the waitress stands behind the counter, her hands firmly in her apron pocket, just in front of her navel, listening to the young woman with the red and purple hair.

"You know, I just got into some social housing, so at least I don't have to be on the streets all the time, especially when the cold weather starts again. The Salvation Army people down on Clark are pretty certain I can have a couch that's been in the back of the store for ages. If you know anyone who's got furniture to give away, tell me, okay? I have a friend with a van."

The waitress's alert, wide-open face doesn't register any surprise or distress even though the young woman continues relentlessly. Francis and I choose the table at the window, nearest the door. The waitress's expression feels familiar, as if I've worn it myself. A look that takes in everything being said, while keeping distance, making sure the emotions of the self are kept well hidden.

The street woman leaves with her cup of coffee. When the waitress comes over with menus, I nod my head in the direction of the door.

"You see a lot of action," I say.

"Oh! I love my job. It's never dull here," she announces matter-of-factly, and places the menus in front of us.

A few minutes later, the two Jehovah's Witness men arrive. When they notice it's us, they glare in unison. They pick the table farthest from us, at the back of the restaurant. It begins as a humming, then when I realize what it is, I start to sing it softly, "What a friend we have in Jesus, all our screams and riffs to bear, what a privilege to bury everyone who hates our guts."

He was so angry! No wonder he can't rest.

"Wu Lan, you've been cranky this morning. What is it?" Francis leans forward and folds her arms on the table.

"Cranky? Nonsense!" I growl, the weight of the hangover becoming even more solidly entrenched between my eyes. I continue, feeling a touch remorseful, "Let's just say I had an incident with myself last night and I'm ashamed of it."

As I recount to her what happened, Francis's eyes take in the information with growing alarm. I pause when the waitress arrives with our dinner rolls.

When I finish, Francis exclaims, "Look, you're a psychologist, you understand these things more than me, but maybe it would help you to go see a therapist yourself."

"I'm not an alcoholic!" I huff, my voice choked with upset. I didn't anticipate that Francis would respond like this, I'd wanted some sympathy.

"I didn't say you are. Hey, I'm just concerned." She reaches out and strokes my hand carefully, tentatively. "Just because you help other people doesn't mean you can't need help." She tears open her dinner roll, places a pat of butter in-between, pressing the two halves together before biting into it.

Doesn't mean you can't need. Two negatives make a positive. It makes sense, so why is it I've been so resistant?

Our food arrives, mine a beef stew over rice, hers a fish burger with French fries. I push at the cubes of beef and carrots and corn swimming in the gravy.

"Sorry. You're right."

"Do you believe your clients have been helped by you?"

"I suppose so . . . some of them . . . but—"

I stare at the backs of the two men. The ones driven by some strong urgency to bear witness to others. They believe they have the key to salvation, and they want to share it. The woman who hurled herself off Block 16. What would these two men have done if they had been there? They would have felt upset she lost her chance at salvation.

"But what?"

"Huh?"

"You were talking about your clients being helped by you...."

"Oh. I was thinking, I don't make any difference in any of my clients' lives unless..."

"...they willingly help themselves." Francis finishes off the thought for me.

She would know. She'd been through it herself with her therapist in San Francisco.

"Okay, okay, I'll think about it," I concede. Why should I resist undergoing psychotherapy? If there's any religion in North America that supercedes Christianity, it's the business of secular confession. I'm part of it all, aren't I? So why not sit in the client's chair? It would be a chance to relinquish anonymity.

I stare out the window. Across the street, waiting at the light is a Chinese woman whose face looks familiar.

"It's her! Tze Cheng," I sit up, more alert, suddenly recalling that first time I met her.

"Who?"

"The woman at the temple, the one who gave me my name. I mean, who explained to me the meaning of my name."

"Go ahead. Say hello," she urges me.

I run out just as the traffic lights change and the yellow figure comes flashing on. She's on her way towards me.

"Tze Cheng, remember me? Wu Lan."

"Oh! Yeah, the dragon eyes."

"Do you still go to the temple?"

"Monday, Tuesday and Friday mornings. Come visit again."

"I will."

I wave goodbye to her and rejoin Francis.

* * *

CHOW CHAT MUI

Have I killed Ah Sek? He's a heap on the floor. I lift up the curtain. No one in the hallway. All quiet. My heart is pounding so desperately it's going to leap out of me! I rush down the stairs and into the street.

What kind of madness? A slave for nearly nine years, and now I'm fleeing. Without thought, without care. An impulse. I must find Ah Loong. I need his help. I try not to run, but oh, I'm walking fast, my heart going ahead of me. Do the people on the street see the fear in my eyes? I must try to hide it. Seven streets to Ah Loong's lodgings. Ten minutes. They will catch me!

Where shall I go? The temple is up ahead, quiet at this time of the late afternoon, when everyone is on their way home. The scholar isn't here with his table and art. Quickly, I'll sneak into the temple, stay until it's dark. No one will guess to look for me here, whereas they might think to send the samseng or the police foot patrols in the direction of Smith Street.

No one here. A few joss-sticks spicing up the air. Never come in here before, always stayed outside, watching others enter. Used to think, see how the people are swallowed up as they cross the threshold from the light outside into the cavernous darkness. Ah Choi was right, there's something soothing about this place. Walking deeper into the temple, I see the altar with its lit candles, a thousand eyes, comforting in their seeing. *We see your fear,* they say to me. I walk up to the altar, my heart still pounding fiercely in my chest. On the left, a large urn topped with a handful of joss-sticks. Underneath the table that supports the urn, concealed by the red and gold ceremonial cloths that rim its perimeter, is a hiding place. I'll crawl into it, lie there quietly, a chance to think. Once the night arrives with its protective mantle, I can venture out into the streets. But where will I go? I must have opium soon.

This hiding place is dark and cool, with a scent of sandalwood and rose. As if the fragrance of the joss-sticks has drifted down and settled here.

Some time goes by before I hear the swishing sounds of a robe. A male voice mumbles, like a gentle stream tripping over rocks. I listen to his odd combination of soft yet exact inflections as he prays. The voice sounds familiar. Can it be him? The scholar. I part the cloths slightly. Blue cotton shoes. So close to me that my breath must dampen their tips. The shoes move away from me to the stool in front of the altar.

How long before they find me? How long before I must be in that chicken cage again? But for now I'm curled up in this dark, welcoming cave, feeling strangely comforted. I could stay here forever, die like this. Ugly and old. Who wants me, truly wants me? No tenderness. I may be alive but I'm a shell. A hollow gourd that houses only a small corner of the wind.

The prayers have ended. I hear him retreat, the footsteps getting softer with distance. I must chance it, I have nothing to lose.

"Wait," I whisper, then I shout, "wait, don't leave!"

Silence. His feet have stopped moving away.

"Who is that?" The voice is startled and tense.

"Here, come here." His padded feet draw closer. Slow, deliberate steps. I lift the cloths. It's the scholar. His eyes squint at me.

"You! Who are you hiding from?"

"I'm afraid. Don't let them find me. I might have killed Wong Ah Sek, my kwai kung." I feel tears welling up. I continue in a more feeble tone, "Help me."

How long this moment of silence is, as I wait for his reply. My worst fears surface. The demons rise up from murky waters to frighten me with their scowls, looking like ghoulish replicas of Ah Sek.

But then the scholar extends his hand to me. My body gains a lightness as I emerge. He leads me to the back of the temple and pushes open a small door. We step into a narrow, wet alley. There must have been a downpour while I was inside. I smell rotting fruit peels, piss, mossy stones under our feet. We scurry under the eaves of the temple, down to China Street. A rickshaw approaches. The scholar hails it and haggles for a few minutes with the coolie over the price. The coolie says he doesn't usually go north of the river, he's afraid of the samseng who control that area. The scholar suggests other routes and promises him extra for his troubles. Finally, the coolie agrees.

Where is he taking me? He said, "East Coast," to the coolie. It is quite a distance away, across the bridge separating Chinatown from the rich commercial districts and beyond. I don't know what will happen, but for one last time I'll trust. There's nothing left to lose.

* * *

MAHMEE

Too much, he not stop coming! I so sick of him kachau me, I went to see a woman medium in her home during Hungry Ghosts Festival. I try to get appointment for first day, but do you know how busy those mediums are? Everyone wants it on same day! We pick next best occasion to call up the ghost. This medium my friend Sylvia recommended, said she helped contact her husband who died three years before mine.

Sylvia and me we went together, all the way two buses, more than one hour, all the way to Balestier Road—so ma fan. One of those very old-fashioned Straits houses. Outside quite dirty, windows needed cleaning, even the doormat dusty, as I wiped my sandals on it. What for? I thought. A young girl opened the door for us, showed us to the living room. I thought, outside so dirty, inside must be too. But no! Everything spic-and-span. So I said to Sylvia, "Huh? Dirty outside, clean inside, how can?"

Sylvia quickly whispered, while slapping me on the arm, "Tche! You don't know? Spirits don't like dirt. Quiet, lah!"

So I shut up. After all, my friend doing me a favour. We went to che sin, so better not be rude, otherwise Yen won't show up. I looked around the room. An altar with the sacrificial food, a pyramid of mandarin oranges, a bowl of coconut candies and mints. Even a bottle of Johnnie Walker. I know then I got right person here to deal with my husband. Incense burning, sticks in a bowl of uncooked rice, quite nice, I don't mind. Hah, if Ah Mak still around, she would laugh at me, finally I go to temple to get help.

Then the medium came. Very old, maybe ninety something, her hair white and tight in a bun, she dressed in black samfu, no jewellery except jade charm around her neck. I felt goose pimples all over and shivered. She looked sternly at me.

"Your husband give you problems?"

I nodded. And what did she do? Straight away, she started to chant, I didn't know what she said. She bowed to the altar a few times, fell on the floor once in a while. The young girl used stick to beat on a tin drum. Noisy!

Took a long time. Sylvia sometimes grabbed my elbow nervously. I thought, she been through this and still she kan cheong. But I admit now, I was also a bit nervous. Then the medium started to shake and flop around on the floor, like a dying fish. Aiyah, I couldn't believe it. An old woman like her doing these tricks, I bet she got blacks and blues all over her body.

"Quick, quick," Sylvia shouted and rushed forward. I followed her. She on one side of the medium, me on other side, we dragged her to one of the chairs at the table. Very strong, like twenty-year-old man. She was sweating and very stinky! Like some juicy pig in the market. I think, now what, how we keep her down? But as soon as she reached the table she flopped down like a piece of nonya kueh. Like she fell asleep, her arms on the table. Then the girl came over and put a black piece of cloth over the medium's head.

Sylvia motioned to me to sit down. "Quick, your questions."

Now, I'm not fast brain and my friend want to rush me? How many times she must say quick? But I did my best.

"Yen, is that you?"

The medium made a few growls, like a bad-tempered dog.

"Why you still bother me?"

The medium shivered, like she just came in from a downpour. Then she rocked back and forth in her chair, tapped the table with her fingers. Finally she spoke, very quiet.

"Not warm enough. Feed me more spices. House needs music and TV."

I tried not to laugh but I giggled softly. This made some sense. Must be Yen, after all. Yen liked TV and spices, but the music? I know he used to sing hymns, but in the last years he never sang at all.

The medium made a sudden leap up, and Sylvia and the girl pull her back down on the seat.

"You ungrateful wife! Make fun of me?"

I was shocked. How did he know? "Okay, sorry lah. I pay attention."

Sylvia poked me in the ribs. "Cry, it will appease him."

How could I cry? Luckily I had brain wave. I thought of our early days when we were happy together, we always want to spend time in bed, in the park, everywhere. It was honeymoon. Until I got pregnant with Wu Lan, and even then, he was quite happy with me. Then what happened? Michael came along. Problem really started then. Why? I began to cry. For the lost Yen, my dear husband! The one who serenaded me with romantic songs, the one who taught me how to dance the cha-cha. I cried even harder, just like baby.

Sylvia looked impressed. A few minutes later, the medium shivered again and grew very still. The girl took the veil off. The medium's eyes were shut tight, but she stood up and walked to the altar. How she know to find altar with eyes shut? She took some uncooked rice from the bowl where the joss-sticks burning, and placed the grains inside both pockets of her blouse. Then she opened her eyes and very sternly stared at me.

Sylvia said, "Your ang pow, now!"

So I fished out the money, all prepared, forty dollars in red packet. Put on table. Very expensive.

Sylvia spoke to the medium, "Eh, Auntie, thank you thank you, hah." What would I do without such a friend?

When I got home, I ran off to market and bought curry rempah and everything to make beef rendang and then I cooked and cooked and put food outside our door. Next day it was gone. Was it Yen or the neighbour's boy? Hope it was my husband or else the boy in trouble. I went to music store and found some old tape, Mormon Tabernacle choir, and played it on and off for a week.

Now I think, worth the forty dollars. Yen not come to bother me any more. I feel very kwee sim, my heart open up and light again.

* * *

She's sleeping on her back, her smooth, quiet breathing occasionally interrupted by brief guttural sounds. Upstairs, Dom and Gerry are still up, the muffled sounds of their TV filtering down through the vents. Must be a very good movie to keep them up so late. Next week I'll have the whole place to myself when they take off to Tofino for their annual end-of-summer vacation. My mind flashes back to that time I brought Stephanie home. Then I had wanted to distract myself from the pain of loneliness, believing that sexual contact would alleviate it, like a drug one takes to soothe away discomfort.

But right now, I'm aware that there's nothing as sharply alone as the presence of another in bed, drifting into her own world of dreaming. Two souls as distant as stars. Will Francis and I become bored with each other?

This was the way my parents slept together for years and years. This was the way in which two strangers began in their loneliness together.

In *Last Tango in Paris,* she was in one room bringing herself to orgasm, feeling despair, while he brooded in the next room, locked in his narcissism.

I get up quietly, careful not to wake Francis. In the living room, I dial the long sequence of digits, hear the space punctuated by a beep. A sound that binds Canada to Singapore, tells me that soon I will reach her. The closely paired rings bring me instantly into her kitchen. After three rings, the receiver clicks.

"Mahmee?"

"Oh-ee! Lan-Lan!"

In her voice I can hear the sounds of her daily market visit, the lunch she's had and the sweet black kopi, her afternoon beverage, buzzing its high through her veins.

"Why you call now?" She sounds worried.

"Just wanted to say hello. How are you?"

"No problem lah. Not to worry."

I hear the restraint. Maybe she had another hard night of poor sleep. As if she's psychic, she continues, "I sleep good this week. Father not come any more. Maybe he's found something better to do, huh?"

"Really? That's good news." Maybe he'll stop bugging me too. "Mahmee, I wonder . . ."

"Yes, Lan?" comes the question edged with a mix of worry and hopefulness.

"I wonder if December is a good time to visit. I know it's only been a year, but . . ."

"Bagus! Good! You come see baby. Soon it pops out. What time is it there now?"

"Midnight."

"So late. Why not asleep?"

"Oh . . . nothing . . . soon." Mahmee never remembers the time difference. But the pleasure shows, about my visit. I would like to welcome the baby.

After the conversation, I feel like tasting that kopi myself, imagine the noisy pasar as the throngs of people bustle through the stalls to buy their day's fresh meat and vegetables. To smell those familiar fragrances and to be reminded once again of the sounds I used to hear every day in my childhood. And oh, the heat. The heat that never lets us forget we are at its mercy. I will be spared some of that, since December is in the middle of the monsoon season. There will be many, many days of rain. It will try patience. It will remind me of that poem I saw at the temple. The rain is not to be controlled. But in that poem rain was seen as goodness that Heaven was withholding. The people craved rain in those desperate times of drought and famine. Everything depends on context and perspective.

Will I tell them about Francis? Only if they bother to ask. Only if they stop acting as if I'm a single woman. I want them to ask.

Back in bed, I let myself breathe through her hair, that veil against which I sense the contours of my own face.

* * *

CHOW CHAT MUI

I climb into the rickshaw. The coolie checks again, "Pergi manah?" The scholar tells the coolie an address, somewhere in Telok Kurau. Then he draws the curtain, even though it isn't raining any more. At times I peer out through the thin space between the roof of the rickshaw and the curtain. The familiar, decrepit buildings of my neighbourhood recede away from us quickly. I don't dare look out when we near the Central Police Station and barracks.

We speed down South Bridge Road, along Elgin Bridge. Cross the Singapore River just as the sun dips under the horizon.

The stinky smells again. The water gleams with the last rays of the sun, the tongkangs with their lamps already lit, swaying from the top beams, the reflections crowded in-between the boats like brightly moving water snakes. No bullock carts out on the Quay at this time of day. I remember that first time, that meeting between Ah Sek and me on that other wharf. He looked so fascinating to me then. Even the ugly side of his face intrigued me.

Is he alive? I couldn't have killed him. I hope not. No matter how angry I am at his wickedness, I cannot forget that I loved him once. They must have summoned the mata-mata by now, and are searching Chinatown. What is that in the far distance, on the other side of the quay? Many kerosene lamps, and the sound of singing. A wayang! With the temporary stage of attap and bamboo, and the cast of characters in their bright costumes, while the audience huddle together below them.

The river divides the mysteries of the world of the rich from the rest of us. I'm struck by the spaciousness of the wealthy area of the British. I have never ventured past the bridge all these years. The banks, the municipal offices, the hotels. They are nothing like the sentinels Ah Loong and I encountered on that bold escape from our village. These buildings are larger here, while the fields are neat, trim squares, unlike the chaotic and natural landscapes of our first homeland. A few men stand outside a very fancy and immense hotel. Their faces are pink and blue under the artificial lights, their eyes hidden under hats, their cigarettes burning red spots. The lot facing the hotel is empty. What a wide space! We pass by a very tall building in the middle of another large field, its sharp, pointed roof looking quite forbidding under the darkening sky.

The scholar instructs the coolie, "Take Middle Road, skirt along the edge of the Japanese brothels, then go along the small alleys to Arab Street."

The sounds around us change. I smell food rich with spices and coconut, and my ears are filled with the sounds of Malay conversation around us. Off to the left is a mosque with its golden minaret. A man's plaintive chanting rises above the common din, an earnest prayer that touches me with its yearning to reach Allah.

Our poor coolie doesn't seem less nervous as the journey wears on. A few times he has to halt the rickshaw and rest his sweating body by squatting on the street. Once or twice he spits violently, globs of white disease splattering on the ground like an explosion under the gas lamps. Then, with a heavy sigh of fatigue or reluctance, I'm not sure which, he gets up and resumes his labour.

"Where are we now?"

"We are passing through the Japanese section," the scholar informs me.

This brothel section is denser than the smaller one near us. I try to see if I can spot a karayuki-san or two. No luck. But I recognize their flags, quite a few of them showing up under gaslight, the white with the red suns stirring lazily in the slight breeze. As we leave this area, the houses are no longer as crowded together. Some of them are set back from the road, fronted by a long piece of land. How luxurious! Occasionally we pass by huts on stilts, kampongs, with washed sarongs still hanging on the line. Then shophouses squeezed together, seven or eight in a row. I feel sick from the journey's twists and turns. Eventually, we stop in front of a three-storey house set quite far back in from the road.

It is completely dark by this time. The scholar helps me quickly out of the rickshaw, and pays the coolie. We walk down a sandy path, and enter a musty hallway with cubicles on either side. Voices trickle out from one of them, two men murmuring languidly to each other, talking about their families in China.

The scholar leads me to the back of the house. There is a tap in the middle of the courtyard. I long to splash my face with cool water. But he motions to me not to, pointing upwards with a finger. I see that the windows of the upper floors open out onto the courtyard. Lights from the inside rooms stream out of the windows. Perhaps he's afraid that the noise would draw the other tenants to look out their windows, and we would be seen. We carefully climb the creaky staircase at the far end, all the way to the top. I feel shaky, my legs almost crumble under me. My hands tremble with that urgency. Opium!

He unlocks a door and goes ahead of me. Inside, even before he finds the kerosene lamp and lights it, I can already sense the size of the room. The breeze moves through the space, rustling a paper here, a curtain there. With the light, I see that the room is quite large indeed, compared to my cubicle. One big bed and a smaller one. Several crates in the far corner stuffed with clothes. A beautifully carved sandalwood trunk. A small table and chair, both of very dark wood. He explains to me he shares this with his mother and younger brother, who are away visiting relatives in Bandung.

"Where?" I ask, still quite dazed.

"In Java. My cousin is pregnant. My mother has gone to help out. Later my cousin and her husband will be coming to Singapore."

"They will move here?"

"No. They want to find a husband for my niece."

I show my surprise. "But how can they know? It'll be a female child?"

"We have ways to predict these things. The mother's face . . . the shape of the belly. . . ."

I shake my head in disbelief. A sudden dizziness overcomes me and I begin to sway slightly. He takes my arm and helps me onto the small bed.

"Rest now." His face is calm, curious. I look up at it for a few moments before I let the words escape.

"Opium, I must—"

He furrows his eyebrows. "I will make you a brew now, to help you sleep."

I close my eyes against the many fears, surrendering to the tremors, surrendering to the wait.

* * *

MAHMEE

Oh Lan-Lan, still mine! After all these years of silence. Blood is thicker than water, I say. Now she's coming back, I must cook her good food, feed her well, make sure she drinks all the cooling things. She too much worrying in the brain, not good for her. Daughter, don't think so much!

Too much. Must be why she had to take time off her work. Never mind. What's past is past. I'll tell her funny stories, try to make her laugh more. She too serious. Takes after Yen.

She wants me to tell her more stories about her Mah-Mah. Why? What does she want to hear? Those were such hard times. Better to forget, better to let go of the bitterness. I say bitterness is only good in medicine, or if you fry bitter gourd with egg, then it's delicious. I told Lan-Lan many times, we have only one life, it's important to kua kwee, to look spaciously. Not keep the eyes so narrowed down to the small despairs.

Those people who say forgive and forget, I say they not right. Not so simple. I say, find right medicine. Bitterness must be just right for problem. Then swallow it, think of good things can do when no longer sick. If got ghost around, have to be very patient. Aiyah! Humour him a bit, feed him favourite food. Then he finally leave you alone. Peace and rest again, heart is light. He gone!

All right, Lan-Lan says she wants to go forward. She wants to welcome her niece. I say, okay, you come home, and let me feed you some good bah-kut-teh and laksa, and make sure you eat all the things you don't get over there in that cold and rainy city.

* * *

I close the book. A small group of newcomers to the library follows the tour guide. He stops in the space between the History and Fine Arts section, ". . . if you all turn and face the escalators, you'll notice the following features common to most levels: the service desks located at the west side . . . photocopiers found on each floor in the red rooms at the east side . . . pillars which are approximately one metre across . . . notice how the light is." He waves his arms in the appropriate directions, uses his hands flamboyantly like flags signalling important clues.

"What do you mean, how the light is?" interjects a young woman whom one might suspect to be sixteen or older because of her height, but who's probably thirteen, guessing from the still-cherubic face, brazenly virginal.

The guide flashes her a rude look. "I mean, the light is reflected off the ceiling, thereby creating a comfortable reading environment."

"I don't understand. That doesn't seem such an unusual thing. Isn't some light in a room always reflected from the ceiling? Besides, the light from these reading lamps at the tables"— she points to the nearest one—"is being directed straight down at the table." The young woman slides her gold-rimmed glasses back up her nose. A couple of people in the group shift their weight uneasily from one foot to the other. The guide's face turns beet-red.

"Well, actually, you . . . you're right," he stammers. "I was given the information to memorize. Never thought of it until now." He shakes his head, as if he were trying to realign his jumbled thoughts. He uses his right hand to flag them to the west, and they trot off dutifully.

The bravura of the young woman reminds me of Stephanie. It seems quite strange that I haven't run into her in all these months. Perhaps she and Dale decided to move elsewhere. Leave Lotusland. Return home, wherever home is.

I follow at the tail end of the group. No one seems to notice or mind. We pass an overhead sign announcing World History, Geography and Travel, and Ancient History. We reach the more secluded area where the reading cubicles are, all of them presently used. We stop at the windows facing the corner of Homer and Robson.

"This is the Reading Arcade. Notice that we came over a corridor of sorts to reach it. Okay, let's retrace our steps. This way, please." The tour guide seems to have regained his confidence. He takes us back to the corridor just in front of the sign. I hadn't noticed before that in fact it's a bridge of sorts.

"If you look down from here, you'll realize that the library is actually a rectangle in an ellipse. Traditionally, in libraries, people were in the middle and the books surrounded them."

"Like in the old one," an elderly man in his off-white Tilley hat offers nonchalantly.

"Correct. But in this library, the plan's inside out, so to speak. Because the people"—he makes a wide circle with his arms, as if preparing to embrace a long-lost friend—"are now on the outside and the books are in the middle."

"Cool," the tall cherub remarks.

The guide puts his hands together and announces that the tour is over. I return to the table I'd been at, and open up the book. The young woman was right. The light from the lamp illuminates the bone-whiteness of the pages. I flip to the middle section where the photos are. I look at the one of the Smith Street brothel that's now a barbershop. If not for the characters carved into the window frame, who would have guessed it had been a brothel? The exchange of sex, disease and opium: all the dark traces of history would have faded into oblivion.

I look around. The light in this new library is stark. One hundred years ago, lighting was much dimmer—the candle flame, the kerosene lamp—and couldn't illuminate as wide a space. In the next millennium, how would the light in buildings change?

* * *

CHOW CHAT MUI

My body shakes with the struggle. Oh the need, the need for this pain to leave me! I scream, wake up confused. What was the dream? The moths came towards me in the hundreds, as if I was the light, and their bodies entered me, burning holes through my skin. Burning through my sores, until they opened up like eyes. I've so many eyes, yet I can't tell where I am. I raise myself slightly up on one arm and look around. In the far corner, a kerosene lamp burns at low flame. He's sitting at a table next to it. His body turns towards me, his face partially lit by the orange glow.

"The brew will be ready soon. It will take away your pain." His eyes are sad, even though they're still looking at me with that rare kindness.

"Thirsty. I'm thirsty," I whisper.

"You must wait. The brew has to be drunk. Nothing else yet."

I lower myself back down onto the bed. The pain shoots up my left leg, claws through my bowels and into my chest. My forehead is damp from sweat yet my lips are as dry as dust. Thirsty, so thirsty. How can I endure this?

The flame in the kerosene lamp is a hot, tempting light that burns inside me as I stare into it. Do any moths escape its compelling power? I hear the rustle of clothing nearby. He's come to sit next to me. His hand slides gently under my head and raises it. A bowl hovers at the edge of my lips. My mouth opens up to a thick, dark liquid. I choke on the horrible taste.

"You must finish all of it. Drink slowly."

I force it all down. Vile. More vile than the waters of the Singapore River. The brew's warmth permeates my insides, settling like sludge somewhere too deep to vomit out. He lowers my head back down. What luxury, to be nursed by a man, to rest my head on his mother's exquisite pillow. Embroidered in silken browns and golds, with exact, square corners, the sound of sand rustling within its rectangular shape as my head moves against it.

The light casts a bright aura around his face from behind.

The contours of his face blur until the boundaries between his expression and the surroundings no longer exist, and everything is a watery illusion. I am swimming in the dark liquid, swimming towards the lamplight. Heaviness overcomes my body, sinking itself into my bones. His voice an indistinct mumble. Can barely keep my eyes open. Soothing. A warmth easing my chest. Ease....

* * *

One hundred years ago, the light was dimmer, and could only illuminate a small space. True enough, but it was a light that was not taken for granted. It was a light that became more precious by its contrast to the surrounding dark.

One hundred years ago, the choices were different, yet still the same—whether one wants to live, and how. I wish they hadn't died in such despair, in their cubicles, taking their own lives.

What does a body feel when it has been taken over by a contagion? Sleeping pills, opium, romantic obsession. Soothing in small amounts, addictive and deadly with increasing surrender to it. What does a body feel, when it has been too blighted by disease and suffering to feel the saving power of its own life force? What does a body know when it has been taken too far for escape to still be a conscious choice?

* * *

CHOW CHAT MUI

I'm awakened by his hand shaking my shoulder. My samfu is soaked through. I struggle to surface from the stupor of deep sleep. Light pierces through the wooden slats of the window.

He's standing over me, a basin in one hand, a towel in the other. He places the basin of steaming water down on the floor and soaks the towel, then wrings it quickly and offers it to me. I sit up and welcome the cleansing heat over my face and my neck. He goes to the sandalwood trunk and retrieves a set of woman's clothes.

"You may wash, I will not look." He places the clothes at the foot of the bed, turns his back to me and sits at the table. "The mata-mata are looking for you. It is not safe to be in the city."

Panic flutters across my chest. "What can I do?"

"I think you must leave the island soon."

I peel off my samfu, my undergarments, piece by piece, carefully considering the scholar's advice. The heat of the towel wakes up my tired skin, and a pleasant cooling sensation follows. I'm free from pain, compared to last night. Slightly numb and dizzy, but nothing severe, just an ache all over. Then I feel a pang of sadness, remembering how Ah Choi loved her daily baths.

"How? Where could I go?"

"I could buy you a passage on a ship."

"Ship? Going where?"

"To Java. Where my family is. I will send them a telegram to meet you."

"But won't you come?" My voice is quivering with fear. To leave this country for yet another place. And this time, alone.

"You'll be safe on the ship."

I pick up the clothes. There's a white cotton blouse, with fasteners all down the front, a cream-coloured undergarment, and a sarong. Why hadn't I realized this before? That's why his family is in Java, why he wears his hair tied up like that, and maybe partly why I was drawn to him. He is a peranakan, part Chinese and part Malay, and he doesn't act like the men I've known.

I stand up and put on the clean clothes slowly, with some awkwardness. "I'm ready but I don't know how...this sarong...."

He turns around and smiles. From the trunk he lifts up a silver link belt. The buckle is beautifully etched with the outlines of a bird. The silver links are delicately fashioned, with a flower shape repeated along the length of the belt at regular intervals.

"This is to hold your sarong up." I wrap the belt around my waist, close the buckle, and tuck the cloth over the belt, leaving the buckle slightly exposed.

"It is my mother's, which is how she'll know it's you." Then he fishes out some slippers from the trunk. Delicate brocade, with the design of two phoenixes entwined. "We call these slippers kasut manik." He blushes again, an even deeper red. "I helped my mother sew them. You may wear them."

I sit down on the bed and place my feet gingerly into the steaming water. Oh, how wonderful! Only after washing my feet thoroughly do I put on the precious slippers. They are a bit small for me, but my feet don't complain.

Should I go? All alone. I clutch my head in my hands. Unimaginable. Yet what other choice do I have? I could stay, risk it. Perhaps all Ah Sek wants to do is make an example of me in front of the others. A slap or two. A shouting fit. Nothing too serious.

No, not true. Ah Sek must be furious. If he finds me, he'll want to kill me. Their patrols are scouring the streets. It's only a matter of time before I'm found. And then the scholar might be in trouble if they discover that he hid me here in his lodgings.

"Do you want to leave?" He squats down beside me so that his eyes are almost level with mine. They narrow in a look of puzzlement and concern.

"What would I do in Java?" My lips tremble with the thought of starting all over again in a new country. I'm too old and ugly. Diseased. What use could I be?

"While you were sleeping, I was thinking." He pauses for quite a while. "You trusted me in the temple. No small feat.

Perhaps because I'd given you that word?" I nod. He continues, "I don't know how long you've been an ah ku, but the first time I met you, there was such bitterness on your face! But that second time, even though we didn't speak much, I saw how your eyes were brighter. But also sadder. Yesterday afternoon, when you looked up at me through the ceremonial cloths, your eyes were wild with terror. I live a simple life. I'm very fortunate, I am healthy. I . . . I don't act on my desires. Not that way."

"What are you saying?"

"This is what I've thought of. If I marry you, you'll be accepted into my family. They respect my decisions. They won't question me even if they might wonder. Marriage will gain you protection on the ship and elsewhere."

"We don't know each other's names!" Why would he go to such trouble?

He laughs, a light ripple through the air. "My name is Koh Tian Chin."

I tell him my name. "Why chain yourself to me? You're a free man, refined, and in good health."

He blushes, then his face assumes a serious look. "If you promise me, I have a secret to tell."

"Yes, yes. Go ahead." I'm relieved to hear that this man has secrets.

"I feel brotherly love towards you. As I do towards many women. And some men. But"—he draws in a quick breath, a fearfulness overtakes his face—"my deepest love is reserved for men." He lets out a sigh and regains his calm. "My family has been worried. But if I marry. . . ."

"I see. I won't repeat what you've told me."

There've been a few instances where I caught sight of this tender love between men. Of course it was not meant for my eyes, but how can I not see? In the small distances between their bodies, there was a subtle language. The way their hands gently touched each other's shoulder or arm in greeting or parting.

"I will marry you. But first, I must go to the cemetery."

"Why?"

"I also have a secret. I loved someone once. Another ah ku. Her spirit will not rest if I don't visit her one last time."

He now sits besides me and folds his hands together in his lap, gazing inwards. "It could be dangerous. Every moment you're out in the open, you risk being caught."

"Yes, I understand. I'm willing to risk it."

He walks to the window, opens it to look outside.

I walk over to a mirror to roll my hair up. It's the first time I've looked at myself carefully in a long while. My skin looks tight and pale, my mouth thin with worry. Even so, there's a vast ocean swelling up in my eyes. I have nothing to lose.

"I have a request to make of you, kind brother."

"What is it?"

"Can you make me another copy of that character? The one you gave me?"

"Oh?"

"The one for thought."

"Ah . . . yes."

He goes to the table and mixes up a small amount of ink on a stone slab, smooth slope gleaming with blackness that pools at the base. Pleasure rushes over me as I listen to the sound of the stick against the slab. One kind of stone moving against another. Nature meeting nature. He talks to me as he dips his brush carefully into the ink.

"While you were sleeping this morning, I went to the Chinese protectorate to apply for permission to remove your name from the list of ah ku. But they require that you appear in person, to tell them you wish to leave the brothel. It won't take long. After that, we'll go to city hall to register as husband and wife. Then perhaps, if we have time, you can go to the cemetery to say goodbye."

I nod my head. He finishes his calligraphy. I go over to look. My heart starts to pound with the thrill of seeing this beautiful character again.

"Drink some more of this."

It's the brew again, now lukewarm and even uglier tasting. I gulp it down. It will be the last time I enjoy its bitter benefits before the long journey.

* * *

I wipe the mirror clean. Only four more days of the leave of absence is left. I look carefully at the reflection. A face says more than words can describe. Wu Lan, the sum of which is greater than its parts. She is neither Ah Choi nor Chat Mui, although they are parts of her. An image seeks itself, the particular truths. Today I notice more details that distinguish me from my parents: the three small moles along the left side of my face, the faint scars from catching chicken pox as an adult.

In a couple of hours, the constant whine of race cars from miles away at the Indy will begin. The roar of mad speed, around and around, centrifugal, spinning so as not to be spun out. Countdown. Four more days before going back to work. I mustn't lose track of myself. I must hold onto a centre, while I re-enter the flux.

I turn around to pick up my shampoo bottle and soap. Time for another visit to the pool. In one corner, a spider spins its lovely web. Beautiful secret life. Dark, hairy body, quiet and private sanity. It begs me not to inflict the cruelty it would on its prey. I use one of my slippers to lift the spider off, intending to escort it to the garden outside, but it jumps off onto the linoleum and scampers quickly underneath the tub.

Will I still feel that occasional twinge of anger towards my clients? Will I still have an ear for suffering that's invisible and wordless? That registers as silence between words? I know what it's like to fall into the abyss where the ground of language gives way.

I'm returning to this place called absence, where in front of me, a stranger talks. Stringing words together. Two strangers who sit across from each other in a small, soundproofed room. Face to face. Truths or lies?

A torrent of words, like a seasonal monsoon, underneath which lies the deepest pain. Aren't all stories true? To intuit the meanings of what is left unsaid.

I am Wu Lan, an exorcist of hidden demons.

I am the discoverer of secrets.

I stir fire into the bones of the dead.

I prepare the dead for release.

Bending into the porcelain whiteness of the bathtub, I lean very close to his embalmed body and whisper one last time.

Goodbye, Father.

* * *

CHOW CHAT MUI

I had to state my intention at the office of the Chinese protectorate. "No, I no longer wish to work as an ah ku." I had to put my mark on a piece of paper. Black ink soaking into the patterns on my right thumb. The inner whorls appeared like magic on paper, the intimately curved paths that pulled me closer and closer into a swirling centre. At city hall, we stood side by side as they prepared even more documents. Again I had to place my mark on these papers. But this time, Tian Chin also placed his own mark beside mine. It was easy, a private ceremony unwitnessed by the brothel family. Is it possible I am finally no longer a tap tang? What about Ah Sek and his mother? I owe them money still.

As if he understands my worries, Tian Chin assures me, in the rickshaw, he will take care of the debts I owe.

"But you will expose yourself to Ah Sek's wrath!"

No, he replies, still calm, nothing bad will happen to him. He will pay the debt anonymously.

We reach the cemetery. Very humid. The cicadas hum with approval. I find Ah Choi's place easily. As I kneel before the stone, I'm aware of Tian Chin's presence in the distance. He's not interfering. No, he's not like the others who have wanted my will and my body to obey theirs.

The piece of paper I'd left is ruined, the character soaked and distorted by the rain and sun. What's left to offer her? Only my honesty. At this moment, the desire for freedom is stronger than my dread of leaving her.

"Ah Choi, my dreams for escape are still strong."

I must risk again. Love for her can't keep me here, love can't tame my will to be free.

When I rise up from kneeling, I feel my heels rock back. I'm dizzy again. Tian Chin rushes forward and holds me steady. We walk back to the rickshaw.

The ride to the shipping district is fraught with worry. Again, we draw the curtain. Tian Chin firmly instructs the coolie which streets to take. This one shows less nervousness, his dark Tamil features betraying only concentration. We cut through the heart of Chinatown, pass all the familiar sights and sounds one last time. The shops, the brothels, the Chinese protectorate. I shrink away from the gap in the curtain, in case....

This morning, it had been so quick, so easy, to walk into the office just north of New Bridge Road, next to Wayang Street. So close to our brothel, and yet, many fears and warnings had kept me from going to the protectorate all these years! I used to pass by and envy those who trusted in the unknown, who believed they could find other means to make a living. Once I reach Bandung, his mother will take care of me. He reminded me, "You can tell them what you wish to do, and say it's also my wish." I can't imagine what the future will hold for me. After all these years, can Heaven suddenly shower mercy on me?

I'll show him my gratitude. I'll repay him by serving his mother. I'll help take care of his cousin's daughter.

The rickshaw bumps along on the older streets, dusty and uneven, until I catch sight of the river with its tongkangs moving lazily. The men working them, with their wizened eyes, their rubbery skins.

We don't cross the river at the usual place, but turn south, follow it along its course until we reach another bridge. There's a lot of traffic here, mostly rickshaws, but also a few cars driven by Englishmen. How healthy and clean they appear, in their finely tailored suits! After crossing this bridge, the Tamil rickshaw coolie slows down, sweat pooling at the nape of his neck and collarbone. Finally, Tian Chin tells him to stop in front of a stone building.

"Collyer Quay. This is where we wait. They'll tell us when the ship arrives at North Pier, then it's time to go." I check the sky as I step out of the rickshaw. Clouds tinged with orange and lilac in the southwest. A good omen. That day Ah Loong and I sailed from Guangzhou in 1900, the sky also had coloured clouds. I look up at the clock. Three PM. Sailors dressed in dark blue tops and white pants rush in and out of the cool insides of the building.

When I ascend the marble steps, peering into the dimly lit hall, I'm trembling with anticipation. A voice announces sailing schedules in several languages, its echoes resounding down the hall, hypnotic and musical. I clutch my cloth bundle close to me, thinking of the word-gift tucked safely within it.

* * *

In the women's locker room, a group of Chinese women in their fifties and sixties are peeling off their swimsuits. They all seem to know each other, gossiping in Cantonese. One woman is drying her hair, tightly permed salt-and-pepper curls. She's wearing loose white panties and around her neck a towel. She's singing some traditional folk song above the drone of the hot-air dryer, a slow, lilting melody, the kind I could imagine a young girl singing, to keep herself strong as she labours in the fields. Another woman joins in, hums a few lines, stops, then a few more lines.

I gaze at their bodies in shy snatches as I take off my swimsuit, as if I'm not supposed to look at the folds of flesh, the greying pubic hair, the bulging varicose veins, the floppy breasts. The realities of women my mother's age, the reality of my own body changing and moving towards theirs.

In the open shower with two others, I turn on the tap, and my body shudders at the icy water. My muscles ease as the water warms up. I begin to hum softly. The water slides over my body, smooth and silky.

The Chinese ladies leave together, a gang of cackling laughter. By the time I'm ready, it's 8:30.

Abruzzo's Coffee Bar is already busy, the large TV telecasting news live from Italy. I stride in for a take-out americano. The news announcer is blonde and sexy, right out of a James Bond movie. The men sprawl out in the green plastic lawn chairs, entranced. Words pour out of her, punctuated with steamy authority.

I feel no urge to stay and admire her. At Charles Street, I cut across Grandview Park. The tall weeping larch near the beginning of the path sways in the breeze. Swaying like a sentinel or guardian spirit, watching over those of us who pass by it each day. I head in the direction of the temple. What will I ask Tze Cheng this time? The meaning of dragon eyes. And if there are any wu shi practising today.

This autumn morning is rich with sublime shades. I taste their honeyed possibilities on my tongue. Light filters through the red and golden leaves of the maple trees overhead. The concrete path is graced with fallen leaves, and the occasional dark imprints of death, shapes of what had been.

I pause just as I reach the tennis courts. From behind me, I hear the squeals and gurgles of a child at play. I turn back to look for her. A child of about three. A woman faces her, pushing the swing. The child's small hands hold the chains with a relaxed confidence. She throws her head back on the upswing, chortling in that rare, spontaneous way only a toddler can. Her hair gleams, lifted light as air in the movement. The swing returns. Just before the push backwards, there's that sweet space in time when the woman's and the child's eyes meet in a dance of mutual delight. The woman leans forward to touch the child's cheek with a kiss.

May this child live to remember and to forget.

When I turn away, resuming my walk along the path, I feel the vibrant energy of her small body follow after me. I hear my own heart beating loudly.

AUTHOR'S NOTES

This novel is a pure work of fiction and all characters are fictional, as are all incidents and journeys described. However, the initial inspiration for the novel came from James Francis Warren's article "The Ah Ku and Karayuki-San of Singapore—Their Lives: Sources, Method and a Historian's Representation" in *Southeast Asian Journal of Social Science*, Vol. 20, No.1 (1992). I have relied heavily on two books by James Francis Warren: *Ah Ku and Karayuki-San: Prostitution in Singapore 1870–1940* (Singapore: Oxford University Press, 1993) and *Rickshaw Coolie: A People's History of Singapore 1880-1940* (Singapore: Oxford University Press, 1986).

A variety of Chinese dialects are used in the novel, as are Malay and "Singlish"—a corruption of the Queen's English—a colloquial form spoken in Singapore. Speakers of Chinese dialects and Malay borrow terms from one another, incorporating them into their speech. I have reflected this tendency across the four voices. Most of the terms used by the ah ku are from the Cantonese: I adopted the transliterations used in James Warren's books. Chinese terms used by Wu Lan and her family are sounded according to the Hokien dialect; Mahmee's speech is her version of "Singlish." Tze Cheng speaks Mandarin, and Wu Lan's explanation of her name is according to Mandarin. I have separated transliterated words on the page to reflect the Chinese language. In contrast, the Malay language is rendered phonetically.

The Religious System of China, Volume V, Book II by J.J.M. DeGroot (Leyden: E.J. Brill, 1907) and *The Religious System of China*, Volume VI, Book II by J.J.M. DeGroot (Leyden: E.J. Brill, 1910) yielded the central ideas about the wu shi, demon possession, and exorcism, including the method of contacting the spirit, che sin (Hokien) described by Mahmee. *Tao: The Chinese Philosophy of Time and Change* by Philip Rawson and Laszlo Legeza (London: Thames and Hudson, 1973) provided information on Taoist beliefs of the universe and the human body. *Climate of China* by Chu Ping-Hai (Washington, D.C.: U.S. Department of Commerce, 1968) outlined ancient Chinese folklore about weather prediction, as well as climatic conditions of south China. *All Under Heaven*, text by Jonathan Porter, photographs by Eliot Porter (New York: Pantheon, 1983) contained descriptions of rice cultivation and agrarian society in pre-Communist China. A chapter by David Pearce, "Sampan ports and the tides of change" in *Journey into China* (Washington, D.C.: National Geographic Society, 1982), was consulted for re-creating the journeys taken by Ah Choi, Chat Mui and Ah Loong from Guangzhou to Singapore. The tale about the Gaos and the Lius was also found in this chapter. The description of an ancient painting of dragons, gnomes and humans was adapted from *The Art and Architecture of China* by Laurene Sickman and Alexander Soper (London, New Haven: Yale University Press, 1968). *Traditional Chinese Medicine* by Sheila McNamara (New York: Basic Books, 1996) was consulted for how a Chinese physician—sinseh (Hokien) or yi sun (Cantonese)—assesses patients.

Two books provided information about opium and its effects: *Opium: The illustrated diary of his cure* by Jean Cocteau (London: P. Owen, 1990) and *Opium Poppy: Botany, Chemistry, and Pharmacology* by L.D. Kapoor (New York: Food Products Press, 1995). I consulted *The V.D. Story* by Stewart M. Brooks (New York: A.S. Barnes, 1971) for the symptoms of gonorrhea and syphilis. I learned a few geological facts about mountains by reading *A Field Guide to the West Coast Mountains* by Stephen R. Whitney (Vancouver: Douglas & McIntyre, 1983).

The article Wu Lan finds while at the Java Cat café is based on an article, "Woman dances with scorpions" in *Southeast Asia Post*, March 26-April 8, 1998. "The Tyger" by William Blake was found in *The Norton Anthology of Poetry* (New York: Random House, Inc. 1975).

Other supplementary materials which were useful for writing scenes set in the early 1900s in Singapore were: *Chinatown: An album of a Singapore community* (Singapore: Archives and Oral History Department, Times Books International, 1983); *Vanishing Trades of Singapore* (Singapore: Oral History Department, 1992); *Singapore Historical Postcards* (Singapore: Times Editions, 1986); and *Singapore Sketchbook*, paintings by Graham Byfield, text by Gretchen Liu (Singapore: Archipelago Press, 1995).

ACKNOWLEDGEMENTS

I am grateful to the B.C. Arts Council, and the Department of Canadian Heritage for providing financial assistance.

Thanks to Nancy Richler, who offered helpful comments on the most number of versions of the manuscript; Louié Ettling, Carmen Rodríguez, Angela Hryniuk and Daphne Marlatt also enriched the novel through their feedback; Anne Jew, Erin Soros and Karen Tee provided comments on early drafts. Dr. Wei-Jen Ng reminded me of important facets of life in Singapore as a peranakan. Thanks to Dr. Lawrence Chan for confirming details of the Traditional Chinese Medicine perspective. The folk belief about hantu tek-tek was mentioned to me by Dr. Gaik-Cheng Khoo. My appreciation to staff at the National Archives in Singapore who assisted with research. Thanks to the Ben Lau Gallery for providing the Chinese calligraphy.

To Manuela Dias, Managing Editor at Turnstone, my gratitude for your enthusiasm and support. Thanks to my editor Jennifer Glossop for smart suggestions and incredible meticulousness; a thank-you to May Yee and Susan Goldberg for editorial comments; and thanks also to Pat Sanders for the copy editing. Thanks to my cousin Dr. Eng-Hwi Kwa for financial support; to Dr. Sandra Parker for tips on how to keep sane in insane moments. My appreciation to Louié Ettling for taking my photograph and for providing the image on the cover of the book. My gratitude to

Katharine Dickinson for many coffee breaks and stimulating conversation.

Excerpts of the novel in earlier versions have appeared in *West Coast Line, Open Letter, Hot and Bothered* (Karen X. Tulchinsky, ed., Vancouver: Arsenal Pulp Press, 1998) and *Imaginings: Drawings* by Ed Pien (Charles H. Scott Gallery, 2000).